By JWCouch

MIK3 D3VON:
CONTINUING SERI3S

Discoveries
Disclosures
Disruptions

MIK3 D3VON:
Disclosures

By
JWCouch
VC3 Publishing

Cover Art by Emily Masters
Cover Design by ViviAnne Brock
Virtual Assistant / Proofreading by Annie Lynn

DEDICATION

THIS book is dedicated to my family and friends, without whose support this book series would have never been completed. Our oldest daughter and my wife spent many hours editing. To those who cheered me on and to those who "always wanted to write a book": you were the fuel when I was running low. Thank you all.

Table of Contents

Now, I don't want to scare anyone, but there is more 'Science Faction' going on in the pages ahead than you may realize…

PROLOGUE

1. In Mike Devon: Discoveries, Mike, Courtney, Danni, Court, Terri and Bill engaged in deception and struggled to survive while they discovered three parallel versions of the world. There is our current reality, one where the Nazis conquered the world during World War II, and the third where Great Britain rules supreme.

2. In an effort to understand what has happened, and stay alive, everyone is struggling with the trinity of realities, and where they fit into the scheme of things. Their mission is to obtain information on what and when the world went wrong, who did it, and if possible, fix it.

Mike, Courtney, Court and Danni were walking down the sidewalk. The four had just escaped to the British dominated world. Mike desperately searched his brain for options. George had been a true friend. How could he selfishly ask George to risk everything again?

It's not about George, or me. It's not even about my George back home. Forget everyone you know, they're nothing in comparison to what you need to do. This is nothing personal. It's about the billions of histories and futures that have been ruined. Mike felt like he had been punched in the stomach. *If it can be fixed, and even if we survive, we'll all be forever changed.*

* * *

UNIT 1: A NEW DISCLOSURE

"George, wake up. Michael's on the phone and it sounds important."

"What? How long have I been asleep?" the groggy janitor asked. "Wait…who?" he said, as he lurched up in bed.

"Well, it sounds like Michael, but he's trying to disguise his voice with a silly accent. Said he was an old friend in town for the day," his wife answered and turned to leave the room.

George jumped out of bed and passed her before she could get to the door of their small bedroom.

Grabbing the phone handset off the kitchen counter, he said cautiously, "Hello?"

"Hello there, old friend. I know I told you yesterday that I didn't want to cause you any trouble, but can you do me one last favor?" Mike Devon asked.

"Do you have any idea what's happening, mate?" George asked and turned away from his wife's inquisitive look.

"No, are they after Michael?" Mike asked.

"Maybe, but the coppers have bigger problems right now. Someone hacked our boss to pieces in a hallway at work. We're all under house arrest while they finish the investigation." George closed his eyes as he listened for Mike's reaction.

"Someone hacked Alec up? George, that's awful. The smell must have been horrendous," Mike said.

"Funny you should say that because the entire building had the stench of burned flesh. Whatever they used cut right through the flooring as well."

"I can imagine."

"You don't know anything about it?" the janitor asked.

"Me? How could I?"

"No, you're right. How could you?" George answered.

"Do they have any suspects?" Mike asked.

"Not yet and no one at work will say a word about what went on with Michael for fear of being arrested themselves. We had one chance to turn him in when we learned about the insubordination and crimes against a higher class. No one did and now they're all scared."

Remembering that Scotland Yard could be listening in, George changed the subject. "What do you need from me?"

"I need a ride. *We* need a ride. Four of us came to town this trip."

"Four of you?"

"Yeah, I'm sorry, George. I shouldn't have called. I don't want to cause you any more problems."

"It's fine."

"Thanks, I owe you, again," Mike said.

"No worries. Do I know any of your friends?"

Mike replied, "No, but you'd recognize one from old photographs. If things settle down, I'll introduce you."

"I'd like that." George tried to sound calm, but his mind raced. *Is it the girl? Old photographs—that must be Courtney! She's here?* "Give me an intersection near you and I'll send my brother-in-law right over. I'm too tired or I'd come myself."

"Looks like Seventh Street and Rollins Avenue," Mike read.

George replied, "You aren't far at all. Hold tight."

* * *

"He's sending his brother-in-law over to pick us up," Mike said to the curious threesome.

"Hacked who up?" Danielle asked.

"Alec, George's boss. Remember him? The jerk that runs the janitorial crew George works on." Mike remembered that she knew the names, faces and habits of nearly everyone around him back home. He added, "The head janitor at Theoretical Applications Corp."

"He has the same job as our George at TAC," Courtney said.

"Yep," Mike replied. "Alec's wounds were cauterized." He watched as Court and Danni glanced expressionlessly at each other. "You already knew about Alec?"

There was no reply from Courtney's parents.

Mike wondered if something had happened during their recent stay in the Nazi-torn world. Being here in Supreme Britain was dangerous, but nothing like they were used to. He realized he had spent very little time trying to understand the emotions and cultures of the three realities, but he knew he didn't have time.

"Remember, no secrets," Mike said.

"None," Court said. "We regularly see cauterized wounds on the Nazis, back in our world."

Danni, who looked like an older version of Mike's Courtney, added, "Sounds like wounds from the Colonel's sword. Michael also brought one to Supreme Britain. It could have been him."

Mike's eyes closed for a moment and he saw the event taking place as if he were there. When he saw the horror in the decapitated Alec's eyes, he jerked and shook himself alert.

Courtney asked, "Everything OK?"

"Uh, yeah. Michael hated Alec with a passion, but he would have gone to the USA after he got his sword, not here. It had to be the Colonel, he was the only one who would have been here with a sword."

"No secrets? Then why do I sense you're hiding something from us?" Courtney asked Mike.

Mike looked into her blue eyes and felt his defenses lower. "It's not a secret, just strange. I had deja vu about the killing. I can picture the body all cut up and something else really disgusting which George didn't mention."

"You weren't going to tell us?" Courtney asked.

"I wasn't sure if it was my imagination playing tricks, so I didn't mention it."

"Really? Like the flashes after we travel?" Court asked.

"Yeah, like that but clearer. Look, this could be bad. They could have a video of it and be waiting for me at Michael's. I think we should split up before we get there," Mike said.

"We aren't getting separated again," Courtney said, as Danni reached out and grabbed her hand. "We'll take our time and if it's doable, we'll get what you need."

Looking over at the three of them, Mike couldn't help but smile. "I wouldn't want to cross that daughter of yours, but this might get ugly, sir."

"We understand," Court said, "but we're in this together."

* * *

"I'm getting another cup of coffee if you want me to stick around," Bill said to his senior partner. He didn't want to admit it, but he was in pain and needed sleep. The pair had been in the data analysis conference room for three hours, looking for clues to Mike and Courtney's whereabouts in the power plant video clips.

"After the tree beating you got last night, you should probably be in the hospital," Terry said.

"Tree beating? That's not a thing," Bill replied, still looking at his screen.

"It most certainly is."

"That tree did not give me a beating," Bill grumbled.

"Then you clearly haven't looked in the mirror," Terry chuckled.

"I wonder how that nice security guard you popped in the face is doing," Bill asked.

Terry looked up from his screen. "He had it coming."

That got his attention. "Would've been nice if you'd backed me up rather than punch civilians," Bill replied.

"You mean, if I dove out a third story window, into the darkness and played hangman in an oak tree like you did?"

"Well, once I blew out the window, you could clearly see the tree. It would have been easy for you," Bill said.

"Real easy, Terry said sarcastically. "How about processing some of the video feed from Military Mike and Courtney's visit, so we can get out of here," Terry said.

Bill tried again, "But there are five teams going through these clips in no logical order, I might add. They can ID every frame

Courtney or Mike are in just as easily as we can. No—better, since they slept last night."

"One more hour, then we'll go," Terry said. "The whole floor is buzzing about the night's events and its good PR for us to stick around and help. The Good Lord knows you need all the help you can get."

"What's that supposed to mean?"

Terry looked up again, "You strangled that Chinese spook over at Mike's place a while back. Everyone's been waiting to see who they'll knock off to even the score."

"Yeah, yeah. But if you hadn't gotten yourself shot—no, if you'd have done your job and shot him first—then I wouldn't have needed to kill him," Bill retorted.

"I did shoot him, which is why you were able to lumber in and lift his little, frail, paralyzed body off the ground without resistance."

"Frail? He tried to shoot me," an exasperated Bill said.

"He shot himself because of the mortal wound from my bullet," Terry said.

"I forgot. You did break his wrist with that deadly barrage of one bullet to the hand." He looked up at his screen on the wall in front of them and started another video clip. "Yet another clip in the control room with Military Mike. Hey, he's a Colonel. I see *COL Devon* right there on his chest."

"Hey, Bill, take a look at these shots, would you?"

Terry transferred three paused clips to the big screen in the center of the wall. They stared at all three frames simultaneously, then looked at each other in disbelief.

"That's Mike? In all three?" Bill asked.

"Sure looks like him to me."

"Are you trying to tell me that he slipped out, lost weight and got a haircut while they were at the power plant?" Bill asked. "Come on, what did you do to the footage?"

"Nothing. This doesn't make sense. I'm putting these aside to see what else I can find," Terry said.

"So far, we have Mike, Colonel Devon and now skinny Mike?"

"Wait, the footage from TAC, why is it locked?" Terry asked.

"Well… I'm still in the TAC files…um…you need to see this," Bill said. He slid his video player over to the large, shared screen. Bill started the clip and watched for Terry's reaction.

"Now watch this one," he said and ran a second clip for Terry.

Terry said, "Wait, now run it again, at half speed."

When Bill moved to restart the clip, his cursor went up to the corner of the player and closed out the program.

"Hey, open it back up," Terry demanded.

"That's not me, someone locked me out," he said, as their screens went blank.

The door to their room opened and a senior agent Bill didn't recognize stepped inside.

"Case closed boys, dump it."

"Roger that, sir," Terry replied without hesitation.

"You're both on paid leave until further notice. Oh, and your project bonuses have posted to your accounts," he said coldly.

"Sir?" Terry asked.

Get us out of here, Terry, something's wrong, Bill thought.

"Speak," the man said.

"How much and how long?" Terry asked.

Bill relaxed slightly after hearing the question.

"You both got the full fifteen percent of your annual and four additional weeks off. We might need you before then, but as of this moment you're both on vacation."

"Thank you, sir," Bill said.

"Double time!" the man barked.

"Yes, sir," Bill replied, doing his best to sound excited at the news.

"Yes, thank you, sir," Terry said, as he stood up quickly and headed toward the door.

Bill followed Terry past the senior agent and knew his every movement was being assessed.

"You heading for the beach, Bill?" Terry asked.

"I'm heading for bed, then to the doc for an X-ray or two, then back to bed. I don't have anything planned after that," Bill answered.

"I hear you. It's been awhile since we had time to think about anything but work."

Bill wanted to talk about the unbelievable footage they had seen, but he kept quiet.

"You should come up to Maine and go out on the boat with me. It will give you plenty of time to heal from your bicycle accident."

"Bicycle?" Bill asked.

"You can't tell the locals you look like that from diving out a window trying to catch a rogue spook, now can you?" he asked.

"True. Thanks, I'm going to use that," Bill said.

"Don't mention it. Hey, I'm hungry. Let's go get a hot dog, Dopey," Terry teased.

"Oh, yeah, that would be great, Hansel," Bill replied.

"Hansel? Okay then, Gretel," Terry shook his head.

"Who's Gretel?" Bill asked, watching for Terry's frustrated response. He loved to play the role of dumb oaf and Terry always fell for it.

Terry rolled his eyes as they walked down the hallway.

Gotcha, Mr. Know-it-all.

Bill hoped their conversation would greatly diminish any suspicions the senior agent had. He knew their superiors would need convincing that he and Terry weren't an issue to be resolved. Bill also knew they had seen too much. He hoped Terry would have a plan to put some time and distance between them and the investigation. If not, they were in serious trouble.

* * *

Mike looked up when Courtney said, "I think our ride is here."

The dark blue sedan pulled up as the right front window rolled down.

"It's nice to see you, but I'm not so sure you should have come back to Supreme Britain," George said. "Toss your things in the boot and get in."

"George!" Mike exclaimed, then guilt washed over him. "I

wish we didn't have to come, but we had no choice."

"Hurry," George said. "We need to get you off the street before someone recognizes Mike."

"What on earth are you doing here?" Mike asked, as he climbed in next to George.

"I wanted to meet your friends, so I borrowed my brother-in-law's auto and slipped out," George said. He looked behind him as Courtney entered and asked, "Is this who I think it is?"

Mike turned sideways in his seat and said, "George, meet Courtney and her parents, Danni and Court."

"I knew it, I just knew it. It's a pleasure to finally meet you folks," George said. He reached his right hand past his left shoulder and shook Courtney's hand.

"Hi, George, thank you for picking us up," Courtney said, taking his hand.

"Do they know?" George asked, looking over at Mike.

"Yep, no secrets here," Mike replied.

Still holding Courtney's hand, George said, "I've seen your picture many times. Michael has talked about you so much I feel like I know you."

"It's nice to meet you, George," Courtney replied. "Finally."

"And you, Mr. Lewis, Mrs. Lewis," George said, reaching for their hands.

Court shook his hand. "It's very nice to meet you, George."

"We need to get you back home before someone starts wondering," Mike said.

"Very true," George said, as he drove away from the curb. "Can you tell me why you are all here?"

"We had some trouble back home," Mike said, "and we needed to find a quiet place to regroup."

"I'm not sure Supreme Britain is that place," George replied. " You aren't safe here, either."

"I agree," Mike said. "Do you think they're watching Michael's place?"

"They could be, I suppose. Michael didn't even show up for work that night and they are still looking for the killer," George answered.

"Michael won't be showing up for work ever again," Mike said.

George turned off the street, went down a narrow alley, then asked, "What happened?"

"It's complicated. Let's just say he tried to kill me, but got himself killed in the process," Mike said. "I'll tell you the details another time."

"Really? You saw each other?" the janitor asked.

"Yeah and it was pretty weird. About Alec…was his uh… was his head there?" Mike had to know if his vision was memory or imagination.

"It was there all right," George said.

"Oh, good." Mike exhaled.

"They found it in the stairwell. Someone threw it clear down the hallway, then rolled it down the stairs," George explained.

Mike heard a gasp from the back seat.

"The only person I know who hated him that much was Michael," George said.

"It was the Colonel, he kicked it down the stairs," Mike said. "But first, he clubbed it down the hall with one of Alex's severed legs."

"That's horrible. How would you know that?" George asked.

"I had a vision of the whole thing," Mike answered, "like I was standing right there."

"That would certainly qualify as—let's see if I remember this correctly—something else really disgusting," Courtney said.

"Indeed, it would," Court murmured.

"If they find out, you're in grave danger," George said.

* * *

Terry had a newspaper waiting on his doorstep when he arrived at his apartment.

I don't subscribe…Courtney? What is she up to now?

Inside the folds was the prearranged slip of yellow paper, made to look like an advertisement. It was for Champion Carpet Cleaning, with a few testimonials about their workmanship. The

11

ad was designed to appear benign and anyone unaware would never notice it. Without the cipher key and reference book Courtney trained them on, it was impossible to discern the real message.

You thought it up and laid out the system while we were working together, as if you were planning for this all along, Terry thought.

Terry let himself into his apartment, closed the door, then walked to his bookshelf. Pulling down the dime store novel Courtney had them each buy, he sat in an easy chair and began to read. He read through the ad for numeric clues. *Seven…teen,* he read in the ad. That gave him the page and line to start on. He then wrote out each word he encountered in the book that had the same starting letter as each letter in the words from the ad that followed. He did it with the skip key she had them memorize: 132312.

Not to keep you dark I am from another place not here there now wish explain tried to keep all safe someday may tell more you are better not knowing unbelievable great risks wanted to go home help my people gift united Philly John Walker account see one baker hotel water fast too same servant.

Terry stopped after he reached the word seventeen again, but without the space as before. He softly wrote out United Bank of Philadelphia John Walker #C1BHWF2SS.

Terry stared at his handwriting until he had committed it all to memory. He then walked over to the kitchen sink and burned the yellow paper along with his own notes. He poked the remains into the churning disposal, then headed for the shower.

When he stepped out of the bathroom, he heard his phone ringing. Looking first at the caller ID, Terry answered, "Hey Bill, what's up?"

"Not much. I've been thinking about your offer," he said.

"Great, you want to go with me then?" *Did you get one, too?* Terry wondered.

"Yep, I'm there. I'm online looking at tickets now. Looks like we can skate out as early as tomorrow. Delta flight 3636, bounces through Philly with a four hour layover if we take Delta 5235 on to Bangor.

Philly? She did send him one, Terry told himself.

"That gives us enough time to grab a swanky sandwich in town before we go out to sea," Bill explained.

"You think that is a good route?" Terry asked, thinking, *Do you trust Courtney?*

"I thought about a few options, and I think this is the best way to go," Bill said.

No surprise there, he trusts her. This could be a setup, but what if it isn't? Terry wondered. He felt himself struggle for a moment, then said, "Perfect. There are some great hotdog stands in the airport though, Gretel."

"I wish I could play hockey like that Gretel guy," he replied.

"Hansel—you mean Wayne—oh, never mind," Terry shook his head.

"I'll get the tickets and you cover the rest?" Bill asked.

"Sure, sounds fair to me," Terry said.

"I'll text over our itinerary in a few," Bill replied.

"Thanks. See ya tomorrow." as he sat and pondered their next moves.

* * *

"We are about five blocks away now, good?" George asked, as he pulled up to the curb and shut off the car.

"Perfect. Thanks George," Courtney said.

"My brother-in-law will take you wherever you need to go from here," George offered. "What time should he pick you up and where?"

"I was thinking, how much do you think he would sell this car for?" Mike asked.

"You want to buy it?"

"Actually, I'll even give it back to him, in a month or two," Mike said.

"I'll ask him when I get back, but it won't take more than three thousand pounds to buy this old thing," George replied.

13

"Here's five thousand. Whatever deal you work out with him is fine, then keep the rest for yourself. Oh, and tell him to drop the car back here in an hour and put the key on top of the right front tire," Mike said.

"I'm sure he'll jump at the deal. The extra money will be a big help, but I really don't need it. That watch was worth a lot of money," George said.

"You found a buyer already?" Mike asked.

"I showed it to a jeweler on my block and he tried to buy it on the spot."

"Excellent," Mike said, "shop around, though."

"I will," George said and shook Mike's hand. "Good luck, to all of you."

Mike and the others got out of the car and watched as George drove off.

"OK, let's work out a plan of attack. Courtney, you should be in charge," Mike suggested.

"To get started, we need some local effects," she said.

"Great idea, they do dress a little different here," Mike replied.

"Can I have some of the local currency I saw in your wallet?" Courtney asked Mike.

"Sure, here are five twenties."

Mike watched as Courtney ran up the block to a little corner store.

"She's good at this, maybe too good," Mike said with a smile.

"I don't think that's a bad thing either," Danni said.

Courtney returned barely three minutes later with two bags.

"Here, put these on." Courtney handed each of the guys a cap. "These are football teams by the way, not soccer. Also, each of us girls will be wearing new windbreakers," she said. Courtney gave her mother a jacket that matched her father's hat.

"Hey, yours matches my hat, too," Mike pointed out with a big grin.

"Oh well, no time to return it now," Courtney replied.

"Hey, that's not nice," he said, as he felt her arm hook into his.

"Off we go," Courtney said while nodding at their arms. "It's part of our disguise."

"Oh. And to think I was starting to like you," Mike said, with a smirk that disappeared when she elbowed him in the ribs.

"Oops, sorry about that," Courtney said, as Mike watched her wink at her mother.

"Courtney, you be nice. Those brainy boys can be quite frail you know," Danni teased.

"Court, I may need some backup. They're plotting against me," Mike said.

"Roger that," Court replied.

* * *

Danni enjoyed watching Courtney and Mike interact, as the two couples strolled along in the late morning sun. She kept Court behind the pair, just out of earshot, soaking it all in. Danni spent twenty years thinking her daughter was dead, but after spending a few hours with her, that pain had faded greatly.

Leaning toward her, Court whispered, "I think they're falling for each other."

She whispered back, "You always were perceptive, dear."

"How long then?" he asked.

"The night we met him in the park, silly," she answered.

"But he didn't even know if she was married, or had kids—"

"Shh, you're going to spoil it, you big dummy." Danni held onto his arm and laid her head on his shoulder. "We have our girl back now."

* * *

Courtney looked up to see two men in plain clothes pretending not to look in their direction.

They both have guns. One's ex-military, the other slouches. Maybe a desk jockey? The soldier must go first, Courtney thought.

"That's Michael's place, the brown one with the white trim," Mike said.

"And those two are looking for him. We need to look for

an entrance in the back." Courtney instructed quietly, as she kept between Mike and the men down the block. "In case you're wondering, they aren't very good at their job."

"I see that. Remember, it wasn't two days ago that I was chased out of here by a couple of those goons. I bet they're on high alert now. Maybe we shouldn't—"

Courtney interrupted, "It's risky, but we can slip in for a quick look."

"Maybe we should come back at night?" Mike asked.

"Nope, this is perfect. Trust me, it's what I do." Courtney slowed and turned, as her parents joined them. "See anything?"

"The two men out front?" Danni asked.

"Yeah," Courtney said. "We're going to slip in through the back and get a few things from inside."

"All of us?" Court asked.

"Yep. We need someone to watch for trouble while we look around, it'll be quick and easy."

Mike said, "There's a tall wooden fence with a gate back there."

"Good observation. I didn't think you paid much attention to your surroundings," Courtney joked.

"You sure like picking on me," Mike said.

"I walked past you on the sidewalk dozens of times over the past few years. I wore wigs of every shape and color, but you never even noticed me."

"Seriously?" Mike asked, as they neared the end of the block.

"Yep."

"Well, it's a new skill I have had to hone since meeting you," Mike said.

"Hey, is that meant to be derogatory? 'Cause it isn't," she said.

"I think it's behind this next house. Stay focused," Court warned.

"Yep, that's it. You're sure you want us all to go in?" Mike asked.

"How am I supposed to keep you safe if I let you out of

my sight?" Courtney asked, as they turned and walked down the gravel of the overgrown alley.

She could feel the pressure of their situation building as they neared the fence. Courtney was far more keyed up with Mike and her parents in tow. She tried to relax, but her usual methods weren't working and she was struggling to maintain focus. The four of them were a huge target and she would need to be on her A-game if she was to keep all of them safe.

"Dad, you bring up the rear, I'll take point," she said softly and released Mike's arm. She immediately felt more alert and focused. *Mike is the distraction...*

Courtney moved the daypack to the front of her shoulder. It was an effort to hide the weapon and provide some protection from gunfire. She glanced back and saw that Court had taken off his cap and used it to conceal his gun.

"Stay alert and remember to breathe normally," Courtney whispered to Mike.

Courtney reached the gate first and carefully lifted its weight off the hinges. Moving it slowly, she made certain it did not alert anyone to their presence around back. Two garbage cans inside the fence caught her eye and she watched them carefully as she eased into the back yard. Once the other three were inside, she repeated the process to close it, then took her place in the lead. She could hear Mike's breathing over everything else and motioned at him.

"Stay here until I have the door open," Courtney said, then walked toward the steps at the back of the building. She pulled a pick set from the front pouch of her weighty backpack and had the door open in a few seconds. The other three immediately joined her inside.

"Dad, you and Mom watch back here in the kitchen. We'll sweep the house," Courtney whispered, as she locked the door behind them.

Courtney had Mike hold onto her belt as they worked their way through the rooms. When she stopped, she felt his body jerk and then freeze behind her. She turned and whispered, "Relax. Your muscles are working overtime, hence the heavy breathing."

17

She knew her tone had given away her frustration.

"Sorry," Mike mouthed.

Glancing into the first bedroom, Courtney saw it was for a young girl. *The other Courtney's room,* she thought, as an eerie familiarity crept over her. Hearing how Michael had pieced it together was strange, but seeing it was very disturbing. She began to feel sad and then memories from her past flashed by, with other images she didn't recognize. Courtney was startled when she realized she had closed her eyes and quickly opened them. She turned to see Mike looking suspiciously back at her, but said nothing. She moved on and finished checking the rest of the first level. Confident the main floor was clear of threats, she led Mike back to the kitchen. Pausing near the living room drapes, she attempted to locate both men out front, but only saw one of them.

"One's gone," she whispered to Mike.

As they walked through the kitchen doorway, Courtney saw her father watching out the rear blinds.

On a hunch she walked up beside her father and looked out the blind in the side window.

"There! Through the bushes, I saw the other one walking down the sidewalk," she hissed. "Stay here," Courtney ordered. She slipped out the door, rushed to the fence and crouched down at the trashcans by the gate.

He's almost here, Courtney thought to herself.

She could hear his feet easing into the grassy rocks, carefully working his way up to the gate. Courtney felt her well-honed senses returning.

Too careful. He suspects something. May have a weapon drawn. Righthanded. Lightweight, fast, moderate skills.

She instinctively flexed her muscles in sequence, preparing them for action, breathing slowly.

A hand reached over the gate and went straight to the latch.

Rookie mistake, dominant hand visible, no weapon drawn—now!

Courtney moved from behind the cans and grabbed his hand just as the latch released. She sidestepped the gate and yanked him through it.

He must have been standing on his toes to reach the latch on her side of the gate. Probably why he lost his balance so easily and nearly fell as he came through the gate.

With her left foot, Courtney drove his right foot behind the other. Then, she quickly shifted onto her left foot and snap kicked him in the throat with her right. Courtney expected the small man to roll around on the ground choking, but he rolled and returned to his feet.

She knew she had hit her mark from the wheezing and gurgling sounds he made as he set his stance to fight. She watched him grab his throat with his left hand and try to adjust his collapsed windpipe. This was her opportunity to strike again. Courtney feigned a left roundhouse to make him think she was a rookie, then swiftly kicked his left elbow. The agent tried to block the second strike with his knee and kept his left hand up to his throat. Lack of oxygen was taking its toll. Her foot easily slipped past his failed block, struck his left elbow and drove his left thumb deep into his damaged windpipe.

Courtney saw his expression change. *Now you know what I'm capable of.*

Falling backwards onto the ground, he rolled on his side, facing her and reached inside his jacket. He instantly fired off a round and his jacket billowed up as the gasses erupted.

Courtney had no time to react as a bullet whizzed past her, missing her by mere inches. Though muffled by his jacket, the percussion was easily loud enough to be heard out in front of the building and alert his partner. Courtney jumped into the air above his head and landed a knee into the base of his skull. Feeling his neck give way, she knew the man had expired.

She opened his jacket to see an open bottom pistol holster on a swivel. A gunslinger's holster? Are you kidding me?

Angry that she had underestimated her opponent, Courtney pulled out her silenced pistol and ran toward the house. The sound of pounding feet was getting closer as she scanned the back yard.

The building! She managed to make it past the corner of the

19

structure when she heard the footsteps of the shorthaired agent.

The younger man plowed through the gate with his weapon drawn.

"Help me please," she called out. "He's over there!"

"Don't move!" he yelled back.

Courtney slowly peeked her head out and made eye contact.

He pointed his gun in her direction, but then panned away as his gaze turned in the direction her eyes lead him to. When he had focused on the opposite side of the house, Courtney slowly exposed the barrel of her pistol and took careful aim. Seeing an easy hit, she squeezed off a round into his upper right torso to disable his shooting hand. She hadn't wanted to kill either of them, but the first man had left her no choice.

His pistol made a dull thud as it hit the grass at his feet. She watched him bend down, to pick it up, but he straightened up when their eyes met. She walked calmly, toward him with her barrel pointed at his chest as the young man stared back in disbelief.

Courtney watched the look on his face, a slight sway to his stance and realized he was considering his gun. She said, "I'm not going to kill you, unless you force me to."

"You killed him," he said.

"Correct. He shot at me, so I had to."

"That's all it takes?"

"More than enough. Look away, I just came for information," Courtney said.

"If that was all why'd you kill him?" he asked, his face tightening from pain.

"I already answered that. Look, you're in a lot of pain and you're scared. I get it, but you need to keep your mouth shut and do as you're told."

"I think you're going to kill me, no matter what."

"If I wanted you dead I would have already pumped a couple more into your chest. You know I'm telling you the truth. Stay calm and live, for your wife's sake."

The young man glanced down at his wedding ring.

"Now walk to the house. We're going inside to patch you

up."

He walked toward the door with Courtney following several paces behind. As he reached for the handle, she saw him stiffen and her finger firmed up on the trigger.

Gasping for air between every few words, he said, "You're an assassin. You'll kill me, too. After all, I've seen your face."

"No, you didn't see my face. You saw your partner fight some man in blue jeans and a gray hooded sweatshirt. When you came in through the fence, that man shot you. The knot on your head was from when he knocked you out. You woke up, staggered inside to stop the bleeding and called for help. That's the last thing you remember." Courtney hoped he would catch on. She never liked killing a good guy.

He reached for the door and said, "He was about five foot ten, medium height, medium build, in his twenties. As I—" The young man stopped and gasped for air. "Sorry. Feels like your bullet...*his* bullet, is lodged under my shoulder blade."

"Cuffs?" Courtney asked.

"Around back, on my belt," he said.

"I need you to cuff yourself, hands behind your back and then we'll go inside and stop the bleeding," she explained. Seeing he was slow to respond, she ordered, "We should hurry this along, there will be internal bleeding."

Obediently, he slipped the handcuffs from his waist with his left hand and managed to get them in place.

"Stand to the side, facing the handrail, so I can open the door," she said, as she walked up behind him. "I'm going to check you so, hold still. Two clips, a spare gun in your pants leg, a wallet and badge. Hmmm...Scotland Yard?"

He stood silent, except for the occasional grunt Courtney assumed to be from the pain.

"Hold still now, I'm going to throw this jacket over your head so you don't see my partner when we get inside. He will kill you if you see his face," she said.

"Whatever you say."

Courtney heard shame and defeat in his voice.

"Now, please keep your head down," she said.

The two of them entered through the back door.

"Walk straight and you will see the legs of chairs. Pull one out with your foot and sit down facing away from the table." She saw her father poke his head around the corner, gun drawn. Holding up a finger to her lips, Courtney continued, "Excellent. Now sit quietly while I get something to stop your bleeding." She turned on the kitchen faucet, then walked up to her father. Courtney whispered, "While I'm fixing him up, I think you should go get our car and park it around back, at the gate. We'll load up and get out of here ASAP."

He nodded.

"Give me one minute, while I get something for our guest," Courtney said, then went into the bathroom. Returning with gauze and medical tape, she walked up to the young man. "I'm going to lift your shirt now and put a bandage over the wound."

"Yes, sir," he whispered.

Yep, military, she thought, as she carefully lifted his shirt and placed the bandage. "Hold these, and get a little blood on them for me." She placed them in his cuffed hands. Courtney didn't want to leave anything behind to look suspicious to an investigator. "There isn't a whole lot of bleeding, you may make it after all."

He replied with a hoarse, "Thanks."

Courtney motioned for her father to get the car, as she retrieved a glass of water for the young agent.

"Here, take a drink," she said and lifted the jacket for him.

He drank the entire glass and asked, "You really aren't going to murder me, too?"

"Awful lot of confidence in that one glass of water," Courtney said. She placed the barrel of her gun to the side of his head and clicked the safety off.

He twitched at the metallic sound. "Wait, I shouldn't have said that."

"Now listen here, there is a big difference between killing and murder. What happened out there was killing. If you want to see a murder, then I could show you what that looks like," Courtney said.

"You're right, there's a difference. I knew him, too well. He would have killed you the first chance he got, or worse."

Courtney answered, "Thanks, but a good assassin doesn't really care either way."

* * *

Courtney was raised in war and had known killing all of her childhood. She had seen many hundreds of dead bodies by the time she was fourteen and killed her first time in college. Early on, it was one of the things about her that had most interested the DIA.

The campus was abuzz over the news that several attractive college coeds had been attacked. It was the same story each time, lone girl walking home late at night, by herself and usually drunk. At first, Courtney was worried about her own safety, then a thought struck her, *hunt the hunter.*

The third weekend of her hunt, Courtney was staggering along through a dark section of campus housing pretending to be drunk. She noticed the faint smell of alcohol and felt her senses heighten. A subtle noise in the bushes followed by a sharp pain in the back of her head and she knew she had found him.

Courtney grabbed his hand and struggled to keep from falling backwards to the ground. She shuffled her heels in the flowerbed to meet his hurried pace. Once she was able to regain her footing, she flipped over to face his back and jumped on him. She grabbed onto his ear, twisting it with all her might until he lost his grip on her hair. Courtney knew she had one chance and buried two fingers into each eye socket, using her legs to hold on. She felt his eyes squirt out into her hands, while he punched and elbowed her repeatedly. She was furious when she dropped off his back. Courtney turned back around to see him staggering, holding onto his eyes. He was screaming obscenities at her, so she stomped his right knee sideways and dropped him to the ground. As he lay there, continuing to scream obscenities, she kicked in his windpipe. As the young man lay there dying, Courtney picked him up by the hair and snarled into his ear, "That will teach you to pick on young girls you piece of—"

"Hurry, over here! I heard screaming in those bushes!" a young woman's voice screeched.

The attacker tried to slap her away from his ear but Courtney was too fast.

"Over there!" the voice screamed again.

You idiot! You're going to save this piece of trash? Courtney thought for a moment, then she realized she had no choice. With all her might, Courtney kicked him in the back of the neck and he collapsed into the dirt at her feet. She then dropped on his neck with her knees, over and over, until she felt it snap. Courtney began laughing as tears flowed down her face. "I got him! I got the rapist!" she screamed into the night.

At the police department, Courtney was interviewed by a detective, who wreaked of cigarettes and body odor.

He's not very smart, but watch out for trick questions. And think about the evidence before you answer, she reminded herself. When the stinky detective brought in an FBI agent, Courtney became concerned.

"Congratulations," the agent began, "you did what the rest of us couldn't."

"That's an odd thing to say," Courtney replied.

"You're clearly good at what you do, but I didn't think I'd need to go along with the whole college student cover," he said. "Is there a number I should call for your extraction?"

"I'm sorry, I don't know what you mean," Courtney said.

"You don't work for The Company?"

"The Company?"

"You don't know what I am talking about?" he asked.

"You must have me confused for someone else," Courtney replied.

The agent picked up his phone and pressed a few buttons. "I have one of yours down here at the police precinct, but she's denying any affiliation. Here's a picture for you," he said, holding up his phone.

Courtney waited in silence, knowing the reply, but interested to see the agent's reaction.

"Are you sure? I see. She singlehandedly beat and killed the Collegetown Rapist tonight." He sat and listened for a moment. "She's sitting here recanting the entire thing like she had planned it out. I assumed she had to be one of yours."

Courtney felt her face begin to smile, against her will. He noticed it while listening to the other end of the conversation.

Finally, he asked, "What's your major?"

Courtney thought for a moment. "You already know the answer to that, or you aren't who I think you are. Either way, I'm not answering any more questions without an attorney."

"Quite an impressive young lady. You weren't afraid at all tonight, were you?"

Courtney was prepared for the question, sooner or later. "I was afraid for my life. I was so scared I couldn't scream to call out for help. I defended myself the best I could, but was sure he was going to kill me."

The agent's face dropped and an annoyed look appeared on his face. "Not exactly a passionate delivery. You think you're pretty smart, don't you?" he said, as the phone slowly lowered from his face.

"Not necessarily, just smart enough to know better than to answer any more questions," Courtney replied.

The laughter on the phone was so loud that Courtney could hear it across the table.

The agent quickly held it up to his ear and said, "Excuse me, I am interrogating someone here."

"That's strange, I thought you were interviewing the victim of an attempted rape," Courtney countered.

The agent jerked the phone away from his ear and Courtney once again heard laughter on the other end. He quickly lowered the volume and put it back up to his head. "Yes. I see. OK. I understand. I will tell her," the angry agent said, then hung up the phone. "You're free to go. You have the full support of the DIA in this matter. Here is a phone number and a name for you to call when you have recovered," he grumbled and scribbled on the back of his card. "Here's my information, if you choose to file a complaint against me," he said, as he flipped the card over. "They'd like to hear from you sometime next week, to schedule an interview with you."

"DIA?"

"Defense Intelligence Agency," he said.

"Defense Intelligence wants to interview me?"

"Yes."

"That seems a bit odd, don't you think?"

"Yes."

Courtney was barely able to maintain her composure.

"Is there anything else I can do to help you at this time?" he asked.

"You seem quite annoyed, I wouldn't dare ask," Courtney replied.

"Anything."

"They brought me here without my purse, so I don't have any money..." she began.

The FBI agent stood up, pulled out his wallet and removed a wad of cash. "Here's a couple hundred. Anything else?"

"Uh, will you be explaining this to them, or will I need to?" Courtney asked, pointing at the one way glass on the side of the room.

"They're good with it," he replied, pointing to a nearly invisible earpiece he was wearing.

"Oh, OK. Thanks. Have a nice night then," Courtney said, stood up and walked to the door.

The full story was never released to the public, as the DIA took control of the case, and 'advised' the FBI from behind the scenes. An intelligent, athletic female, with a killer instinct and one under her belt, was a draw for the recruiters. Courtney also had a natural ability to resume normalcy right after a major trauma. It put her miles ahead of every other new recruit in the DIA. Not having a military background provided her with other advantages. Courtney didn't need to be trained how to walk, talk and act 'normal'. She was identified as a top candidate for fieldwork and taken into the fold the following year.

* * *

Courtney moved the gun away from the young Scotland Yard agent's head. "I need some extra cash, wallet please?"

He leaned over to his left and said, "It's in my right, back pocket."

Pulling out his wallet, Courtney removed the money as well as his identification card. Showing it to him she explained, "I have not read this yet and hope I won't need to. Understand?"

The agent lowered his head and nodded.

"Remember, stick to the story. I do not want you to make this a personal problem."

"I won't do anything stupid, I give you my word," he said.

"The truth will be harder to tell anyway, don't you think?"

"Yeah, that's for sure," he replied.

She only needed enough time to get out of town, at that point he wouldn't be dangerous to them. The thought of him explaining to his superiors how a young woman killed his partner then shot and captured him, made her smile. She wished she could be there if he did decide to tell the real story.

"Excellent. Now just relax while I make sure your testimony is believable," she said, holding back a smile.

"What does that mean?" he asked, turning his head slightly toward her.

Courtney gave him a sharp punch to the back of his neck and lowered his body to the floor. "You'll know soon enough."

* * *

As they drove down the road, Mike looked over at Courtney and asked, "Everything OK? You look like you're thinking about something."

"Oh, just that Michael managed to draw some serious attention to himself."

"What do you mean?" Mike asked.

"Those two were abnormally well-trained for Scotland Yard. Not exactly Special Forces, Spetsnaz, or SAS, but better than CIA, KGB or MI6," she explained.

27

Mike chuckled, "How can you tell that from a quick tussle?"

"The Russians play for keeps. Fight one of them and you'll be lucky to come out with everything intact. Joints, throat and eyes are all fair game. The Brits and Americans are far too civilized. Until they've had their butts kicked on the street a few times, they fight like technicians."

"Really?"

"The older guy had been around, he was seasoned. You don't put a top guy like that on something small time."

Mike glanced back over at her and said, "Thanks for the situational assessment." He chuckled. "I was thinking about you—you seem sad."

"It's just that, I really thought I was done with the killing. It does something to you, makes you go numb. I had just started to feel somewhat normal for the first time in my life and then that happened."

"Hey, you did what you had to. You protected all four of us. I should be the one protecting you, after all." Seeing he hadn't gotten through to her, Mike said, "We would all be in jail right now, or worse, if it wasn't for you." He reached out, took her hand in his and felt her tension drain.

Danni said, "Let your father and I handle the dirty jobs in the future, sweetie. We don't like you taking all the risks. Besides, he likes beating bad people up. It's an ego booster."

"I'm sitting right here you know," he said, as the four of them laughed.

"Pull over there, I need to dump the junk down that alley." Courtney jumped out as the car came to a stop. She was careful to handle Michael's things with her sleeves, as she stacked them on the fence.

"That should confuse the case, at least for a little while," she said and pulled her door shut.

"Eighty miles to go," Mike said.

"Then wake me in an hour," Courtney replied. She leaned over, placed her head on Mike's left shoulder and closed her eyes.

The four of them sat in silence while Mike headed out of the city. He was driving to a farm belonging to George's aunt, where they could prepare for the next leg of their journey. The only movement Courtney made the entire time was to slip her hand on top of Mike's, curling her fingers into his palm.

Mike enjoyed the quiet closeness so much, he pondered passing their destination. Squeezing her hand softly, he leaned over and touched his cheek to her head. "We're almost there," he whispered.

"Looks like we are getting close, everyone ready?" Courtney said, as she sat up, instantly alert.

"We are ready," Court replied.

"Whoa," a startled Mike said. "I thought you were all asleep."

Courtney laughed, "Sorry, it comes with the profession. How are you doing?"

"Good here," Mike said, "a little stiff, but that's it."

"Work as many muscles as you can and get some blood flowing, we may need to fight," Courtney warned.

"You're expecting trouble?" Mike asked.

"Yep. Don't know these people, the area, or if somebody talked. Too many unknowns and not enough prep, this is how amateurs operate," Courtney said.

"Sorry, I guess I'm pretty new to all of this. I felt like we were going to be in good shape from here on," Mike replied.

"No need to be sorry, but we need to be ready for anything. This whole thing could blow up on us," she replied, as Mike turned into the driveway. "I don't see any recent tracks in the driveway, so that's a good sign."

The lower level of the farmhouse was lit up and the porch light was on. As they got closer, a short, thick woman in a long, country dress stepped out onto the porch. She had a double barrel shotgun in her hands, held across her body, watching them approach.

"Yikes, granny's got a gun," Mike said.

"And combat boots." Courtney let out a soft laugh.

"You two be nice," Danni said.

Mike pulled the right side of the car up to the end of the sidewalk and cranked his window down. "Good evening, ma'am, George sent us."

Leveling her barrel right at his face, she said, "We don't like trouble out here. You running from the law?"

"We are in a bit of a bind, uh, I think we'll be moving along. Sorry for disturbing you this evening." Mike held his breath as he eased the car ahead.

Lowering the weapon, she said, "At least you're honest. Bring your things inside," then she motioned over to the barn, "then pull it into the second bay." With that, she turned and walked back into the house.

"I guess that was a test?" Mike said, as he exhaled.

"Looks like you passed. Good call," Court replied.

"I was thinking the innocent route would play best myself," Danni said, "I wonder what she would have done then?"

"She was just trying to scare us a little, show us who's boss," Courtney said.

"Well, I was just too scared to lie to that lady, that's all," Mike said, letting out a nervous chuckle.

They got out and unloaded their belongings onto the sidewalk. Mike got back in and drove the car up to the barn, with Court walking beside it. He opened the second bay, then watched Mike drive in.

"Let's go see what Annie Oakley has to say," Court said with a grin.

"You know about Annie Oakley?" Mike asked.

"Sure, she and Bill Cody were some of our earliest snipers. They did training and exhibitions across North America in the early Nineteen hundreds," Court said, as he closed the barn doors.

"Interesting. They were exhibition shooters where I am from, too. Cody was military, but I don't think she was." Mike paused in thought. "There are so many similarities between our two worlds—I suppose I shouldn't be surprised anymore, but I can't help it," he said, as they reached the girls on the front porch. He smiled at Courtney and pushed on the partially open door, stepping into the house.

"Don't stand there, come in and get that door shut," George's aunt called from the kitchen.

"Something sure smells good," Mike called back to her, as he stepped aside to let the others in.

"He's too trusting," Courtney said.

"Sweetie, that is a sign of a trustworthy person. You don't meet many like that."

"I know you're right about him, but what I don't know is if I can keep him alive like that," Courtney replied to her mother.

"Better like that than like the rest of the world," said Court.

"Uh, I'm standing right here, in case you would like to talk to me," Mike said.

"The upstairs is all yours, so get your things put away. And hurry it up, dinner will be ready in fifteen minutes," George's aunt ordered.

"Yes, ma'am," Mike called back.

"Call me Aunt Margie, would ya?"

"Yes, ma'am—I mean Margie," Mike answered. "Let's hurry it up," he said, smiling.

Courtney looked at her parents as if to plead her case, sighed and rolled her eyes.

"Did you two see that?" Mike asked.

"How could I miss my thirty three year old daughter acting thirteen all over again?" Danni replied. "You didn't forget that attitude, did you?"

Court shook his head, "No, I guess not."

"You lead the way, you're the only one who appears to feel right at home," Courtney said.

"Roger that," Mike said and walked up the stairs.

Mike heard Danni say, "Get moving soldier," and turned to see Court leading the other two up the stairwell.

They took turns looking in the doors of the three bedrooms. Courtney said, "You two should take this big room here, on the left, by the bathroom. I'll take this room across the hall from you. That leaves Mike in the first room, on the right. Sound good?"

"She already sorted that out in ten seconds, huh?" Court asked.

"More like five, she's already washing up," Mike said, nodding toward Courtney entering the bathroom. "Isn't she amazing?"

"Oh, she's amazing alright," Court said and walked into his

31

room. "Reminds me of her mother."

* * *

They had been upstairs less than ten minutes when Courtney heard, "Hurry it up! Dinner's gittin' cold!"

Courtney stepped out of her room to see Mike skipping down the stairs. Court and Danni walked into the hall as she was pulling her door shut.

"Something sure smells good, "Court said.

"Evidently Mike thought so, too," Courtney said with a chuckle. When she reached the bottom of the stairs, she could hear Margie and Mike talking in the dining room.

"Ah, now that the rest of you have finally arrived, we need to go over the house rules. There will be breakfast at seven—sharp—and lunch is served promptly at noon."

"Yes, ma'am," Mike said.

Courtney watched her cut a look at Mike.

"I mean, Aunt Margie."

"I expect each of you to do your fair share of the chores as well," she continued.

"We are more than happy to, Aunt Margie, after all you're doing for us," Danni said.

Courtney could see that Mike was soaking it all in. One of the things Courtney found endearing was his attentive and carefree nature.

Courtney felt herself losing focus. Her vision began to blur and she took a deep breath to counter the feeling. Guilt washed over her.

That was mean. Micah would be so sad if she knew you were thinking about Daddy that way. Wait, who's Micah? Courtney thought, as she tried to shake off the dreamy trance.

Her thoughts were interrupted by Margie's comment, "What? You're not married?"

"No, but I'm in the first room on the right and she has the second." Then Mike added, "We only met a few days ago."

George's aunt looked over at Courtney, so she nodded in

agreement.

Margie then announced, "All right, but I have my eye on the both of you, so don't get any funny ideas."

Courtney noticed Court's shoulders were shaking and his head bowed low.

"What's wrong with him?" Margie demanded.

"Court?" Danni leaned forward to see his face.

Taking a deep breath, a teary eyed Court looked up, "We're married, anything I should know?" he asked, struggling to maintain his composure.

Aunt Margie nodded toward Courtney. "Looks like you managed to figure that out for yourself, at least once anyway."

Court broke out in laughter, then one by one the others joined in. *Wow, even Margie laughed.*

"So, how long have you been here?" Mike asked.

Courtney liked that he was talkative and engaging the others, since it gave her time to think. But as soon as she started to think, Courtney fell into a dream like state and watched as memories flashed by.

Wake up Courtney. You're asleep, she told herself, trying to fight off the mesmerizing dreams. Regaining her concentration once more, she thought, *those aren't dreams, they must be memories from the other Courtneys.* The sound of chairs sliding on the floor caused her eyes to focus. She saw an empty plate in front of her, then looked up to see the other two women walking into the kitchen. The men got up and shuttled the dishes and pots until the table was cleared, but Courtney didn't move. *Why aren't they saying anything to me? It's almost as if they don't even know I'm here...*

Courtney heard their hostess order everyone out of her kitchen and up to bed.

"Breakfast is at seven, not a minute later," Aunt Margie reminded them. "Now get some rest."

"Thank you for dinner, it was wonderful," Mike said.

What was so wonderful? What did we eat? What did we talk about? Courtney was dazed and confused as she followed the others up the stairs.

33

After getting her things out for her shower, Courtney walked out, then turned back and tapped on Mike's ajar door. She found him lying across his bed, shoes still on his feet, sound asleep.

That was fast. How? Courtney shook herself alert once more, then took off his shoes and pulled the blanket over him as best she could.

"Goodnight," she said and kissed him on the cheek.

"Nite, beautiful," he mumbled.

* * *

"George, there's someone here to see you. George, wake up."

"How long…wait, what's going on? Why won't you let me sleep?" George asked.

"It's the police," she whispered.

George launched out of bed and yanked on his clothes.

"Maybe they know something about Michael," he said.

"Or maybe you do," came a voice from the other room.

"Wow, you startled me. Sorry, I didn't know anyone was in here," George said, as he looked into the living room.

The man said, "I can see that."

"Oh, let me get a shirt on," George said and stepped back into his room. Grabbing a shirt, he yanked it on and walked out into the living room. "What can I do for you?"

"We have some problems and you're one of the only people who knew the source of these problems," he answered.

"Michael?" George asked.

"Son, I want to give you a chance to come clean," the investigator said. "You seem like a nice guy. Your wife is pregnant and they're making you the head janitor at work. That is, if you don't go to jail for helping a fugitive." He watched George closely.

George felt his stomach drop and his face go red. He wondered, *does he know about Mike?*

"I can see you know something."

"Sir, I don't want to go to jail. If this is about Michael, I haven't seen him for two days. I heard he was dead."

"That's funny, your brother-in-law said you talked to him

yesterday. He also said you talked him into selling Michael a car."

"Sir, you have it all wrong. Michael's half-brother called me yesterday and asked about Michael. I told him I was under house arrest and didn't tell him much more. He asked me if Alec's head was cut off and gave me the feeling he knew something."

"Yeah, the rumors are already out," the agent said. He looked down at some papers in his hand and said, "I have the transcript from your conversation here."

George felt the blood drain from his face.

"You should have called us," the detective said.

"Sir, there were some people watching Michael. At least, that's what he thought. Michael told me that if anything should ever happen to him I was to stay away. I don't know anything, really, I don't. Just ask and I'll answer any question you have. Please help protect my family. I'm afraid those people who were after Michael's invention could be the ones who killed Alec."

"We were watching Michael," the policeman said. "So, tell me what you know about the invention."

"Uh, sure. It has wires that run from a box to a circle of crystals and hums a little. I saw it once, but Michael quickly covered it up when he saw me walking down into his basement."

"Once?"

"Yes, sir. He told me never to go down there again," George said.

"But you drove him to and from work for over a year."

"I didn't go inside after that. I waited outside." George felt his eyes tearing up.

"Nothing else to say?" The man asked.

"No, sir. Nothing that I can think of." George hoped it would be enough.

"How about the brother's name and where can I find him?" the detective asked.

"I only know him by Ike, sir."

"Ike? Interesting…"

"Yes, Ike. They were raised worlds apart and only met once or twice." George felt the stress begin to subside as he transitioned into the truth.

The man stood still, staring at George. After what seemed like minutes, he walked up to George and slapped him on the shoulder. "Congratulations on your promotion, George, but act surprised when you get to work. That's a big deal, a step up in class and double the pay. You might be my boss someday if you keep making leaps like this."

"Thank you, sir. I was in the right place at the right time," George said.

"You were dangerously close to a bad outcome there for a minute," the man said, as he looked George square in the face.

"I know it, sir. It could have been terrible if I had been in that hallway the other night." The thought sickened George.

Laughing, the man said, "That's true, but not exactly what I meant. You'll call me at this number if anything else comes up, won't you?" He handed George his card.

"Absolutely, sir, but I sure hope you figure this out before someone else gets killed," George said.

"Yeah, we lost a man over at Michael's place yesterday. Some kind of pro, got one of our best agents and knocked another out cold," he said, staring into George's eyes again.

"Oh, no. Won't you please post a guard here? What if they're coming for me, too? Maybe they think I know something," George said worriedly.

"George, calm down. You're moving up one class, not three. Keep a butcher knife by the bed and you'll be fine. Enjoy going back to work tonight," he said as he opened the front door and let himself out.

George's wife grabbed hold of his arm.

"Please, could you stop yanking on that arm," George teased.

"You think this is funny or something?" she whispered.

"No, I'm just relieved I guess."

"Is it true? What he said, is it true?" she asked.

"I guess so. I'll find out tonight I suppose."

"You don't look so scared now. What are you up to?" she asked.

"Oh, you mean that little show I put on for the detective?" George smiled.

"Show?"

"Yeah, to get him out of here. Michael's dead and I don't know anything about it, but I had to convince him of that."

"George, I'm worried," she said, "you don't seem like yourself."

"I'm fine. Now you sit down, relax and forget about the whole thing."

"But I'm not sure I can."

"You have to. Look, I'm exhausted. Wake me around seven, okay?"

"I suppose so."

"Thanks. Now don't forget, seven," George said, as he gave her a kiss.

* * *

"Morning there, big guy!" Terry called out, as the cab rolled to a stop. He watched with a smile as Bill ambled down the sidewalk, with a large duffel bag slung over his shoulder.

"You sure you're all right with me tagging along?" Bill asked, lowering himself into the cab.

"Wouldn't have it any other way," Terry said, handing Bill a notebook.

Bill gave a crooked looking smile through the bruises on his face.

"That looks like it hurts," Terry said.

"And that's not the worst of it. I almost stayed in bed this morning until I remembered those little pills they give us," Bill said as he closed the door.

"Those are only for emergencies—last resort—not everyday injuries."

"I know. Cost something like a grand a pop they say, but I can't feel a thing now so they're worth it."

"I believe they're still experimental," Terry said.

"I didn't know they had made it that far," Bill said, chuckled, then reached up to hold his side.

Motioning for him to open the notebook, Terry began

37

telling a story about a fishing trip. Bill read, occasionally asking a question to go along with Terry's act.

"I found the perfect place for a Philly sandwich, but after that we'll be eating peanut butter and jelly." Pointing to the notebook, Terry asked, "What do you think?"

Bill replied, "Sounds good to me. Besides, I'm used to following you around and I haven't died yet."

The two chatted about sports all the way to the airport, passing the notebook back and forth, while the cabby drove. When they arrived, Terry took the notebook back and tucked it in his carry-on. They kept their conversations benign since they were likely being monitored via cameras by their DIA brothers. Terry knew Bill wanted to talk about the notes from Courtney, but was pleased he kept quiet.

They put their phones in the trunk, then got into the rental car. Terry said, "We'll go inside the restaurant and get a seat in the back. Once we're sure we aren't being followed, we'll slip out the back."

"You think they're still watching us?" Bill asked.

"They could be. If so, we're in a bigger mess than I thought," Terry replied.

"I think we'll be fine, as long as we do as we're told."

"I hope you're right," Terry said, then paused. "The bank is about five blocks from here, so we can get there and back without being missed. We'll wear caps and sunglasses to make it tough for the NSA's facial recognition program to spot us."

"Sounds good."

"So, you're in?"

"Absolutely, but why should both of us go to the bank?" Bill asked.

"For backup, but it's not necessary," Terry replied.

"Shouldn't one of us stay here and order some food? Hold down the fort, so to speak?"

"Probably wouldn't be a bad idea," Terry replied.

"Good, I'll stay behind. Besides, if something went wrong, I'd only slow you down."

"You have a point," Terry said. "You're becoming quite the

spook."

"These past few months, Courtney's been drilling me more than ever. That girl sees angles I never even thought of."

"I'm still not sure what I think about all of this. She lies to us for years, nearly kills us both, but she's also trying to help us?" Terry said.

"She kept us in the dark to keep us safe?" Bill suggested.

"I suppose it's possible," Terry replied. "You're sure you'll be OK if I go to the bank alone?" Terry asked, as he pulled up to the curb.

"If I can't trust you by now, then who can I trust? Besides, I'm starving and will go cannibal on you if I don't get some food ASAP."

"Have it your way then," Terry jumped out of the car and went around to the sidewalk.

As the door was closing behind them, Terry caught sight of two men in sunglasses driving past.

"Looks like your reputation precedes us," he said.

"Seriously?" Bill asked.

"Yup. Great call on separating to keep the smoke screen going."

"Wish I was wrong," Bill murmured, as they walked up to the door.

"I'm heading straight out the back. See you in one hour, tops," Terry said, as he slipped past Bill and made his way through the restaurant.

* * *

Micah? Is she real? How could she know how to work the spud? Mike wondered, as he lay in bed. *Is it even possible? Theoretically, sure, but... if I adjust the synchronization of the fields, like she said, I'll know.*

"Morning all! Rise and shine!" Margie's voice called up the stairs.

Mike climbed out of bed and was getting dressed when he heard footsteps in the hallway.

"Mike, are you awake?" Courtney asked, as she tapped on the door.

"Yep, be right out."

"OK, I'll wait."

Mike quickly finished and opened his door. "Morning. Let me wash up really quick," he said as he walked past her.

"If you make us late, Aunt Margie won't be happy," she said.

"I heard that," Danni said.

Mike looked up as he ran water over his hands and saw Courtney had jumped slightly.

"That wasn't funny," Courtney said, then began to smile.

"Just keeping you on your toes, dear."

"You're like a pair of teenagers," Mike said, chuckled, then turned and splashed water on his face.

Within minutes, the four of them were seated at the table as Margie instructed them where to sit.

"I need to know what you've gotten me into," Margie began. "George said you needed the workshop for some project. Nothing too dangerous I hope?"

"No, mostly some small electrical stuff, the workshop in the barn is all I need for now." Mike didn't want to lie to her, but he was fairly certain that he could use the sword's power supply to run the spud.

"Good enough, that works for me," Aunt Margie said.

"I'll take my breakfast out there and eat while I work, if you don't mind," Mike said.

"I suppose I could make an exception this once, but don't make a habit of it," Margie said.

Mike excused himself, went out to the workshop and left Courtney behind with her parents.

* * *

Mike heard the workshop door open. He looked up from the bench and saw Courtney carrying a sandwich and glass of milk.

"Wow, you smell nice," he said.

"Wow, you smell awful," Courtney replied with a grin.

"Wait a minute. You can't repeat things you heard while spying on me. It's an unfair advantage, and I'm fairly sure it's unethical."

"I'm not sure what you mean. I was merely pointing out that you have been in here for hours, sweating over your project. Just stating the facts, sir," she replied.

Mike reached around her with his sweaty arm and pulled her in closer.

"Okay, now you're doing that on purpose," she wrinkled up her nose as he kissed her.

"Now get back in the house before I completely lose my train of thought," he said.

"You haven't already? Guess I'm losing my touch." She turned and walked toward the door.

Mike couldn't help but noticing how gracefully she moved.

"Are you staring at me, sir?" she asked without turning around.

"Yes, ma'am," Mike said and looked back down at the bench.

Take deep breaths and keep your mouth shut. She doesn't want a drooling schoolboy, he thought, as he heard the door click shut.

* * *

Terry stayed on the back streets until he reached the block the bank was on. He used the storefront glass to help increase his field of view, as he made his way. He paused a few buildings before the bank and pretended to look at a display in the store to scan his surroundings. Convinced he was clear, Terry continued, timing his cadence to match a pedestrian in front of him. At the bank entrance, he turned to approach the door and checked for a tail one last time. Still clear, Terry walked inside and took a seat in the waiting area.

Relax, no one was following you, Terry told himself. He then began to mentally rehearse his conversation with the man seated at the desk. When it was finally his turn, the man motioned for Terry to approach.

Terry said, "Safe deposit box for John Walker."

"Certainly, sir. Can I see some ID please?" he asked.

"I have a passcode on it, not identification. Check the notes," he said, still standing.

"That would be highly unusual, sir, and not very secure. You should consider—"

Terry cut him off, "Can I see your manager please?" Terry knew Courtney wouldn't have given them a name they didn't have ID for. Then a thought crossed his mind. *What if this is a setup? One more 'gotcha'?* He felt a growing uneasiness while he watched the man make a call.

"I need an escort to the viewing room please," he said, then looked up at Terry. "Go ahead and take a seat in the waiting area. Someone will be with you shortly."

"Thanks," Terry said, then walked back to his chair to wait for the escort.

Terry was only in his seat for a moment when he saw the man at the desk nod in his direction. When he turned and saw the man walking up he felt himself stop breathing. *Six foot four, two fifty plus, probably been a street fighter since birth. Why did I let you talk me into coming alone?*

Terry was ready to make a run for the door when the guard asked, "Deposit box viewing room, sir?"

"Yes, please," was all he got out before he felt his voice nearly waiver.

"Follow me please," the big man said, as he lead Terry past the desk and to a door on the back wall. Pushing and holding it open with one hand, the guard said, "In and to your left."

Terry obediently walked through, feeling himself tense up as he passed.

"Step into the scanner please." The man pointed to a machine on the right side of the hallway.

"I have personal items I need to put aside before I step in there. Do you have a locker for me?"

"Personal items?" the man asked, as he stepped back to watch.

"Yes, personal. Trust me, you don't want to ask any more questions. I'm not hiding anything, just not showing, that's all."

"Lift your arms and lock your fingers behind your head. I'll take them out myself. You need to stand very still while I do," he instructed Terry.

Get ready for it…

"Standard issue Glock, under my left. Safety on, chamber empty, seventeen in the clip," Terry said, trying to sound like a cop.

"Thanks, already made you for a fed. Am I right?" he asked, as he removed Terry's gun.

"You're pretty good. You aren't looking for work, are you?" Terry asked.

"You don't need someone like me."

"I wouldn't be so sure," Terry replied, "you seem to have some valuable skills."

"Yeah, but your people don't like felons much," the man laughed, showing two gold teeth.

"We can work around those things. You have a number?"

"Sure." The man pulled out a card and handed it to Terry.

"Samuel J. Rodman, Tire Iron Security." Terry laughed. "Subtle, Samuel, I'll give you that."

"Freelance stuff," he explained, "I don't take the Hollywood bodyguard gigs."

"You're exactly the kind of help I need from time to time," Terry said. He pocketed the card, then walked through the scanner.

"Let me know when I can be of service. Now, stand over there and they'll buzz you in when they're ready," the guard said. He walked back toward the far wall and took his post near the outer door.

"I'll do that. Thanks, Samuel."

Within moments, Terry heard a voice over the intercom say, "Come on through."

Terry opened the door and walked into the outer chamber of the deposit box safe.

"Enter your passcode please," the lady behind the bulletproof glass instructed.

Terry typed C1BHWF2SS and the lady immediately disappeared from the window. He stood and waited several

43

uncomfortable moments for the hulk of a guard to come tearing into the room. Terry relaxed when the lady returned to the window and slid a security drawer out toward him.

So, it is real after all…

Taking the drawer, Terry walked over to a booth and drew the curtain behind himself. Looking at its face, Terry saw a small, reddish, biometric scanner. He placed his thumb on it and jumped slightly when the latch popped.

Pop, goes the weasel, he thought to himself and chuckled.

Inside were two thick, unmarked and sealed envelopes. Terry looked at them for a moment and then tucked them inside the front of his jacket, zipping it part way.

Terry walked back out to the clerk and said, "Thanks, I'm finished." Then he walked toward the buzzing door.

"Mind if I take you out the rear entrance? I can give you back your heater once we are outside the secured area."

"Not a problem," Terry said, happy to use the much quieter alley.

Terry returned to the back entrance, locked his fingers and stood still. The guard held his nearest arm and replaced the pistol with his free hand.

"Thanks, Samuel," Terry said, as he stepped out the door, a wave of relief washed over him.

"No sweat, G-man."

That is exactly the reason we use Bill for these things, Terry thought to himself.

When he reached the back of the restaurant, he glanced at his watch. It was just over twenty five minutes from the time he left.

"Hey there, you all good?" Bill asked, looking past him for any sign of trouble.

"Yep. Let's roll," Terry said.

"Excellent. You eat while I drive," Bill said, handing Terry a white paper bag.

As Bill drove them back to the airport, Terry opened the envelopes one at a time. "Looks like ten grand a piece and a love note for each of us."

Bill smiled, "That girl has been planning this for a while."

"You aren't just now figuring that out, I hope."

"Yeah, yeah," Bill said, looking in the rearview mirror.

"It just keeps getting stranger though. Listen to this, I hope that neither of you were injured in my escape. I did my best to keep you safe, but even the best plans get screwed up when the game is underway. I will explain someday, if I can find a way back there. Best wishes, Courtney. Can you believe that?" Terry asked.

"She almost got us all killed and thinks it was a game?" Bill said.

"How about the fact that she would have killed both of us to win it?" Terry replied and laughed when he saw the annoyed look on Bill's face.

"Man, you are one twisted pair of sisters," Bill said, shaking his head in disbelief.

Terry laughed even louder.

"Uh, don't look now but our tail has returned," Bill said, without moving his lips or body to arouse suspicion. "Good thing we tossed our phones in the trunk, big brother was listening."

"Yeah, we better pull over for a pit stop and see if they want to dance."

"Roger that," Bill said as he turned on his turn signal. "That's odd, they're not exiting with us. Looks like we might be fine after all."

* * *

It was dinnertime when Mike finally looked up and relaxed.

"Now to see if you power up," he said, switching on the sword's power unit.

A sphere of fog engulfed him. Off to his left side he could see a wall of haze, like they were now accustomed to. To his right was a wavy pattern he had never seen before, like ripples on water. Mike rotated the spud and the two patterns moved with it.

* * *

"Shh! Listen. Is that a chopper?" Courtney asked.

45

"Whatever it is, it's big," Court replied.

Jumping up, they peeked out three different windows. Courtney motioned to her parents.

"Uh, come over here, you need to see this…" Courtney mumbled slowly.

They were looking at two bubbles of fog that appeared to be stuck to adjacent sides of the barn walls.

"Mike!" Courtney exclaimed, then scrambled out the door to the barn. When she was within reach, she realized she couldn't go in without entering the edge of a hazy sphere protruding through the building. Stepping several feet to the side of the door, she banged on the barn wall.

"Mike! Are you okay in there? Hello?" Courtney pounded and shouted with all her might, but he didn't respond.

The deep, pulsing hum continued to reverberate and she felt herself begin to worry. Infuriated by the feeling of helplessness, Courtney headed straight for the front door. She reached through the fogginess and felt a strong tingling sensation. She gasped as she watched her hand pass through the door handle.

Everything went eerily silent and Courtney realized she was standing outside. It was nighttime and she was holding onto the shop door handle. The only sound she could hear was crickets chirping all around her. Turning around, she looked back at the house and noticed the lights were off. Courtney made her way back to the house and let herself inside. She walked up the stairs as quietly as possible and eased open the first door on the right.

Mike was sound asleep.

She then went to the end of the hall and opened her parent's door. "Dad, you asleep?" she whispered.

"Not now, what's up?" he asked.

"How long have we been here?"

"Two days. Why? Is something wrong?"

Courtney heard herself gasp.

Court jumped out of bed, grabbing for his gun. "What's wrong?" he asked.

"Something happened out at the barn," she replied.

"Something?"

"We need to talk. Sorry, I know it's late," Courtney answered.

"It's fine, but let's talk in your room so your mother can sleep," Court said.

"You two think someone could sleep through that?" Danni asked.

Flipping the light on, Court turned around to see his wife with a gun in her hand and eyes squinting.

"Hey! Put that thing away," he said with a nervous laugh.

Mike's door opened. "Everyone all right?" he asked. "Courtney, is that you?" He sounded surprised to see her.

"Yes, but why are you surprised to see me?" she asked him.

"Don't know, sleepy I guess," Mike stuttered.

"We were all right, until a few minutes ago," Court chuckled.

"What's going on up there?" Aunt Margie called up the stairs.

"Sorry to wake you, too, Margie. I had a weird dream and it seems I woke everyone," Courtney answered.

"Come down here so I can hear what all the commotion is about," she said and turned on the stairwell lights.

They all filed down the stairs, like children in trouble. Margie was sitting in her favorite chair with her shotgun propped up against the wall.

"Boy's got something stuck in his gut. What happened to you? You caught tumors or something?" she asked.

Mike laughed and said, "Hey, I worked hard to get these abs. They call it a washboard."

"I call it repulsive. Get a shirt on already," she demanded.

Mike spun around and trotted upstairs.

"Phew! I thought I might make a pass at that boy there for a minute," Margie exclaimed after he left.

Court and Danni burst out laughing and Courtney smiled. Seconds later, they heard Mikes footsteps on the stairs.

"What did I miss?" he asked, as he walked into view.

"Nothing you need to hear, Tumors," Margie answered. "Tell me about this dream, they can be very important you know," she said.

"It started yesterday at dinnertime, about twenty hours after we got here," Courtney said.

47

"You've been here over two days now," Margie corrected.

"Perfect. That makes it even better." Courtney went on, "Let me back up. I only remember the first night and the next day, up to the middle of the afternoon."

"She's right, we've been here two days," Danni said.

"The first afternoon I saw these huge fog bubbles on the sides of the barn. I ran out to check on Mike, but when I reached through the bubble to grab the door handle, everything went crazy. The next thing I knew, I was standing out in the dark. That was a few minutes ago."

Courtney watched as the four of them glanced around at each other.

"What is going on here?" Courtney asked cautiously. "Why do you have such suspicious looks on your faces?"

"Not sure about them, but I guess I don't remember you being around since yesterday afternoon. What about the rest of you?" Court asked.

"I don't remember her being around either. Do you, Margie?" Danni asked.

Margie shook her head. "She didn't eat dinner with us tonight either. I would remember. Go count the plates in the drying rack if you don't believe me."

"I remember you bringing me lunch that first day and we talked a little," Mike said.

"Yeah, I remember. That was yesterday, right?" Courtney asked.

Mike answered, "No, that was the day before yesterday."

"She wasn't around, but I never noticed she was missing?" Danni asked. "How can that be?"

"Something happened when I was testing and tuning the spud that has confused you," Mike suggested. "The fields it creates and amplifies could disorient anyone around it."

"Yeah, I heard a funny noise and went out to check on you," she said, "but that doesn't account for the missing day."

"No wonder the authorities are after you, you have a brain muddler. They'd kill us all to get their hands on that," Margie said with a chuckle.

"In the wrong hands, it could do a lot of harm," Mike said.

"Oh, don't you know it," she said and they laughed together. "Alright, that's enough excitement for this old bird. I'm going back to bed now." She reached for her shotgun and headed back to her room. "Nite."

"Goodnight," Court said. "Let's get back to bed."

"See you kids in the morning." Danni said, taking Court's hand while walking up the stairs.

Mike looked over at Courtney and patted the couch beside him. She got up, walked over and sat down next to him.

"I'm confused, Mike. I feel like something very bad almost happened to me, to us."

"You'll be all right, you just need some sleep."

"No one is taking this seriously?" she asked.

Mike said, "No, but we're exhausted and no harm was done."

"I feel like there is something you aren't telling me."

"There's nothing important you don't know," Mike said. "Promise me you won't go poking around in dangerous energy fields anymore?"

She punched him in the arm. "How about you promise not to make them? Then I won't get zapped trying to save you."

"Sorry, I'll do my best. I know you're upset with me, but I didn't mean to put anyone at risk, especially you," Mike replied.

Putting his arm around her shoulders, Mike pulled her up against him. He leaned back so she could lay her head on his chest. Courtney wrapped her arms around him and they sat in silence.

There is something you're holding back and I will find out eventually, Courtney thought to herself as she dozed off.

* * *

It was a warm, calm night out on the water and the small waves lapped at the hull of Terry's boat. The second leg of their journey had been uneventful and they had made it out just before sundown. Terry was elated to get out on the water for their much needed R&R.

"This view is amazing! It's no wonder you keep coming back," Bill called out, from the top of the cabin.

"Yeah, I've been doing it for half of my life," Terry said. "You can really unwind out here, with no one around for miles."

"I get it now."

"I'm gonna call it a night," Terry said, as he headed down into the cabin. "I'll wake you before sunrise so we can get our lines in the water."

"I'll come down in a bit."

"Bring that blanket and pillow down with you. They came off your bed," Terry called up from below.

"Roger that."

* * *

Terry gasped awake. *Three long taps and there it is again! Three long, three short, three long—S O S—Bill!*

Terry quickly slipped out of his bed, reaching under the pillow for his pistol. His heart was pounding, but he was able to calm himself as he struggled to see Bill's bunk in the dark. He reached under his bed and pulled out a small gun safe. Careful to keep his Beretta pointed at the door, Terry blindly worked the combination. He was glad his habit was to set the four discs to zero after each use. Once opened, he pulled out the silenced .22 caliber semi-auto Sig Sauer and a night vision monocle.

No more taps. *He's either dead, or they're too close now.*

Terry felt the big cabin cruiser nudge so slightly that most people wouldn't noticed, especially in their sleep.

We have company.

Terry forced his heart rate down even further and crouched behind the foot of the bed. He slipped the monocle strap over his head, placing the scope in front of his right eye and closing the left. If the intruder were to use a flashbang, or fire his weapon, it would blind one eye, but not both.

Breathe. Breathe. This is a pro, there won't be a second chance, he told himself.

Terry watched the handle on the door at the top of the stairs.

The handle moved slowly and he trained his weapon right at the door jamb where he expected a head to appear. Three soft taps sounded on the door. Terry wanted to call out to Bill but he remained quiet.

The door eased open and Bill's head poked through at ground level. "It's me," he whispered.

Bill slipped in and closed the door, then retrieved the sidearm from his bunk.

"There's a slick about a hundred yards out, two on board, all blacked out," he whispered. He smoothly chambered a round, then stuffed the spare clip into his back pocket. "Had to wait until they came around far enough that the door was out of sight. Sorry."

"No, you did good. I got your S.O.S."

"Looked like one of them was getting ready to swim," Bill said.

"Right. One slips aboard to kill us, while the other has his six."

"Or the swimmer sticks a bomb on our hull and they detonate it when he's clear," Bill suggested.

Terry winced. "Now why did you have to go and do that?"

"What did I do?" Bill whispered back.

"Made me feel stupid, again," Terry teased.

"I've been paying attention," Bill said.

"If he comes on board, I'll pop him with my quiet, little Sig. Then we go after his partner and clean up."

"Ten four. What if there's a bomb?"

"I'll go after it while you break out the flare gun and rifle from the chest at the helm. The code is sixteen thirty seven," Terry said. "Now tuck in behind your bunk and relax."

"I'll have my own private turkey shoot."

They both chuckled softly, then waited in silence for their visitors.

These guys are patient or they have already planted a bomb and we are as good as dead, Terry thought to himself. One more minute and then I'm going swimming.

Terry was ready to head up top, when the door handle started to move again. The door opened several inches, but no one was visible. Terry continued to sit without breathing and watched through the night vision. Finally, Terry had to breathe. As he did, a black face with night vision goggles peered around the corner of the doorjamb. Terry fired three shots, the first striking the goggles and the other two struck just under the chin.

"Direct hits," Terry whispered, "Hold tight while I check."

Terry crawled up the stairs and placed his barrel to the man's head as he carefully turned it. An earpiece, Mil-spec even. *These guys are pros,* Terry thought. He slipped it into his own ear and heard a man breathing on the other end.

"Status!" the voice demanded.

"Done," Terry said, feeling himself tense up for the response.

"Roger that. Now hurry back or they're going to think these idiots got us instead," the voice said.

Terry switched off the com and said, "Let's search him." He pulled the body over to Bill.

Bill pulled out a small, Chinese military spec explosive, a knife and a small pistol.

Terry's heart sank. "It's a bomb, so they're expecting a show tonight."

"No detonator," Bill said.

"Strip him, I'm going for a swim."

"But—"

Terry interrupted, "You're too big for this suit. Here, put on the monocle, I have his now."

"Wow, that's better," Bill said, as he put the night vision in front of his eye.

"Stuff him back there, behind the beds. I need the floor to get into this," Terry said.

Bill grabbed the corpse by the feet and yanked it out of the way.

"Tie the bomb to the life ring and when I hit the water, toss it out to the end of the rope," Terry instructed.

"Why not sink it?"

"We need to pull it back in so we can blow the boat, once I have the detonator," Terry answered.

"Seriously?"

"What if there are people watching these guys? Maybe they came out in a bigger boat. We have no choice, so let's get it done."

"Roger that."

"OK, I'm turning the earpiece back on, in three, two…" Terry said, then switched the com on.

Terry headed up the stairs, stepped out the back of the boat. He found a set of flippers, right where the intruder had left them. He slipped them on then turned to see Bill looking at him with the ring in his hands.

Thumbs up, here we go, Terry told himself as he dropped into the water. He heard a thud as he started to kick. *Bill did his job, now it's your turn again.*

Terry looked in the direction of the boat and waved, then he pointed at his head.

"I see you. Com trouble again?" the man's voice asked.

Terry raised his thumb as he swam, then put two fingers in the air, continuing to approach the rubber raft.

"Confirming, two done?" Terry heard him ask.

Terry put his face into the water and spoke so his voice would distort.

"Confirmed, two done, package in place," Terry said. He hoped the man wouldn't blow the charge until he was safely in their boat.

Terry swam the last fifty feet with his legs and eased his pistol from the knife belt around his waist. When he reached the side of the dingy, the man reached down and grabbed Terry's left arm. Terry kicked with all his might, thrust his body out of the water and came face to face with the man. He placed the pistol to the man's left temple and squeezed off a round. It was over before the would be killer had a chance to flinch. His grip on Terry relaxed and he fell into the bottom of the raft, letting Terry slip back under the water. With a hard kick, Terry launched himself into the raft. He checked the man's jugular, then he searched his body and the raft. Finding no detonator, Terry started the small motor and headed for Bill. He cruised toward the boat, wishing he didn't need to blow it up. When he got close, he shut the motor off and coasted in.

"Man, you did that like a pro!" Bill exclaimed when he returned.

"You thought I wasn't?" Terry asked.

Bill said, "You are getting old—"

"Yeah, yeah."

"So, what now?" Bill asked.

"Strip this one and suit up," Terry answered. "I wanna know who's pulling the strings."

"Seriously?" Bill asked as he helped Terry get the body on the boat.

"Yep and hurry up. I can almost guarantee there will be someone waiting on shore for these two," Terry said.

"How can you know that?" Bill asked, as he tore the suit off the body.

"No detonator on either of them. Someone else wants to do the honors," he answered.

"Great, another round tonight?" Bill asked.

"At least one more. Now get the necessities and jump in. One change of clothes apiece and the envelopes from Courtney, that's it."

"Roger," Bill said.

"I need to turn this thing back on, so don't say anything," Terry said, as Bill disappeared into the cabin.

Bill was ready in less than two minutes and when he started to climb over the side Terry switched the com back off. "You left our wallets, phones and credit cards, right?"

"Come on, I just got that stupid phone last month," Bill said.

"Yeah, yeah, and you were already looking for a new one. Pull in the ring and toss the bomb down there too."

"Are you sure about this?" Bill asked.

"I've already bet my boat on it, now pull in that line."

Bill disappeared back inside the boat. A minute later, he appeared with one backpack and joined Terry in the rubber raft.

"His goggles and com," Terry said as he reached out and placed his hand on his pride and joy for one last time. "She's insured, but it's still gonna hurt."

"Sorry buddy," Bill replied, as Terry fired off the outboard.

"Thanks. No more talking." In his best imitation of the second man's voice, Terry said, "Two asleep. Package delivered."

"Roger that," came a voice on the other end. "See you in a few minutes."

Terry could tell by the expression on his face that Bill had heard the reply. Pleased he was right, Terry then remembered that his boat was going to pay the price. He twisted the throttle as far as it would go, noticing it was also military spec, fast and quiet.

Two minutes later, the night sky lit up behind them with a bright flash. A few moments later, the sound of the explosion reached them. Within a few minutes, there was nothing left to see.

It had to be done. Either the FBI or DIA are after us. Maybe both…

Terry thought back to getting kicked off the case and realizing things were going to be bad for them. *The DIA got us into this mess—or did they? Courtney is the real puppet master, but for how long?* He thought of the notes and money she left for them and felt his anger toward her start to weaken. She had been training them and planning this for a very long while. Realizing there was no more time to think about it, Terry focused on the land looming up ahead.

"Can I get a marker?" Terry mimicked the voice into the com again.

Two headlights flicked on and off, about a half mile further up the beach, so he nosed the raft in their direction.

"There you guys are. Hold that course, you're coming right at us," the man said.

Two men were waiting for them at the water's edge as they slid to a halt on the beach.

"Nice work," one of them said. "Double time now," he said, as he and his partner grabbed the front corners of the raft.

Terry and Bill jumped out of the raft and lifted on the back corners. The four of them ran the raft up the beach to a big, black, four door pickup and slid the raft into the back. The two men got into the front as Terry and Bill jumped in behind them.

"I didn't hear either of them make a peep, you guys were well worth the money. We may even have another job for you," the driver said, "but she won't go down quite as easy as those idiots did."

"Good ol' plausible deniability gets us a lot of work," Terry said.

"Us, too," the driver added, then both men up front chuckled.

"Thanks for letting us push the button. Hopefully one of them was still breathing when she went up," the passenger said.

"Doubt it," Terry said, "I cut 'em both up pretty good and put a couple in each."

The men up front laughed louder.

"Watch it there, you're starting to make me nervous," the driver said, then both men laughed again.

The driver slowed to a crawl when they reached the sharp edge of a paved road.

Without disguising his voice, Terry said, "The next two are free."

The two men spun around to face pistol barrels. Bill and Terry fired in unison and the two men slumped in their seats. Terry reached over and turned off the truck. There were a few twitches from each, then the passenger groaned once.

"Good thing you had me use that little peashooter," Bill said. "My forty would have splattered brains all over the place."

Working together, they pulled the bodies out. They patted them down to find wallets and car keys on each.

"Both of them worked for an insurance agency not far from here. Should we check it out?" Bill asked.

"Nah, those identities are probably just sheep dip. Maybe the office exists, maybe not. Either way, we need to get as far from here as we can," Terry said.

"They were sloppy, there might be something there we could use," Bill said.

"Not sloppy, cocky. They didn't know about your stargazing stamina," Terry said.

"Actually, I fell asleep on the roof. One of them made a noise in the raft and woke me up. Dumb luck saved our skins."

"We can't rely on luck anymore. Grab the cash but leave everything else since there are RFID in everything," Terry said. "Here, help me lift them into the raft."

When the second body flopped into the raft, Terry said, "You drive."

Bill pulled out onto the road, then asked, "So, were those guys dirty?"

"If those two were sent to kill bad guys, why did they think it was funny they were hacked up?"

"Enough said," Bill replied.

"We need to get a new ride ASAP, something pre-GPS. After we're sure we aren't being tracked, I have a place we can go for a day or two and prepare for our next move."

"Roger that. I have nothing to hold me back," Bill said.

"Same here, partner."

After several minutes, Terry broke the silence, "The sun will be up soon so keep your eyes open for a new vehicle."

"Roger that," Bill said, "I'll pull off at the next town."

* * *

Mike awoke to the sound of a rooster crowing and looked down at his chest to see Courtney's auburn hair.

"Hey, you awake?" he asked.

"Sure, is everything okay?" Courtney asked and lifted her head.

"As far as I know," he replied.

"Why is that not reassuring?" Courtney asked, as she sat up.

"Because I'm not the most observant person you know?"

"I like you just the way you are, so don't think otherwise. Right now, I need you to be a killer, but I don't want you to change."

"Then what should I do?" he asked.

"Do what you do best and get that thing ready for the next leg of our journey. Let us handle the rest," Courtney said and laid her head back on his chest.

"That I can do," he said. "Or should I say, have done."

Courtney lifted her head again. "What do you mean? Is it ready?"

"We can go anytime you like."

"Today. We go today," Courtney said and jumped up. "Let's pack, eat breakfast and then go." She leaned back down and kissed him on the cheek. "You're amazing."

"Thank you, kind maiden." Mike sighed loudly. "My work here is done."

"Here, maybe, but I have big plans for you back home," Courtney said, then rushed up the stairs.

* * *

"Hospital," Bill said, as he pointed to the right, "and a bunch of houses."

"Perfect. We'll find something there."

"Caps on and eyes down. There's no telling where the cameras will be," Terry said, driving slowly down the street.

"Here's yours," Bill said, handing him a cap off one of the dead agents.

"The parking garage is right down there," Terry said. "We'll ditch this truck in there after we find...there it is, a late 90's Toyota Camry."

"The choice of car thieves, for nearly two decades," Bill chuckled.

"You get the car and come around the block. Make sure you don't get close to the hospital's cameras. Park on the other side of those bushes at the Southwest corner of the garage. They left us with a lot of gear, so it'll take a couple of trips, but I don't want that car inside the garage," Terry said.

"Roger that," Bill replied and stepped out of the truck.

Terry immediately drove the pickup into the uppermost, interior level of the parking structure. He backed into a space near the rear stairwell, then jumped out and grabbed his first load for the car. When he opened the back door, Bill was already there.

"You look surprised to see me," he said.

"I must admit, that was an impressive theft," Terry replied.

"I had a little help. They left it unlocked with the key under the visor."

"I thought it looked like a good one," Terry said, as he handed him the bags. "I should at least get half of the credit."

Terry let the door close and sprinted back up to the truck. He quickly worked the front license plate until he was able to tear it off, then threw it in the back seat. He then grabbed the last two backpacks—heavy with equipment and ammo—and muscled them out of the truck. Finally, he locked the truck, tossed in the keys and closed the door. Terry was breathing hard when he reached the bottom again.

"I was starting to wonder," Bill said, as they each put a bag in the seat behind them and jumped into the car.

"Yeah, didn't want to take the time to dig out a knife, so I tore the front plate off instead," Terry said.

"I thought you were slowing down."

"Yeah, yeah. Get in and drive. And keep it on the speed limit," Terry said, as he got comfortable in his seat and pulled his hat down over his eyes.

"Roger that. Where to?" Bill asked as he drove toward the highway.

"We're going home," Terry replied.

"Home? Serious?"

"Yep."

"Have you gone crazy?"

"Yep, now keep quiet so I can get some rest," Terry said.

* * *

"What's all the excitement about?" Court asked. He poked his head out of the bedroom door and saw Courtney rushing up the stairs.

"We can go home now. Get ready and pack, we're heading back to town in an hour," she replied.

"He got it working already?"

"I told you he was amazing," Courtney answered, flashing a proud smile.

59

"Yes, you did. Give us five minutes and we'll be down," Court said, then closed the door.

Danni looked at him and said, "We should have told her."

"I know, but it's too late now," Court said, as he packed his bag.

"Or do we risk it?" she asked.

"What do you mean?"

"She can't go back to the USA and we can't stay here," Danni said.

"We're not going without her, so I guess it doesn't matter."

"We're going home?" Danni asked.

"If that's where she wants to go, then yes," he said.

"I say we tell her and make the decision together."

"And what if she chooses to go where we'll be safe?"

Danni shrugged, "I guess we should make sure we go back home then."

"So, there's no reason to tell her."

"You'll upset her if you don't, she'll lose faith in you, Court."

"I suppose you're right." *Perfect, our first family quarrel will be in public.*

Five minutes later, he and Danni joined Courtney and Mike downstairs.

"Can you...fill us in?" Court asked.

"The device is ready and we can leave anytime. Wait, why do you both seem worried?" Courtney asked.

"It's a bit complicated," Court began.

"Out with it," Courtney ordered.

Great, here it comes...

"Tell her, Court," Danni said.

"I am, but give a guy a minute, will ya?"

Danni said, "Sorry, I thought you changed your—"

"The Colonel killed a guard at the lab so we could get to the crystal altar. Actually, he ordered another soldier to do it."

"One guard killed another? That's not going to help us," Courtney said.

"Then he committed suicide," Danni said.

"The Colonel put the deaths of two SAF soldiers on your

hands. Perfect," Courtney said, shaking her head.

"It was horrible," Danni said.

"Were the two of you involved?" Courtney asked.

"We were there and that's enough to get us executed," Court answered.

"Geez, Dad. Why didn't you guys tell me this before?" Courtney asked.

"We couldn't stay back there with your people and I wasn't exactly sure Mike would be able to get that thing working. Certainly not in a day or two, so I thought we had some time to talk to you about it," Court said.

"Well, you were wrong. What now? Stay here with Margie?"

"Sweetie, we didn't mean for it to happen this way," Danni said.

"You realize Mike and I are DOA, right?" she asked.

"What does the Department of Accountancy—" Court began.

"Dead on arrival," Mike said.

"Oh, sorry," Court said.

"If they catch me back there, I'll wish I was dead," Courtney said.

Perfect, they're upset and think you're an idiot.

"They wouldn't give Mike a chance to explain or show that machine to them?" Court suggested.

"Maybe, but he wouldn't see the light of day for years even if he did survive." Courtney got up, walked over to the front door and stared out across the road, into the fields. "You know how the warriors think, kill first, ask questions later."

"I'm sorry, I guess I thought it was more civilized there," Court said.

"No matter how uncivilized they are, every culture thinks they are the civilized ones," Courtney said.

"You wanted to be with your parents. Why don't you do that, at least until things cool off?" Mike asked.

Court walked over to her and put an arm around her shoulders.

"Please don't, I'm angry," Courtney said.

"No, you're not angry. It's called disappointment, sadness, maybe even fear," Court said.

Courtney turned toward Court with her mouth open.

Uh-oh, she's really mad now, Court thought. He braced himself for an outburst, but instead Courtney began to sob. He put both of his arms around her and held her while she cried. Danni and Mike joined them and the four of them stood there, consoling each other.

"Knock it off already, I can't take much more of this mush." Margie said. "Bunch of pansies."

Courtney let out a sobbing laugh, then everyone else did, too. "OK then, let's sit down and figure this out."

Court took a chair, watching Danni to make sure she was holding up.

"Thank goodness. The sight of you four was making me queasy," Margie said, causing them to laugh again.

"Aunt Margie, I think you may be a bit of a softie," Mike said, walking toward her.

"Back off, Tumors, I don't want to hurt you," she said, holding up a fist.

Court watched Mike smiled and put his arm around Aunt Margie. *That boy is definitely a keeper.*

"What's the plan then? Find work somewhere?" Courtney asked.

"Well, there is one more option," Mike offered.

"What are you thinking, Tumors?" Courtney teased.

"Nice," Mike said sarcastically. "I've been experimenting with a new, uh, feature these past few days. When the spud frequencies ride on the front of the pulse, we move forward through the three places, in the current order. If I shift the waves so they ride on the backside of the electrical pulse, we'll go in reverse order. Also, the better I synchronize it all, the less nausea and blindness we have. With a little tweak I can step back and forth without any side effects."

"No side effects?" Danni asked. "How do you—you've been traveling without us?"

"Hold on, he said the last few days," Courtney said. "As far as

I know, he was only out there yesterday, but the rest of you were saying two days. Mike seems to think it's been more than that," Courtney said.

"Exactly what did you do to test it?" Court asked.

"I went to the SAF, then I came back here, then I went to the USA, then back again. Did it a couple of times and felt great afterward," Mike explained.

Court asked, "How long did that take?"

"Well, it definitely took a while," Mike admitted.

"Interesting. Especially since you still had the thing in pieces around two in the afternoon. You were miles away from completing it at dinnertime," Court replied.

Courtney said, "The dinner I never had."

"It turns out that the wave sword and its power supply are far better tuned in to the magnetic and gravitational fields than my system was. With the massive amplification I give it, the power cell won't keep up for long, but it opens up options."

Court asked, "How long did it take?"

"I tested it for two days, off and on."

"We lost two days? Or did you gain two days?" Court asked.

"I sort of relived a day, so no one lost a day, except Courtney," Mike answered.

"So, how long have you been here?" Court asked.

"Probably five days, but I'm not exactly sure since I've been working most of the time."

"Balderdash!" Margie exclaimed. "You're losing your marbles, every one of ya, that's all there is to it."

"Court, that's not possible, is it?" Danni asked.

"I don't know," he replied.

"Let me show you. Everyone sit down and keep your fists out where everyone can see them. Give me about ten minutes and you'll see it's real and safe," Mike said and walked out of the house. A moment later, he walked back in, "let me write something in each of your hands." Mike wrote something on every hand, closing them as he went.

"This is absurd. This boy is touched in the head," Margie said.

Courtney laughed, "Yeah, we already knew that, but this is something new, Margie."

"Look at him," Margie said. "Wipe that fool grin off your face, young man. It isn't nice to mess with an old woman's mind, especially one that's already starting to go."

"Then you'd better brace yourself, Auntie. I want everyone to think about your first pet's name, then open your left hand," he instructed.

Court heard the others gasp in unison.

"Now, think of your favorite childhood friend and open your right hands," Mike said.

"This is amazing," Court said.

"I know," Mike said, still grinning from ear to ear.

"How did you do that?" Courtney demanded.

"Would you believe I slipped back in time a few minutes?"

"Maybe…" Courtney said.

"Tell us," Danni said.

"Well, I went out to the barn and got everything ready. That took almost ten minutes. Then I came back in to ask you those two questions." Mike paused. "You all gave me a bunch of flack for it, I might add. Then, I ran back out to the barn and slipped back to a few minutes before I came in to ask the questions."

"That is amazing," Court said

"Can you take me back to see Earl, before he died?" Margie asked softly.

The room was silent for a moment.

"Maybe, but I'm not sure," Mike answered. "The power supply is running low after all my testing. I went back a day, twice and accidentally left it on for a while. I can't do anything else until we decide what to do about the power source."

"Wait a minute. Is there enough power to go back?" Courtney asked.

"Yeah, I'm pretty sure there is. Especially if we wait, it seems to regenerate a little as it sits."

"Will we be trapped here if we don't go back home?" Danni asked.

"Only until I build a power supply and locate a high voltage source to run it," Mike explained.

"Will you take me back to see Earl, someday? Promise me you will," Margie asked again.

"I'll take you to see him if I ever have the ability. I promise to do my best," Mike said.

"Very well." Margie slowly got up, then made her way to her bedroom and closed the door.

Courtney said, "I'm the only one who can do this. The rest of you will be shot, or at least jailed for years. I have a second copy of the files to deliver to the SAF and when I get my hands on a sword, I'll return."

"I don't like it," Mike replied.

"Me neither," her father said. "You're a stranger without credentials. If you get caught, you'll be executed on suspicion of treason."

Mike said, "We stick together and go straight to the authorities when we get there. It's the best chance we have. They know you two and Courtney has the information they need. I'll say my actions were to help collect it for the SAF."

"Your actions?" Courtney asked.

"Remember, my DNA will be a match for the Colonel's," Mike replied. "We leave after breakfast." Then he got up and walked out toward the barn.

"I'm not sure I like it," Courtney said.

"What? That he took charge? Or the plan?" Court asked. "You need to back off. That boy's right and you know it."

Danni interrupted, "Dear, why don't you take our things out while Courtney and I have a talk."

"Yes, dear," Court grumbled. *Keep your mouth shut Court, keep it shut…*

* * *

"Did you notice she didn't sound like herself in the safe deposit box letter?" Terry asked.

"What?" Bill started slightly. "You laid there for an hour without making a peep and then just start talking?"

65

"She was trying to tell us something. Half of the letter was the same as the first. Though, the wording was a bit off."

"She was in a hurry when she wrote it. At least, that's what I thought when I read it," Bill replied.

"Nah, she has been planning this for too long. There has to be another message." Terry sat up. "Pull over, I want to take another look at it."

"Did you bring a copy of the book?"

"No, but that's why she chose that book, they're easy to get," Terry answered.

Terry jumped out, grabbed his packet from the bank and was back in his seat in moments. "Thanks."

Pulling it out he read it over again.

"Yep, she did it again. She put a number in it—twenty three—and only a sentence later it starts to sound odd again. You wouldn't notice it if you didn't know her," Terry said. "That girl is amazing!"

"You're kidding? I didn't even catch it," Bill said as he pulled back out onto the road.

"Hey, stop off at the next superstore so I can get one of those book readers. No reason to waste time driving around trying to find an old book when we can download it off the web."

"Don't you think that's too risky?" Bill asked.

"Not if you do it right."

"But you have to set it all up—"

"I'm not that old and I'm not an idiot."

"Okay, but don't say I didn't warn you," Bill grumbled.

"There's our store, up ahead and on the right."

"I see it. I'll park off to the side, over by the bushes." Bill dropped Terry off in the parking lot.

Terry watched him park along the outer edge as he went inside.

Nearly an hour later Terry walked back out, and wandered through the lot. He worked his way past the large vehicles and vans, pausing occasionally to check his bag.

When Terry reached the car, Bill said, "No tails. What took you so long?"

"I had to get the darn book loaded."

"A bit too complicated for a seasoned person like yourself?"

"It would have been easy, if I had a credit card or online account. I had to wait until the punk behind the counter went on break, so he could buy an online gift card for me to open the account with."

"How much did that four dollar book end up setting you back?"

"Almost three hundred. It wasn't such a good idea after all, now drive," Terry said.

"Yes, sir."

Terry started reading the book as he worked through Courtney's note. "It's an address, about an hour north of the office, on the edge of the slums," he said with interest. "She says to use the place in case of an emergency."

"She had a personal safe house? One we didn't know about?" Bill asked. "Where the heck did that girl get her money?"

"Are you kidding me? She was a workaholic and her base salary was over a hundred grand for at least ten years. With all the hazard pay, plus comp, I bet she grossed two hundred a year," Terry replied. "The girl drove one of these cars for Pete's sake, that should have clued us in."

"They don't pay me that kind of money, I barely made half that last year."

"Yeah, I know," Terry answered.

"What? They told you what I was making? Why would they do that?"

"I've worked with the audit team a few times when they suspected someone was on the take," he explained.

"No way, someone in the office?" Bill asked.

"Remember Tyler Forney?"

"Sure, he died in a car wreck a couple of years back. We met his wife and twin sons at the funeral," Bill replied.

"Tyler took a bunch of money from a crook in New York to pay for his girlfriend's apartment there."

"Tyler?"

"Yeah. The situation was handled—in-house," Terry said.

"You didn't?" Bill asked.

"Look, kid, this is a dirty business. When we were shown the door the other day, I expected them to send someone after us. What Courtney and Military Mike did on that video is way above our paygrade. We became loose ends when we saw it. It's nothing personal."

"Why was it so funny to those two jerks they sent after us?" Bill was becoming irate. "Because that felt pretty personal!"

"Easy big guy. That was to make it easier on their consciences. It works pretty well, most of the time," Terry answered.

"I think I'm going to be sick," Bill said. "I mean, I knew this was a tough business, but it's getting awfully hard to tell the good guys from the bad guys."

"I know, but sometimes you have to make tough decisions and good people die."

"Yeah, well I'm not convinced that makes it right," Bill growled.

Terry looked over at him and said, "Swing in there, I'm getting hungry. Their hot dogs are a bit greasy, but the relish is to die for." Terry watched Bill roll his eyes and smiled.

"You're never going to let me live that down, are you?"

"Why should I? We had to call in a professional cleaner after you puked all over Mike's bathroom," Terry replied.

"No, we called in the cleaner to clean up the Chinese spook. Remember, the one that shot you while you sat on the floor in Mike's bedroom?"

"He had intel I needed. Plus, I had him right where I wanted him until you Rambo'd in and strangled the nice little man," Terry said.

"Saved your life and you know it. End of discussion." Bill pulled into the drive through. "Six deluxe dogs, with extra relish please."

"You can't be serious?" Terry said, "There's no way I want three of those hotdogs."

"Oh, you're hungry, too?" Bill asked.

"Cheeseburger, please. I might be sick this time," Terry said.

"Don't look now but we're being followed," Bill said. "They

took the exit with us and just turned again. Looks like two men, but they're staying back a bit."

Terry kept his head from moving around while he pulled two pistols from the backpack at his feet.

"Safety's on, one in the chamber," he said, as he slipped a gun into Bill's lap.

"I'm going to see if they follow again," Bill said and turned at the next intersection. "Yep, still there."

"Pull into that driveway, beside the red pickup," Terry ordered.

Bill stopped alongside the truck, while Terry turned around in his seat to return potential fire. The car drove past and a garage door opened several houses down the street.

"That was a close one," Bill said.

"Yeah, it was. Nice work."

"Thanks. We only have about twenty blocks left before we get there, you want me to find a quiet spot to park?" Bill asked.

"Sure, let's find someplace dark. I'll hike in to the address she gave us and see what we are dealing with."

"You sure you don't want me to go?" Bill asked.

"Nah, I need some fresh air anyway, I'm going stir crazy," Terry replied.

"Yeah, sixteen hours of this has wiped me out."

"Still sore?"

"Stiff as heck. I'm gonna stretch my legs while you check it out."

Terry spotted a dark alley, "There, pull in."

"Looks like a good place to hide," Bill said, as he turned the engine off.

"Give me one hour. If I'm not here by then, I want you to leave and come back at midnight. If you don't see me then, you're on your own," Terry explained.

"What if you're just late?" Bill asked.

"If I can't make it eighteen blocks, twice in two hours, you don't want to be around to see why not. Am I clear?" Terry asked.

"Crystal."

* * *

Mike walked in as Danni, Court and Courtney were finishing breakfast.

"Everyone get their things packed?" Mike asked.

"Yep, put them by the front door," Court replied.

"We should make the shift to the SAF with the power we have left. Not sure after that though…"

After a brief silence, Court asked, "If you came back a day or two ago, then where is the other you right now? You know, the one that should be here with us."

"Yeah, about that. It seems that the area, people and objects inside the field remain unaffected by the time change. Well, other than going backwards or forwards, of course," Mike explained.

"Is there something else?" Courtney asked.

"You don't want to pass in and out of the field once it's generated," Mike said.

"Why is that?" Court asked.

"Because you are moving back and forth between timelines, or staying in both at one time. That'll mess you up." Mike realized he had a concerned look on his face when he made eye contact with Courtney.

Courtney concluded, "Which is what happened to me. Right, Mike? That's how you know, isn't it? Tell them."

"Uh, well," Mike started to consider what to say, then saw the determination on Courtney's face and knew he no choice. "I slipped back the first time by accident. When I realized what had happened, I didn't want to alarm anyone, so I put the finishing touches on the new system. That's when you came to check on me, but got in the field at the barn door. I looked for you for a couple of hours, but at that point I had been up for two days and couldn't even think straight. I wanted to go back again, but had to wait for the power supply to regenerate for a couple hours. I took a quick nap and when I woke it had enough juice to take me back to the time before you disappeared."

"I vanished and you went to bed? Seriously?" Courtney asked.

"No, I tried but it was dark and I was exhausted. The power

supply—"

"And you went to bed," Courtney repeated.

"Well—I guess. I don't know what else to say." Mike stood up and walked his dishes over to the sink.

"I think he did the right thing. It would have just upset us for nothing. What could we have done but search and worry?" Court asked. "I don't like it either, but it's done now."

Danni added, "Court would have done the same thing."

Courtney said, "I suppose you're right."

Mike was looking out the kitchen window and saw Courtney's reflection approaching him. *Great, here we go again.*

She placed her dishes on the counter next to the sink and put her hand on Mike's shoulder. "Thanks for keeping a clear head. You did the right thing and I see that now," Courtney said quietly, as she reached up and gave him a kiss on the cheek.

"It was one of the hardest things I've gone through yet. I thought I had lost you." Mike glanced at her.

"I know and I'm sorry," Courtney said.

Mike looked past Courtney and saw Margie walk in.

"Get out of my kitchen, Tumors," she demanded.

Mike turned, walked toward her and said, "Yes, ma'am." He then gave the stern-faced woman a kiss on the cheek. "Thanks for everything. I will do my best to keep that promise."

"All right already. Now hurry up and get this bunch of crazies out of here before I call the authorities on the lot of you," Margie demanded.

Mike watched as each of the crazies walked up to her, kissed her on the cheek and thanked her. They then picked up their bags and filed out through the front door. Mike packed the spud and straightened the workshop, while Court pulled the car into the driveway and loaded their things. When he finished, Mike jumped into the car with them. As he drove them down the driveway, Mike looked back at Margie on the porch with her shotgun in hand. He rolled down his window and waved to her, smiling when she returned the gesture.

* * *

Terry wormed his way through the darkest streets and alleys as he approached the apartment building. He entered through the parking garage and found the storage unit. He worked the lock, entering the combination Courtney coded into the letter.

Box of books, Terry recalled, as he opened the door.

He saw what he was looking for up on a shelf, inside was the familiar blue book. Opening the book, he found an industrial looking key with very deep cuts. *That would be hard to pick. No wonder this girl was single, all she did was work and plan for this— whatever 'this' is.*

Leaving the unit and locking it behind him, Terry went over to the building entrance and found a keypad. *So that's what the other code is for.* Terry went inside, climbed the stairs and entered the hallway. He felt his pulse quicken as he walked up to the door. Carefully sliding the key in the lock, he heard the pins click one by one. As he slowly turned the latch, he heard a solid sounding clunk and froze.

She either has a big, electric bolt of some kind, or I just armed a nuke, Terry thought. *Relax, she wouldn't have done all this just to kill you. She's had too many opportunities already.*

Terry winced as he turned the handle, then he stepped inside. He checked the rooms and decided it was safe. He stepped back out into the hall and locked the door, hearing a similar clunk. Terry then worked his way back toward Bill, arriving with twenty minutes to spare.

"It looks good. Let's drive closer so we don't have to pack all this gear the whole way," Terry said.

Bill drove the car closer, then the pair made the short hike in, carrying everything they could manage.

Back at the front door to Courtney's apartment Terry said, "Don't screw around with this door." Then he turned the key.

Bill's eyes widened.

"Yeah, I know, it freaked me out, too," Terry replied, as he swung the door inward. "You make some food while I go ditch the car. I'll be back with the last of our stuff by the time it's ready."

"Looks like canned ravioli tonight," Bill said, as Terry stepped out the door.

Sometime later, Terry tapped three times on the apartment door, inserted his key and opened it. "Something smells good," he said, as he stepped inside.

"Yeah, but I hope your expectations aren't too high." Bill smiled.

"Sweet. I loved Chef Boyardee ravioli as a kid," Terry said.

"Funny, I liked Spaghetti-O's myself."

"Hey, it looks like you've been busy. Nice work," Terry said.

"Yeah, got through every room but one," Bill replied.

"We'll tackle it after dinner."

"Uh, no," Bill said, "we have everything we need."

"Seriously? Why not?" Terry asked, as he took his first bite. "Mmmm good," he said, smiling at his own joke.

"It's Courtney's room. I'm not going in there and you shouldn't either," Bill answered.

"You saw the video of them vanishing into the fog, just like I did. They may not even be alive, for all we know," Terry said, between bites.

"I'm not going in there, not after what she tried to do for us."

"You read minds now? That's amazing! To top it off, you have Stockholm Syndrome. You're kidding right?" Terry asked.

"I don't have a birth defect and I'm not kidding," Bill replied.

"Birth defect? Oh, 'Stockholm Syndrome'. I swear, the public school system has become a complete laughing stock," Terry said. "Look, Bill, you may not realize it, but she got us into this mess. Remember? People are trying to kill us thanks to her. Any of this ringing a bell?"

"She tried to protect us, that's why she kept us in the dark. To top it all off, she opened a bank account for us along the route to your boat! Heck, if it wasn't for you and the data recovery team, we wouldn't be in this mess," Bill said. "Now who has 'Stockade Syndrome'?" Bill demanded.

Terry choked on a mouthful of food as he laughed. Seeing Bill's angry look, Terry said, "OK, Bill, I give up. Courtney is a sweet girl with our best interests at heart."

"Real sincere, Terry."

"I'm sorry. I didn't mean to make you mad. I'm a little punchy after everything that's happened."

"Whatever," Bill said.

"Fine, we'll leave her room alone for now."

"You mean it?"

"Yes, I mean it. But, if things get crazy around here for some reason, I will tear her room apart," Terry replied.

"Deal," Bill said. "I'm gonna take a shower."

Terry watched Bill awkwardly get up, then take his holster off, wincing in pain.

"Here, let me help you," Terry said and got up.

"I feel like a complete wimp right now," Bill said.

"You've been a trooper so far, but you need to get lots of rest now that we're safe.

When Bill returned from his shower, Terry said, "I put a little of everything in each of these bags, in case we need to bug out."

"Excellent," Bill said and walked over to pick one of the bags up. "Fifty?" he asked.

"Close, forty six each," Terry replied. "I'm gonna get cleaned up and hit the rack. I'll see you in the morning."

"Roger that."

* * *

UNIT 2: PLAN B

"There's the city," Courtney announced from the back seat. *Time to get back in the game.*

"Where should I park it?" Court asked.

"We need to come out somewhere we'll be safe and close to the SAF lab," she said.

"That park across the street would work. We'll walk right in the front door and turn ourselves in," Mike said.

"I should go in first, then bring you guys in when I know you're going to be safe," Courtney said.

"We aren't going to have this discussion all over again," Mike said. "I'll do most of the talking since they'll think I'm the Colonel."

"That may not be a good idea," Danni replied. "You won't know procedures or protocol. You will fail every test they give you."

"Except facial recognition, fingerprints and a DNA test," Mike reminded them.

"Except those," Danni conceded. "You got hit on the head or something? Wait, the video feed will record you getting shot and bleeding all over the place. We could play that up."

"One small problem— no bullet hole," Court said.

"No, he has a scar on his chest from when he had a mole removed last year. It looks a lot like a bullet hole," Courtney said.

"I don't remember telling you about that," Mike said, turning to look back at her.

"We've all seen you with your shirt off."

"But you can't see the scar, unless I shave my chest," Mike replied.

"We get it. Everyone knows I spied on you for over a year,"

Courtney said.

"Only one year?" Mike asked, "Are you sure about that?"

"It might have been three or four years," Courtney answered. "But the last year was the most intense."

"Three or four years? That's a bit much," her mother said.

"Coming from Spookette, that seems a bit disingenuous," Courtney joked. "He was working on something the government wanted to protect. I was interested in the technology, so I got myself assigned to the case. I didn't mean to fall for the guy when I took the job."

"So, you fell for the guy?" Mike asked.

Subject successfully changed, thought Courtney.

"I don't think I said that," Courtney said.

"No, I'm pretty sure that's what I heard," Mike answered.

"But not positive? Then you could have misunderstood."

"Wait, no, I'm positive that was what you said." Mike added, "And I'm positive he's fallen for you, too."

"Alright you two, you're embarrassing Court. Keep it up and he may end up in tears," Danni said from next to Courtney in the back seat.

Thanks dear, you're always watching out for me," Court replied.

"You're welcome," Danni said, as she reached up and rubbed Court's shoulder.

Courtney smiled. *Now if I can just keep all of them alive.*

* * *

Mike was sitting quietly, with his eyes closed, watching random images flash in his memory. He noticed that when he thought about the crystal altar, the images of it increased. Some, he knew were not his own memories.

If I know what I need to think about, the Colonel's memories will help.

"We almost forgot something," Court said, bringing Mike back from his daydream. "What are we going to do with the spud? We can't let them get hold of it or we'll never get it back."

76

"True, and if that happens, we'll never leave again," Mike said.

"Do we need to leave?" Danni asked.

"What if something goes wrong and we need to escape, or if I need to fix it? Without the spud, if they capture or kill one of us, I can't undo it," Mike said.

"You're talking about playing GOD, Mike," Court said, "I'm not sure you should undo anything."

"We've already been doing that. Even taking a breath in either of the other two places, changes the future there," Mike said. "It's a part of Chaos Theory, called the Butterfly Effect. Basically, it says that even the slightest change can have serious ramifications. Like, a butterfly could cause a tornado."

"So, we've already altered the future, in all three timelines?" Danni asked.

"Yes, but things will be exactly the way they're supposed to be," Mike replied.

"Differently than they have been?" Danni asked.

"I suppose," Mike said. "Look, I don't think there should be three separate timelines in the first place. I think something happened long ago that fractured the true reality. It created two extra, parallel realities."

"What are you suggesting? We shouldn't be alive?" Courtney asked.

"Everyone would think their reality is the right one. The thing is, if the split never happened I'm not so sure our lives would be much different," Mike said.

"What about the Butterfly Effect? If a butterfly can cause a tornado, what are we causing?" Danielle asked.

"I don't know, but most of the buildings are in the same locations and the same people work in those buildings. Why is it that I can get around in this city about as good as I can back home? Because, almost everything is exactly as it should be."

"But there are many differences, too," Courtney argued.

"The Colonel and I lived in the same building, on the same street, in the same apartment. Fate, destiny, karma, call it what you will. I think things were set in motion and we have an effect on them, but that effect is absorbed by the force of time. All these generations along three different timelines and you're still her parents? Some people will never have been born and people will die for different reasons. Even so, time continues forward, heals its wounds and maintains its original course."

Courtney replied, "Then you want to pin this down to one specific event and go back in time to fix it?"

"In theory, we could stop the original fracturing of the timeline and keep the advanced technology away from the Egyptians. That's where the Nazis in your world and the British in Michael's world, got it from to dominate the world," Mike said.

"Won't that damage the stability of your world?" Court asked.

"A lot of this tech doesn't exist in my world. I only invented the spud because of what I experienced with the crystal altar twenty years ago, when Courtney was transferred here. Maybe others have been given similar advancements. They shouldn't have them, so losing them seems appropriate to me."

"How do we figure out when this bad event was, exactly?" Court asked.

Courtney answered, "We already know to within ten or twenty years. It has to be in Egypt and it seems to be likely that it could even be what ended Sneferu's reign. It was at the end of Sneferu's reign and the early years of Khufu, about 2595 BC to 2575 BC. We could get close and then wait it out until we recognize the divergence."

"How do we know all that?" Mike asked.

"From reading the history books you brought from your journey and comparing that with the information I have in my tablet," Courtney said. "A little more research in an SAF library and I could verify it."

"You already read the books I have, in my things? The books you never asked to borrow and I never loaned to you?" Mike asked.

Court started laughing. "She was burning through those books when you were out in the barn working on your project."

Courtney looked at him, "I read fast."

"Fast? You can't read that fast, can you?" Mike asked.

"The DIA has training that every field agent takes. Average people read up to 350 words per minute, after the training the average is 1,500 per minute. I can do up to 2,500 words per minute if I'm interested," she explained.

"I take it you were interested?" Mike asked.

"Very."

"That must be some kind of record."

"Not even close," she replied.

"I wonder who…"

"Howard Berg, twenty five thousand words a minute."

Mike opened his mouth to ask another question but didn't get the question out.

"Because he's the person who designed the classes used by several alphabet agencies. Trust me it isn't rocket science, lots of people can outread me," she said.

"All right. Then let's get some detailed history from there for a comparison and see if we can learn some more," Mike suggested.

"Exactly," Courtney said.

"Change of plans?" Court asked.

"Yep, plan B. We need to get into some history archives and do some digging. Also, we need at least two more pulse sword power supplies, to make this journey," Mike answered.

"We can use the information I have, trade it for a couple of swords and a visit to the SAF archives," Courtney suggested.

"That might work," Mike said.

"It'll be a piece of cake, if we can secure a safe place to work," Courtney said.

"We have a good friend that's well connected with the SAF. He may be able to get access to the archives without raising any suspicions," Danni suggested.

"Also, we want a listing of any unusual technology from that region, near the time of the Fourth Dynasty, 2650 BC to 2525 BC," Mike said.

"Do they have enough room for the four of us to stay with them?" Courtney asked.

"That shouldn't be a problem, it's a fairly big house," Court replied.

"Oh, the Skwiras?" Courtney asked.

"Yes, they still have that big house on Powell Hill and they'd love to see you," Danni answered.

"Everyone out, the park is right up there," Court announced, as he brought the car to a stop along the curb.

"Court, would you carry my bag?" Mike asked, as he got out to open the trunk.

"No problem."

"We'll need to go as fast as we can, since the power level is so low. I'll be coming right on your heels so keep moving when you get there."

"That looks like a quiet spot over there behind those trees," Court said.

"Back home, there's a small fountain right there, with some bushes on the other side."

"And what if someone sees us come through?" Danni asked.

"Be ready to defend yourselves," Mike said. "If we do this right, no one will even notice."

Mike powered up the spud while the group readied themselves for the quick maneuver. Once the haze formed in front of him, Court rushed through, followed closely by the others. Mike powered down the unit and dove through after them. Standing in shrubbery up to their shoulders, the group quickly found each other.

"We made it," Court said.

"Good choice, sir. Now let's call your friends and invite ourselves over for a visit."

"The Skwiras are some of the nicest folks you will ever meet. Unless they're on vacation, I know we're welcome to stay there," Court said. "Wait right here and I will ring them."

Mike led the group over to a bench while Court talked on the phone.

When Court returned to the bench, he said, "They sent a car to get us. I told them we'd be up the street, at the next block. With that Court turned and lead the group up the sidewalk to a restaurant parking lot.

Mike whispered to Courtney, "Do you think this is safe?"

"I suppose so, but I'm not going to let my guard down," she said as a man stepped out of a waiting limousine, waving at them.

"Mr. Lewis, how nice to see you! Mrs. Lewis, you, too! It has been at least a year since we had you folks up for a visit. Who are your…" the driver paused and stared at Courtney.

Uh-oh, he recognizes her, Mike thought, feeling his stomach tighten.

"Perry, I think you may remember our daughter, Courtney?" Danni asked.

"Why yes ma'am, I do. You're all grown up and absolutely stunning!" The driver reached out his arms and Courtney hugged him.

"So nice to see you again, Perry."

"How long has it been?" he asked.

"I've been away for almost twenty years now," Courtney said.

"Perry, our friend Mike here is running incognito, you remember him, of course," Court asserted.

"Certainly, we have met. You're looking good, sir," Perry said.

"Thank you, Perry."

Perry loaded the bags while the four guests climbed into the back of the eight passenger limousine.

"That was speedy service Perry, how did you manage that?" Mike heard Court ask.

"I had just returned from dropping a guest off at the airport this morning. I walked in and Mr. Skwira handed me the address while he was talking to you, so I jumped back in and here I am."

Mike leaned over to Courtney and Danni. "You think that's true?"

"Mike, you're being paranoid, there is no way he could have known we were coming," Courtney whispered back.

"Maybe not," Mike said.

"We'll be in the driveway in two minutes," Perry said, as he pulled out onto the street.

* * *

Court looked up at the front of the house and saw Brian Skwira waving at them. "There he is. I'm surprised we caught him home this early," Court said as the car rolled to a stop. He opened his door and called out, "Brian! How've you been?"

"Court, great to see you! This will be quite a treat. We never seem to have enough time to hear about your adventures," Brian said, as he reached out to shake Court's hand.

"We appreciate your hospitality very much," Court replied. "You know Danni, of course, and this is our daughter—"

"Dear Lord, it's Courtney! But...but..."

Here we go, Court thought.

"Yeah, she's been away for nineteen years and just returned today," Court said. "We took a bit of a trip to get her. Another adventure to share."

"I'm sorry, I didn't mean to pry. I'm surprised to—I'm very pleasantly surprised!" He reached out his arms and gave her a hug.

"It's very nice to see you again, Mr. Skwira," Courtney said.

Holding her by the shoulders, he held her at arm's length and said, "Call me Brian, Mr. Skwira is too formal. My goodness you are beautiful! And you look so much like your mother, it's amazing. Speaking of your mother, how have you been, Danni?"

"I'm doing very well now, as you can imagine," Danni said, accepting Brian's hug. "I'm reliving my excitement with you now, all over again. It has been an amazing week to say the least."

"I can only imagine," Brian said. "It's been almost ten years since our boy, Denny, died in battle. To see him now would be overwhelming."

"He was an amazing young man, Brian. We are truly sorry," Court said.

"Thanks, Court. Who is this stout looking young man hiding behind you?"

Court watched Brian's reaction as Mike took his hat off.

"Colonel? Is that you? Court?" Brian looked back and forth between the two men.

"Brian, this is Mike Devon. He was injured and has been

staying with us while he recuperates."

"We heard you were killed in an accident at the lab, Colonel. You and a couple of soldiers with you," Brian said.

Brian knows, Court thought. *He's covering it up, but he knows.*

"Actually, I don't remember much from the past Brian. I'm still putting the pieces together," Mike said, pretending to be Colonel Devon.

Court said, "The General thinks he was killed, too. Brian, we'll need some help from you to make contact. The Colonel and Courtney risked life and limb to retrieve some valuable technology."

"This is all very intriguing. Let's go inside and have a chat," Brian said, as he motioned for the group to enter the house. "It's wonderful to have you all here. Perry, show them up to their rooms and find out what they need. Court, you come with me so we can catch up."

Court followed Brian into his study and took a seat in front of the large, wooden desk.

Brian closed the heavy doors and said, "I need you to shoot straight with me, Court. That is not the Colonel. Oh, he looks like him all right, but that's not him. Those eyes don't belong to the killing fiend I knew."

"Brian, the problem is—" Court began.

"Now see, that's not what I'm after. If you want my support, I must know everything. I didn't get to where I am because I'm easily fooled, Court. Out with it."

Court noticed that Brian's smile was gone and he had a serious, businesslike manner. "Brian, what I'm about to tell you is unbelievable. I guess you'll have to take me at my word until I'm able to show you."

Court laid it all out for Brian. He explained Mike's surprise phone call, that Courtney was alive. When Court relayed their visit to the Colonel's apartment, watching Mike vanish and the Colonel reappear, Brian's eyes widened. After he told Brian about the crystal altar and traveling to the other worlds, Court stopped. "I've said too much and you think I'm crazy."

"No, you told me what I demanded. I'm sorry to put you on

the spot like that, but I had to hear it for myself. I was told that the Colonel, Danni and yourself had used that crystal altar and vanished into thin air. The SAF has that thing under scrutiny again and has been bringing in captured Nazi scientists to restart the testing. Everything you told me fits with the incredible stories that surround that thing."

"I'm not sure the SAF can be trusted with it. We need to make sure they don't misuse it and keep it out of the wrong hands."

"Court, I have friends in very high places and they're pretty secretive at times. But, when it comes to R&D and manufacturing, I'm usually in the loop. It's my company that builds the machinery, to make the parts for their prototypes."

"I hope we haven't brought any trouble into your house," Court said.

"On the contrary, if Courtney's tech is of value to us, I can easily negotiate your safety."

"That's great news."

"We'll need to contact the General right away and let him know we have something for him. That will buy us time to figure this out," Brian said.

"Thank you."

"Not at all, I'm pleased you trusted me enough to come here with this. I won't let you down," Brian said.

"But I know there's a limit to what even you can do." Court reached out and shook his hand.

"True. Now go get yourself cleaned up and we'll eat as soon as you're ready."

"And the call?"

"Let's make it after supper, when I've had some time to process all of this."

"Great, thanks again." Court left him in the study and headed upstairs. *Wow, that went better than expected.*

* * *

Brian stood in silence, staring at the picture of his son on the wall for several minutes. Finally, as if he awoke from a dream, Brian went to his desk and sat down. Picking up the phone he slowly pressed its buttons and then held it up to his ear.

"General Bradley speaking," the voice on the other end said.

"Good afternoon General, Brian Skwira here. I have some folks you're looking for, here at the house with me."

* * *

Court ate his food, carefully observing their host's behavior. *Something's wrong with him. Something changed.*

"Did everyone get enough to eat?" Brian asked.

"I may have overdone it a bit," Court answered and pushed himself back from the table.

"It was wonderful, thanks so much for putting us up," Danni said.

"It's my pleasure."

"Yes, thank you," Courtney added, "it's very kind of you to help us so much."

"I'm happy to do it. Court, Mike, we need to have a talk. Will you ladies excuse us for a bit?" Brian got up from the table and led the way back into the study.

There it was again. He's lying or covering something up. He knows I'm on to him, Court thought.

"So, let's hear the request and see what I can offer you," Brian said.

Mike was quiet and glanced over at Court.

"I'm used to negotiations and business deals with friends, so don't let that bother you," Brian added.

"We brought a valuable collection of technology with us and would like to turn it over to fight the Nazis. Courtney knows a lot about it since she was the one collecting it for the past decade or so," Mike said.

"Mike can help the scientists with it, that's his area of expertise," Court said.

"Sounds pretty interesting, to say the least. Let's say this collection has game changing stuff in it, what are you hoping for in return?" Brian asked.

"We're certain this is game changing, as you put it, but someone would need to view a sample to be certain. Our problem is that I'm not about to hand it all over to the SAF. Once they have it in their possession, they will never return it nor pay for it.

"You're right about everything so far. That makes me your liaison?" Brian asked.

"Maybe, or you buy it from us and we can get back on to our own projects," Court said.

"I would prefer that, of course. What's your price?"

"We were hoping for a few things like clemency, a little money to support our research and a few wave sword power supplies," Court replied.

"That's pretty cheap, for what you described. Show me a sample," Brian said.

"Right now?" Mike asked.

"Yep, no reason to waste any time."

"I have my cell phone on me. Is this something you have here?" Mike pulled out his smartphone and explained how it worked.

"That is what I'm talking about, something real I can put my hands on. I will give you twenty five ounces of gold for that," he said, without blinking an eye.

"Uh, sure, I'd do that," Mike answered, handing it to him. "I have a few accessories upstairs that go with it."

Their host walked over to his desk, unlocked and opened the top drawer. He then pulled open the bottom right drawer to reveal a strongbox.

"Military issue?" Mike asked, "Looks like the Colonel's desk."

Court saw Mike's expression give away his slip. "It's OK, Mike, I explained it to him," he said.

"Yes, we make them for the military, but you can't be too careful these days. We have a variety of other military grade security features scattered around the place," he replied. Reaching out with a small bag, Brian said, "Now that we broke the ice, where's the good stuff?"

"I have a sample upstairs, but the actual collection is not here," Mike said. "What is the typical family income around here, say for one month's wages?"

"About one ounce of gold," Brian answered, as Mike jiggled the bag of coins. "Aren't you going to count it?"

"I wouldn't insult you by counting it in front of you," Mike answered.

"That's polite of you, but here's a scale. Some folks will read that as weakness and that will get you ripped off some day," he said. Brian turned the balance to face Mike and slid it to him.

"Thanks," Mike said, as the scale leveled out at twenty seven ounces.

"The bag is overweight two ounces." Recognizing that he was being tested, Mike opened the bag and dumped the coins out onto Brian's desk. Placing the empty bag on the scale, Mike said, "Yep, exactly one ounce. I owe you one back, sir." He then scooped the remaining gold coins up and poured them into the bag.

"That boy learns fast, Court." Brian laughed out loud. "You passed that one with flying colors, young man." Brian stepped around the end of the desk and slapped Mike on the shoulder. "Now go get me something that I can use to get the rest of your needs met," he said, as he sat down on the desk.

"Yes, sir. I will be right back down," Mike said.

Mike hurried upstairs with his payment.

When he got to the top of the stairs he saw Courtney poke her head out of the sitting room.

"What's going on down there?" she asked.

"Well, I sold him my phone for twenty five ounces of gold and he wants to see something big now," Mike said, lifting the bag. "What do you have that we can show him?"

Courtney paused, "I guess we can show him some of the plans on the tablet, but I'll need to be there."

"Grab it and let's go see what he says."

He stepped back from the doorway and followed Courtney to get the computer from her room.

Mike asked, "So, when this is all over, do you think we can

have a different kind of relationship?"

"I guess I would need to know what you're asking, Mr. Devon." Courtney glanced at him, as she grabbed the tablet case from under her bed.

"I guess I'm asking you to marry me, when this is all over."

"You guess?" Courtney asked, with an eyebrow raised.

Mike dropped to one knee, "Miss Courtney Danielle Lewis, will you marry me?"

Courtney walked past him, then replied over her shoulder, "I guess." She stepped into the hallway with Mike in tow.

* * *

"Courtney, come on in. Would you leave your firearm on the shelf, there by the door, so my men will relax?" Brian asked.

"Sure," she replied. *How did you know, Mr. Skwira?*

She placed the gun high on the shelf. Courtney turned to head toward the large, wooden desk Brian was now seated behind.

"I'm sorry, but the knife, too, please?" he asked. "But bring it over here so I can take a look at it."

"Oh, sure, almost forgot about this little thing." Courtney reached down and pulled up her pants leg revealing a scabbard strapped to her calf. "It's Kevlar and carbon fiber, no metal in it, to circumvent metal detectors. It only shows up if you X-ray someone." As she approached, she noticed several small mirrors in the bookshelves behind him. Hidden X-ray, one way glass with gun ports.

That's very nice Mr. Skwira, but where's your two-way?

As she leaned over the front of the big desk, she handed him the knife handle end first. Looking down, she noticed one of the pictures was actually a small monitor and it had text scrolling on it.

Bingo.

"Very nice weapon, for a spy or an assassin," Brian commented, watching her eyes.

"Yes, it is. A little too flexible going in, but they all seem to pull out a bit harder than you like," Courtney said.

"Interesting. I'm assuming you're able to keep yourself safe?" Brian asked.

"I can hold my own." Courtney smiled.

"Excellent. A beautiful girl like you is not safe without some toys, skills, or both. Let me see what you have that could be worth clemency for people in your particular situation."

Courtney unlocked the tablet, then handed it to him.

"Here's a slideshow I prepared," she said. Numerous photographs of weapons, electronics and their detailed plans scrolled by. Courtney paused on a couple of them and zoomed in on the drawings to show the intricate detail of manufacturing plans.

"My goodness, this is quite a collection. I see I should keep you out of my factories, if I want to keep my information safe that is," Brian said, looking up at her.

"I would definitely recommend it. Though, these folks tried to keep me out as well," she smiled. *Didn't think that was funny, did you?*

"Yes, I suppose they did. The electronic subcomponents?" Brian continued to study the images as she scrolled through them.

"They're included, but not in this demonstration. I have many, very complicated plans and most include subcomponents," Courtney said.

"I see. Yes, this is exactly what you suggested it was. I suppose you want letters from the General himself, clearing you of any wrongdoing to date? Also, some fresh ID cards with clean numbers to go with your letters?" he asked.

"Yes, that would be exactly what we are looking for, plus enough money to keep us comfortable for a few years," she added.

"Would fifty ounces of gold every year for ten years suffice?" Brian asked.

Knowing she could get far more out of him, Courtney smiled and remained silent.

Without batting an eyelid, Mr. Skwira said, "Two hundred and fifty ounces per year for five years?"

"Could we do the first year up front?" she asked.

"Today?" Brian offered.

"Deal. That and everything in it is yours. Here is the combination to it. The failsafe will destroy it if you misenter it three times, so use caution," Courtney said. "I owe you one solar charger, so don't let me forget."

There was a knock at the door.

"Come in, Ronald," Brian called out.

In walked a burly security guard with an aluminum attaché in his left hand and a heavy-duty backpack in his right. He walked past everyone and went right up beside Mr. Skwira with his delivery.

"Thanks, Ronald, you can go now," Brian said and punched a combination into the case. "Your IDs and letters of clemency. Court, I'll give you Danni's also," he said. "Mike, here are your power supplies. I took it upon myself to get you six of them. I hope that is acceptable?"

"Excellent. That will keep me in business for a long time, thank you," Mike said.

"I guess you're realizing by now that I don't like to waste time," Brian said with a smile.

"I can see that. Thank you very much, this means the world to us, sir," Court said, as he accepted his documents.

"No, thank you, all of you. You have brought things which will save many lives for our country. This collection is truly a game changer. Being the sole manufacturer of these will also beef up my personal reserves. It's likely one of the best deals I have ever made," Brian said. "Who's going to carry the twenty pounds of gold?"

"Me," Courtney answered. "I wouldn't want either of them to get hurt." She picked the bag up off the floor with little effort and slung it over her shoulder.

"You can pick up your gun and knife from Perry, whenever you leave the house."

"Thanks, I'll do that," Courtney said.

Reaching out to shake Mike's hand, he said, "You have yourself a keeper there, son."

Courtney looked at Mike to see his reaction.

"I agree and thank you again," Mike said.

"Pleasure doing business with you all. Now let's close up shop and have a relaxing evening," Brian said as he patted Court and Mike on the shoulders, walking them out of the study.

* * *

Courtney walked up to Mike's door and listened for a moment, then tapped on the door. Hearing no reply, she knocked again.

"Come in."

Courtney walked in, smiling. "I should have known you were working on that."

"How?" Mike asked.

"I knocked twice before I got a reply."

"Oh, that. Sorry, didn't hear you the first time," he replied. "It's ready."

"Great news and just in time since we need to go soon."

Concerned by the urgency in her voice, Mike spun around and looked into her eyes.

"You know something?" he asked.

"I have a hunch our stay will end tomorrow, if not tonight," she whispered as she reached him.

Mike stood up and put his arms around her.

"I agree," he whispered back. "Inform your parents. We'll pack at the last second and take off when everyone is ready."

Courtney pulled back from Mike to look into his eyes.

"That was nice, thanks for the hug," Mike said aloud. "Now, let's go see what everyone wants to do tonight."

"I'll meet you downstairs in a few minutes," she said.

Courtney went into her room, scrawled out a note, then took it to her mother.

"Here's my list for when you go shopping tomorrow," Courtney said.

"Oh, why don't you come with me?"

Courtney waited for her mother to read the note.

Danni glanced down, scanned the paper, then said, "Looks pretty self-explanatory. We're planning to stay in tonight. Why don't you two go out this evening? Might be fun for you to have a night alone and check out the town." She continued, "Besides, it would be rude for all of us to go out the first night. These are good people, Courtney, they'll keep an eye on us."

Courtney asked, "Are you positive you want Mike and I to go out tonight?"

"Absolutely. Don't be gone too long in case we need you for something."

"Three hours?" Courtney mouthed days afterward, hoping there was no camera facing her.

"Oh, that's fine. Three, four, five, somewhere in there I suppose. I'll tell your father when he gets out of the shower. You kids run along now and be careful." Danni gave Courtney a strong hug and kissed her on the cheek. "You're an amazing woman and I love you very much."

"I love you, Mom. I would love to stay a while longer and visit more, but we need to go before it gets too late," Courtney said.

She walked out of her parent's room and poked her head back in Mike's door. "You ready?"

Mike was looking out the window and when she saw his face, she knew they were out of time.

"Looks like we have visitors. We should go now," Mike said as Courtney dashed out of the room.

I had to leave that gun and my knife in the study! Courtney was furious as she stuffed some of her things into the bag with the gold. Thirty pounds total—that'll be fine. Entering the hallway, she glanced through the railing and down the swept staircase. Four troops were at the bottom, but before she could get away, one of the soldiers looked up. She ran into Mike's room and locked the door behind her. "They're coming up the stairs!"

"Into the closet," Mike ordered, throwing his bag over one shoulder, then picking up the spud. Mike began adjusting it as he ran in behind her as the bedroom door was kicked open.

A voice yelled, "SAF! On the ground now!"

Courtney looked at Mike across the large closet as he frantically worked the spud. The haze appeared and Courtney dove through.

* * *

Mike watched Courtney dive toward the relative safety of Supreme Britain. He immediately switched off the spud as he jumped after her. He heard the guard yell and felt a hand hit his side as he cleared the portal. Someone squeezed him around the middle, then landed on top of Mike as he hit the floor. He glanced up and saw Courtney coming at him with a look in her eyes that said death. Her foot flew right at his face and made a sickening thud right past his ear. Mike felt a pain in the back of his head, but wasn't sure what had happened. He felt panicked as he lost consciousness.

"Can you hear me? Mike, can you hear me? There you are. You all right?" Courtney asked.

"Yeah, what happened?" He slowly opened his eyes. "Wait, why did you kick me?"

"I didn't kick you," she said.

Mike stared at her in silence.

"Is that what you think happened?" Courtney laughed.

"What's so funny?" he asked.

"I'm sorry, the look on your face is hilarious, that's all."

"If that wasn't your foot that hit me, then what?" Mike demanded, rubbing the back of his head.

"Let me get this straight, Sherlock. I kicked you in the back of the head when I was standing in front of you?"

"When you ask it that way…"

"You brought a friend through with you. He headbutted you in the back of your head when you guys landed in the hallway. I made sure he felt appreciated," Courtney said, as she nodded over to the other side of the room.

"Handcuffs and a gag? You came prepared."

"Nah, he came with his own hardware," she said as she waved a pistol and wave sword.

"Ah, I see. Glad I could be of assistance, yet again," Mike

said.

"Hey, you did great, saved us both from capture. You're my hero." Courtney leaned over and kissed him on the cheek.

"That all a hero gets these days?"

"Not married, are you?"

"That's not exactly what I meant," Mike chuckled, "but I plan to fix that soon."

"Really? Are you sure your fiancée knows about your plans? I think she would have told me."

"Well, all my fiancée has to do is pick the time and place." Mike replied, attempting to get to his feet. "In fact, I'm on my way to the jeweler now."

"Easy tiger. There won't be any wedding until that concussion wears off. Give it a day and we'll talk again," Courtney said.

Looking at Courtney, Mike asked, "What do we do with your latest conquest?"

Her face went cold and she answered, "Kill him."

Is she serious? Let's see…

"Throw him out the window?" he asked.

"Sure."

Mike kept a straight face when he looked over at the soldier. "We could leave him gagged and cuffed to the chair. That would give us plenty of time to get away."

"I said kill him."

"You sound determined," he said.

"Yep. You sound like you actually care what happens to the guy that tried to snap your neck."

"Would you have done that?" Mike asked him.

"Tell the truth, you puke," Courtney said, threatening him with his own gun.

He sheepishly nodded his head in acknowledgment.

"See?" Courtney asked.

"How about we beat him up a little and make him promise to keep his mouth shut?"

"He won't keep his mouth shut. He'll go straight to the SAF and tell them what he saw. You know, that we jumped through fog and landed in a different place. Then they'll be mad at us for letting him know the secret and kill us all."

"He's smart enough to know that if he tells people he witnessed top secret technology, he's a dead man. They'll probably kill his family and friends, too. It can't get back to the Nazis," Mike said.

"I'm glad you brought that up, I never thought about it that way. He's going to cause way more trouble than I thought. We need to kill him and burn the body, in case there are traces of the radiation left on him."

Mike finally realized she had been playing him all along and nearly broke out in laughter. "I guess you're right. Should we toss him down the incinerator chute? There's one at the end of the hall and that way there won't be any blood to clean up."

"Yeah, that's a great idea. I got to do the last two over at your brother's house, so it's your turn."

Mike saw fear growing in the man's eyes.

"I don't remember it that way. You killed the one by the back gate, crushed his windpipe, then broke his neck for trying to shoot you. The second one you only bashed over the head a couple of times and he could have survived," he said.

"Even if he lived and I don't think he did, he won't remember enough to cause me any trouble. Especially since I had him blindfolded the entire time. Notice anything wrong with this picture?" She nodded at the man. "No blindfold, and he keeps looking at me."

The young soldier quickly closed his eyes and lowered his head.

"You are cute, so you can't blame him for looking at you," Mike said.

"Heads or tails?" Courtney asked.

"Not that again," Mike said. "Heads, I suppose."

"Tails. You lose, I get to kill him," she said.

"Crud. You always get the easy ones," Mike teased.

"It's not my fault you suck at coin tosses. Besides, the last guy you killed suffered for hours before I finished the job myself."

"You make a good point there." Mike looked toward the soldier, who was peeking up at him, "I did botch that one." The soldier dropped his head again and closed his eyes once more.

"On second thought, you can kill him. I'm going to take a shower before we get dinner. Hurry it up, I'm getting hungry," Courtney said. She handed Mike the gun and handcuff keys then left the room.

Mike walked up to the young man and whispered, "Are you going to cause trouble if I take you home?"

The soldier mumbled and looked up.

"Eyes!" Mike hissed.

The young man squinted his eyes shut and said something. The gag muffled his words and Mike almost laughed at the sight.

"You're going to kill my mother?" Mike demanded.

The soldier shook his head furiously. Mike removed the gag and the young man's face contorted as if he expected to be hit.

"I won't tell them anything. Please, I just got married and my wife is pregnant," he whispered.

"We hear that a lot in our line of work, but I'm not sure I believe you," Mike said.

"Please, I swear. They know who you are already, all I know is that I jumped after you and hit my head on the wall. I have a knot to prove it, right where our heads collided."

"But I'm so sick of men groveling about wives and children on their deathbed. Oh, it is so annoying," Mike said, loud enough that Courtney could hear if she was listening.

"I'm so sorry," the young man sobbed.

"Now the whining starts. I should have known . . ."

Walking over to the bathroom door he knocked. Courtney opened it, but kept back out of sight. He could tell from her red, swollen eyes that she had been fighting back laughter.

"Can I take this kid back? He's really sorry and promises to keep his mouth shut about what he saw. Plus, they already know who we are, so there's not much to hide."

Courtney had tears dripping off her flushed cheeks and couldn't say a word.

"Great, thanks for understanding. I'll kick him back through and we can take off for dinner as soon as you're ready."

Making sure his smile was gone, Mike turned around and walked over to the soldier. "Look, if you deserve to die, you deserve to die. You need to be a grownup and accept it." Mike paused, but the guard didn't say a word. "All right. If you promise to keep your mouth shut, stop the whining and be a good boy, I'm prepared to send you back. Can you do that?"

"Yeah, I will. I swear," he said.

"I suppose I will then." Mike reached back and punched him square in the nose. "There, we're even now." Mike turned him around and faced him toward the wall. "You only get a second or two, so when the wall gets the slightest hazy look to it, jump through it. Understand?"

He nodded.

Mike turned on the spud, but left the power low. A faint haze formed in front of the soldier.

"Go now," Mike urged.

The soldier turned and ran toward it, jumping headfirst at the wall. His head fell backward from the impact, half knocking the young guard out.

The sight and sound of it forced Courtney and Mike to burst into stifled laughter. Setting the spud on the table, Mike turned the power up and walked over to the sprawled soldier. Picking him up by the belt and collar, Mike got the dazed guard to his wobbly feet and pushed him through the haze.

"Done!" Mike called out.

Courtney threw open the door and ran at him. "You nearly killed me! I couldn't breathe and almost choked to death in there!" Courtney's eyes were swollen and her face was wet with tears. "I have never laughed so hard in my life!"

Mike burst out laughing with her, "You started it. I was just going along."

They laughed as they walked over to the couch and dropped onto it.

"That poor kid will have nightmares for the rest of his life," Courtney said, continuing to laugh.

"You want me to believe you're worried about him? Need I remind you that he gave me this huge knot and a splitting headache? He almost bashed my skull in!" Mike said, trying to control his laughter.

"I thought that happened when I kicked you, in the back of the head, from the front, somehow. Remember?" Courtney burst out laughing again.

"Yeah, yeah. Very funny." Mike remembered how certain he was that she had kicked him and chuckled. "That was kind of funny, I guess."

"Not as funny as you sending him sprinting into the wall. I thought I was going to pee myself!" Courtney gasped for air between laughs. "I opened...I opened the door...you gave him a push and..." She fell over sideways, laughing so hard she didn't make a sound.

Mike laughed as he watched Courtney gasping for air.

"Enough already! You're trying to kill me, I swear it." Courtney got herself up, stifling her laughter as she walked toward the bathroom.

Mike sat on the couch enjoying the moment. *Who knew an assassin could be so much fun?* he asked himself and smiled. *Yep, she's the one. No doubt about it.*

* * *

Courtney looked in the mirror. *You need more of that and less killing. No killing, unless it's an absolute last resort. Now, let's go see what Mike thinks about the new look,* she thought as she opened the door and saw Mike asleep on the couch. "You awake?"

"Oh, yeah, sorry. Must have dozed off," Mike answered. "Wow, you look nice."

"Thanks, but I'm trying to keep a low profile," she answered.

"Not sure it's going to work," Mike said, as he got up.

"I still haven't been out of the room. What is this place anyway?" he asked.

"A mansion turned into a small, posh hotel."

"How did you do that, with me unconscious and the soldier, too?"

"I broke into this room, cuffed him to that chair, then slipped past the front desk and rented this room for the week."

"What if they were booked?" Mike asked.

"They weren't."

"I realize that," he said.

"I suppose I would have stayed in the room until they discovered us, or until you woke up," she said.

"Does any of this make you nervous?"

"Not really. Should it?" Courtney asked.

"It would me."

She smiled at him. "I'm sure it would. Oh, you won't be surprised to hear the floor plan is nearly identical to the Skwira's mansion."

"I guess I should expect it by now," Mike said.

"Enough talk, I'm starving. Get ready for dinner before I starve."

"Yes, ma'am," Mike said and headed for the bathroom.

"Mike, one thing, do people normally laugh like that? Like we did?"

Mike looked back and said, "People who are in love do."

"Oh, is that right?" she asked, as he continued.

"Yep, that's right," he said over his shoulder.

"I guess you spilled the beans then," Courtney said. "You were laughing pretty hard yourself, there for a while."

Mike closed the door until she could only see one of his eyes.

"Yeah, I guess I did. Did you pick a date yet?"

Courtney remained quiet and smiled.

"I don't need an answer now," Mike winked at her and closed the door.

"Tomorrow," Courtney whispered. "Does that work for you?" she called out.

"That works great, whatever it was," he replied.

* * *

"What are we going to do? It's been several days and still nothing," Terry asked.

"Is this another one of your tests? Cause I don't feel like flunking another one," Bill said. "This show is so good," he changed the subject, "it makes you think."

"Perry Mason is one of the greatest detective shows of all time," Terry replied.

"He's a lawyer," the younger agent corrected.

"Yes, I know. As a kid, I watched it every summer while I ate lunch with my grandfather."

"Then why did you call him a detective?" Bill asked.

"I didn't call him a detective, I—never mind." Terry took a deep breath. "No, it isn't a test."

"OK, good. Did I pass?"

Forget it, Terry, or he will drive you nuts. "I'm thinking we should go through her room and see what else she has put away."

"Yeah, I should have guessed. What is it, two days to the second?" Bill asked.

"No, we're over by several minutes," Terry joked.

Bill looked up, "The show is almost over, can I have a few minutes."

"Seriously, Bill, we need to look in there."

Bill turned off the TV and sat up. "That girl is spooky when you think about it. She could have the entire building rigged to blow."

"Oh?"

"Especially after that mess she made of the stairwell at TAC last weekend," Bill said.

"Yeah, but look at everything she did for us," Terry teased.

"Yeah, yeah. You don't need to remind me," Bill said and rolled his eyes. "If we haven't heard from her by seventeen hundred, then we go in there and poke around."

"Deal." Terry pointed at the clock and said, "Two minutes 'til."

"What? Already?" Bill looked down at his watch. "Time flies when you're on vacation."

"Yeah, vacation is over until further notice. I want to get out of here, but we can't risk being seen until things cool down."

"How long are you thinking?"

"Maybe a week or two, but we can't stay here longer than that."

"I'll go in first," Bill said, as he hurried past Terry.

"You take the bathroom, I'll take the closet," Terry called out. "Oh, and don't forget the tank."

"I always check the tank."

"Always? Like the time I found two pistols and a half pound of cocaine in that hotel, after you searched the bathroom?" Terry asked.

"I was testing to see if you'd find it, too," Bill said, as he removed the lid. "See nothing, just as I suspected."

"Did you look under the lid?" Terry asked. He heard a slight groan come from the bathroom.

"Just a Kevlar and carbon fiber knife, that's all," Bill replied.

"Glad you had your eyes open," Terry chided him. "Hey, phone's ringing. Blocked caller," Terry announced.

"Answer it, it's her," Bill said.

"Ello?" Terry answered with an accent, then paused to listen. Pushing the speakerphone button, he said, "Could you repeat that, so my friend can hear you, too?" Terry watched Bill's face to see his reaction.

"I said, why are you in my bedroom?"

"Where are you? When are you coming over? Are you all right?" Bill fired off.

"Not too far away. You guys are OK then I take it?" she asked.

"Yep, all good. The bruises are mostly gone now, but I still have some cuts healing." Bill answered with enthusiasm.

"Cuts? How bad was it?" Courtney asked.

"Not too bad, just skin," Bill said.

"And a couple of light fractures, a perforated eardrum, a black eye and a sprained ankle. Other than that, he's tiptop," Terry said.

"I'm sorry about that, Bill. I tried to keep you guys as far away from it as I could and give you deniability," she explained.

"I know, thanks for not killing me," he said.

"Sure thing, anytime partner." Courtney laughed. "So, I see you guys figured out my little treasure hunt. I hope you're comfortable."

"We're good, now. They tried to off us the other night, but we're keeping a low—"

"We shouldn't talk about it now, buddy," Terry said.

"I want to see you guys. Are you up for some company?"

"I suppose so," Terry replied.

"We can meet somewhere else if you'd rather," Courtney offered.

"If you wanted to do something, I doubt you would have called to warn us. We haven't had any trouble since we got back to town, so I think we're in good shape here," Terry answered.

"That works for me, I have some things there in my room I want to get. Did you find the good stuff already?" she asked.

"Actually, the big oaf wouldn't let me come in here until a few minutes ago." He looked at Bill with annoyance.

"Aw, that was very nice of you. I owe you a big kiss when I get there," Courtney teased.

"Deal," Bill said immediately.

Courtney laughed and Terry looked at Bill to see if he had also noticed the change.

"What do you guys want? Chinese? Italian? Maybe some hotdogs from a lunch truck?" she asked.

"Italian would be great. He ate a half dozen hotdogs the other day and was sick for hours," Terry chuckled.

"I'd kill for a plate of chicken fettuccine right about now," Bill joked.

"Getting tired of my pantry already?" she asked.

"Well…"

"Just teasing. We'll be there in one hour," Courtney said, "and close my door behind you, please."

"Roger that. See you soon," Bill said.

Terry hung up as they filed out of her room. "Courtney teasing?"

"I told you we should have stayed out of her room," Bill said, as he closed the door.

"I'm not sure that was a coincidence, her calling right then. My gut tells me she has the room wired and linked to her phone," Terry said.

"Yeah, you're probably right. You realize she's been three steps ahead of us all along?"

"Yes, Bill, I'm very aware of that. Thanks for the reminder

by the way."

"Don't mention it," Bill said.

"Let's get ready for our guests," Terry said as he picked up a shotgun.

"Roger that," Bill said and pulled a second pistol out of his bag and pocketed one extra clip for each.

"And who do you think she meant by 'we'?" Terry asked.

"Mike and her, of course."

"Yeah, me too, but you can't be too careful," he cautioned.

They took turns watching the street from the edges of the curtains and listening at the front door. When they heard three knocks at the front door, Terry moved away from the window to watch Bill at the front door. The internal bolt clicked and Terry pointed his pistol at the door. Safety off and finger on the trigger, he didn't breathe as the door opened.

"Guys, it's me, Mike. Can I come in?"

"Come on in," Terry called from across the room.

Both of Mike's hands came through the thin opening first and he said, "I have a gun in my belt, under my jacket."

"Turn around, walk in backwards and keep your hands where we can see them," Terry instructed. "Who's out there?"

"Only me. Courtney, you in here?" Mike asked, as he closed the door and bolted it.

"We thought she was with you," Terry said. He spun around to look back out the window and then toward the bedrooms, feeling his pulse quicken.

"She was, but she came in a few minutes ahead of me. She texted me that Bill was at the front door and I should knock. It sounded like she was already in here with you."

Terry and Bill looked at each other as the toilet flushed in Courtney's bedroom.

"What in the heck?" Bill asked.

"She came in ahead of him to make sure we were alone," Terry said. "Must have been in here for a few minutes now."

Courtney walked out wringing her hands like they had not quite gotten dry after washing them.

"Hey, how are you guys?" she asked, with a big smile on her

face.

Terry set his gun down, motioned for Bill to do the same and said, "You can relax, Mike, thanks."

"I guess you got the drop on us again," Terry said with a smirk.

"Not that I needed it," she answered.

"But how did you know for sure?" Bill asked her.

Courtney walked up to him and gave him a loud kiss on the cheek. "Like I promised."

Terry watched Bill's face turned red as he broke out into a boyish grin.

"To answer your question, I watched you guys on the TV above the tub while I used the facilities. You were preparing to defend yourselves rather than attack someone, so I texted Mike to come on in," she said. "I put your dinner on the bed. Thought you would have smelled it by now."

Courtney walked back into her room as Terry quickly thought back over the past few minutes. *The windows were locked, good latches, too. There's no back door. Fire escape and then slipped one of those latches somehow?*

"Fill me in on the past few days," Courtney said, as she tore open the double wrapped plastic sacks with their take out order.

"No wonder Mr. Ravenous didn't smell it at first," Terry said.

Courtney smiled as she set out plates for everyone. "Fill us in."

As they ate, the two agents took turns recanting the past days since Courtney and Mike had vanished.

When they finished, Courtney said, "Nice work. They underestimated you guys."

"We don't seem to be able to hold our own with you, though," Terry said. "Like to share a few more of your tricks?"

"A girl has to have a couple of secrets you know," she said.

"You seem...well—happy," Bill said.

"It's that obvious, huh? I suppose I should come clean, but some background is in order," she said.

Courtney took them back to the night she arrived in the USA via the crystal altar and the events that followed. When she recanted her story of stalking the stalker in college and killing him, the men were in shock.

Terry looked at Bill. *Great, she won him over. Looks like you're on your own, for now.* Terry watched closely to see if Courtney gave a hint that she was lying to them. *Maybe she has changed.*

"When I realized that they would kill anyone who was connected to me, I knew my exit would need to be very convincing. I guess it wasn't good enough?" she asked.

"You did a great job, actually. Had both of us ready to shoot you on sight after you set off the bomb at TAC," Terry replied.

"So, why did they turn on you guys then?" she asked.

"They had a bunch of us processing video clips recovered from TAC and the power plant security system. Everything was scrambled, thanks to you, so there were hundreds of pieces to identify and catalog," Terry explained.

"I even had a utility timed to rewrite the drives repeatedly, for a clean wipe. They must have gotten to them quicker than I expected."

"We saw you and a military looking Mike, walk through a wall and vanish. Evidently, we became a liability at that point."

"This thing Mike created, it spooked them. We're all a liability now," Courtney said.

"It's cool," Bill replied. "He couldn't have known this was coming."

Terry looked at Courtney and asked, "What are you planning?"

"I guess I need to know what you want first," she said.

"To leave the country and see if we can survive the rest of the year I guess. Why, did you have something else in mind?" Terry asked.

"I see two options for you guys," Courtney said, as she walked off into her room. "I took the liberty of getting you everything you would need for your first option, in case you were unable to. So, I should let you have these first." She walked back into the living room and handed each a wallet and passport. "Had these made up a while back, just in case. They're both clean, with simple backgrounds you'll find inside," Courtney said.

"I feel really bad now, Courtney. I was so mad at you the other day, but I was sure you had tried to kill us," Bill said.

"I don't usually miss, you guys know that," Courtney said.

"We know, but you've always kept us at a distance, so we doubted you at first," Terry added.

"I understand completely, but I don't think I could have made it all come out any other way."

"So, what's option two?" Terry asked.

"Option two is a bit crazy, any way you look at it," she replied with a smile.

"Crazy? Compared to everything else that has happened? That sounds a bit scary to me," Bill chuckled.

"Let's hear it, I doubt it could be any crazier than this past week," Terry said.

"That military looking Mike you saw was Colonel Devon," she said.

"Mike has a brother we didn't know about?" Terry asked.

"Not exactly," she said.

Terry asked, "Why do I get the feeling this is going to get even crazier?"

"Intuition?" she asked.

"Come one, let's have it," Bill said.

"Mike's spud has allowed us to travel between my home world, my version of here and a third one, too. In my home, the Nazis won World War Two and conquered the globe. In the third world, the British took over and similarly enslaved everyone. We believe something happened in history that caused reality to fracture. That's what broke It into three, parallel timelines," she explained.

"I—I just can't wrap my head around it," Terry said.

"I know. Actually, it's hard for me to believe, too, but I saw each of the other two versions of Mike in person. I have been to see the other two places," she admitted.

"So, option two is—" Terry began for her.

"Come with us to ancient Egypt," Courtney said.

"OK, that is crazier," Bill said.

"Ancient Egypt? Not just Egypt?" Terry asked.

"We think the problem began back around the time they were building the great pyramids. The three different realities all converge back on that time frame. From what we can tell, everything was the same before then.

"Something very specific happened that fractured the world into three parallel timelines and we need to undo it," Mike added.

"Yep, that is way, way crazier," Bill said.

"I agree with stupid," Terry said, pointing his thumb at Bill.

"Now, that's not nice. At least I didn't think I outsmarted her. She not only fooled you, but she managed to make you think she hadn't," Bill said.

"Can you show us? I mean, this is really hard to believe," Terry said. "Three worlds and time travel all in one conversation is way, way more than I was prepared for. Though, it does help to explain what we saw on those video clips."

Courtney hissed, "Follow me!" as she jumped up.

Terry grabbed for his shotgun as Mike chased Courtney into her bedroom. When Terry got into the bedroom, everyone was gone except for Bill. The bed had been shoved aside, exposing a hole in the bedroom floor.

"Get moving!" Terry demanded.

Mike called up from below, "There are people out in the hall, in the street and on the roof."

Bill scrambled into position above the small hatch and glanced up at Terry.

"Now how did she know that?" Terry asked.

"How should I know?" Bill asked, then dropped into the room below. "Eight feet to concrete. Hurry up, we're leaving!"

Hearing glass shatter behind him, Terry jumped, feet first through the hole. He grabbed onto the bedroom floor, then dropped the last few feet to the ground.

"Hurry, I have to go last," Mike ordered.

"Oh no—" Terry said. "I'm not going to like this."

Three grenades went off overhead and Terry felt the percussions in his chest.

"Flash bangs," Terry called out, then dove headfirst into the haze.

"Woo! What a rush," Bill said, as Mike bumped into Terry.

"Oops, sorry. I wanted to warn you," Mike said.

* * *

"Where are we?" Terry asked.

"Supreme Britain," Mike answered. "It's a little sketchy for us in the other place. There, the military is looking for us."

"How is he so calm?" Terry demanded. "I thought you were just a lab rat. This is just a cakewalk for you?"

Courtney laughed, "Easy, Terry. Mike has been using this thing for a while now. Plus, knowing you can get out of somewhere in less than ten seconds gives you a feeling of security."

"I must admit, he's looking like a pro now," Terry said.

"Come on, we should get moving," Courtney said, as she turned to go.

"So, we're in a different place and no big deal?" Terry asked.

"Look, you're a bit shook up—I get it," Courtney said, "but, you need to relax and trust us. We're on the same team."

"Are we? Everything was fine until you two showed up. Maybe you set us up."

"Echelon got us. We said way too much on that call. Bill even mentioned the two of you were still alive after a hit had gone bad."

"I never said that," Bill replied.

"Look, the system is way smarter than you realize. It doesn't just watch for keywords, like it did in the 80's," Courtney said. "With the new AI and voice print technology, I'm surprised they weren't there when Mike and I arrived."

"You knew they were coming?" Terry demanded.

"I suppose. Look, I knew we could get out, but hadn't had a chance to tell you guys. Besides, if they had kicked in the door, the dozen flash-bangs I have in the front walls would've knocked them off their feet."

"So, we were more like bait then?" Terry asked.

"Sure, if you want to look at it that way." Courtney smiled.

"Look, guys, this thing is way bigger than us," Mike said. "Everything we know is part of a mistake made several thousand years ago. Somehow, someone did something very bad and fractured our reality. Millions have suffered and died at the hands of the Nazis and the British."

"We know all about World War Two," Terry said.

"I'm talking about the seventy years after that. There are two worlds where it never ended. In this place we're at now, the British completely rule the world. The entire globe. That's not right," Courtney said. "Where I came from, the war against the Nazis is finally nearing the end. You want to start whining about almost losing your skin then go ahead. We are more concerned with global atrocities than our own insignificant lives."

"That's enough, both of you. We have a lot of talking to do, but for now, you'll just have to trust us with what you know," Mike said. "Come on, we'll get a couple of hotel rooms down the street and do our talking there."

As Mike and Courtney walked toward the side door to leave the garage, Terry nodded toward the pair.

"The two of them have become close pretty fast, don't you think?" Terry said, looking at them walking side by side.

"How long have they kept that under wraps?" Bill asked.

"I have no clue."

"You think it really is them?"

"It's them, for the most part but I'm not sure about either one. He seems a bit too adjusted to this craziness for my liking and she's far too nice. Something is not right here and I'm not going to be turning my back on either of them for a while," Terry said.

* * *

Courtney was becoming frustrated by the wait, so she joined Mike at the front desk of the cheap hotel in Supreme Britain.

"I'm sorry sir," the hotel clerk said with a thick British accent. "You must prove you're at least a second class citizen to stay in this hotel. Plus, I can tell by the way you talk that you aren't from around here."

Courtney glanced back to give Terry a warning look and saw he had already picked up on their situation.

"I don't have ID. I told you, my wallet was stolen. All I have is some cash," Mike explained.

Courtney touched his arm, motioning they should leave.

"Look, we're from up north—Michigan," Mike said.

"Michigan? Where is that?" she asked and reached one hand under the counter.

Courtney watched as muscles flexed in her forearm. Diving onto the counter, Courtney drove her fist into the woman's jaw and knocked her unconscious.

"What the heck was that for?" Mike demanded, as he pulled her back off the counter by her belt.

"She pushed a silent alarm, or didn't you notice?" Courtney turned and faced Mike, "Why did you keep on? She wasn't going to rent us a room no matter what you said."

"I thought I could talk her into it."

"You were wrong. Let's go before the people on the other end of that button show up."

Courtney picked up her bag and turned toward the door, freezing in her tracks.

"Get to the elevator," she barked at Mike and yanked a pistol from underneath her jacket.

Terry and Bill were already on the elevator and Bill was holding the doors open for them. Mike took off running for the elevator as the first volley of gunfire erupted through the lobby. Terry reached out with his pistol and returned fire. Courtney saw three pairs of officers dive for cover behind furniture.

"Two hit, six total, pistols," Terry called out.

Courtney saw the closest officer look out from behind a half wall and shot him in the forehead. "Front right is neutralized," she called out as she ran toward the elevator.

Mike was nearing the elevator when she saw him grab his hip, arch his back, then fall to the ground. She turned, planted a bullet in the shooter's face, then ran to help Mike.

"Two hit, two dead, two unknown!" Courtney hoped it

would slow the remaining officers and buy enough time to get Mike in the elevator.

Bill and Terry took turns firing toward the officers to provide cover.

Courtney reached out and grabbed Mike by the jacket, dragging him the remaining few feet into the elevator. As the door closed, Courtney looked into Mike's eyes and realized that he was worse than she thought.

"Mike, where are you hit?" she asked as the elevator climbed the building.

Gasping for air, Mike wheezed, "In the…back…right side."

"Hang on, we'll get you out of here," Courtney said, as she stood up. "The SAF has medical capabilities that are far more advanced than back home. I have to take him there. Do you want to come with us or would you rather return home until I can figure this mess out?" Courtney asked, as she pulled the spud out of Mike's bag.

Terry said, "I don't think we should get separated. Plus, you have the only one of those I know of."

"I don't blame you, but I don't want to force you," Courtney said.

"Can we do it from inside here?" Terry asked.

"Don't try it. What if…the other building…no elevator? Or…a floor above?" Mike managed to say.

"What if there is no building?" Bill asked.

"There's that, too," Courtney said.

"You mean to tell me you had us come here with you not knowing what we might hit on the other side?" Terry asked rhetorically. "That's just plain stupidity!"

"Risky, but not stupid. Things are very similar and in some cases identical," Courtney said.

"We need to get out of this building and back on the ground before I'm going through that thing again," Bill said.

"Terry, you lead. Bill, you carry Mike and I'll carry the bags," Courtney ordered.

"The roof," Mike gasped, "we need…to look around."

"Good idea, but it might get us killed," Courtney said.

At the top floor, Courtney flipped the alarm switch to hold the elevator in place. The foursome worked their way down the hall to the stairwell and climbed the last flight of stairs to the roof. Courtney saw Terry shoot the latch twice to get the door open and jerk his head back, putting his hand to his face.

"I knew I was going to regret that," Terry said, then kicked the door open.

Mike lifted his drooping head. "I know this building in the USA, but I have no clue about the SAF," Mike said softly.

Courtney ran over to the edge and looked around. "Yeah, it's back home for sure. I've been in it a few times scouting around. There's a police station, down there, no wonder they responded so quickly," Courtney said. "I think it's even the same height as the one back home," she added.

"You think so?" Terry asked.

"Yeah, but it could be one or two floors different."

"How can you tell?" Terry asked.

"From the buildings around it."

Terry took his hand off his face. "Is it bad?"

Courtney reached out and pinched the piece of metal sticking out of Terry's cheek. She gave it a tug and watched a small spot of blood form and dropped the piece into his hand.

"Not bad at all," she said.

Terry nodded and flicked the shard aside. "We're out of time," Terry said.

"I know," she said. Holding the unit in front of Mike she said, "Set it up to go forward, Mike."

"Forward?" he asked.

"Absolutely. We have to go, now."

Mike turned a dial, flipped the power on, then handed the spud back to her.

"We're ready. Go on through, but watch your step on the other side, it may be eight feet down," Courtney warned.

Mike glanced over at her and mouthed, "Forward?"

"It's our only chance. Now hold on to Bill." She leaned forward and gave Mike a kiss. "I'm right behind you."

* * *

Courtney watched Terry go first. Bill followed with Mike half in his arms and half thrown over his shoulder.

"Please, let them be all right," Courtney said, then turned off the spud and jumped after them. She felt herself fall for an instant, then landed on something firm as she dropped to one knee. She noticed a small, red glow off in the distance as her eyes focused.

"We are in an apartment," Terry said.

"Hello, is somebody home?" Courtney asked in a kind voice. Pausing for a few moments, she said, "Turn on some lights and search it."

Bill laid Mike on the couch in front of her, then pulled his pistol and walked into one of the rooms."

"Clear!" Terry called out and Bill did the same a second later.

"Food in the fridge looks pretty fresh, we could have company any time," Bill said.

"I have to get Mike to the hospital. You guys should try to find us a place to hide out."

"We'll go together," Terry said. "Lead the way."

They left the apartment and headed down the hallway.

"These buildings are very similar in both places," Terry said.

"All three places, actually. We didn't go to the USA, this is where I was born."

"But Mike said—" Terry started and then realized what she had done. "You aren't the Courtney we know. What have you done with her?"

Courtney almost laughed at his reaction. "Terry, it was necessary and calculated. I would say that roughly ninety percent of the major buildings I've seen are in the same place. Of those, well over two thirds of those are about the same height."

Bill stood in front of the elevator doors, holding Mike in silence.

"He doesn't seem to care, but I do," Terry warned. "What you did was reckless and you endangered all of us."

"We were nearly guaranteed to be caught in the USA. I made the decision to take our chances here."

Terry groaned and rolled his eyes. "Unbelievable."

"You aren't the Terry I know," Bill said.

"Now he speaks," Terry said, "Thanks, partner."

"It's kinda nice to see you have some emotions in there, too." Bill continued to face the doors.

"Now you're starting to get all warm and fuzzy, too? What the heck is happening to us?" Terry asked.

"I know a lot has happened. We're in uncharted territory, so we have to stick together," Courtney said, hearing the elevator chime.

As they were heading into the lobby, a middle-aged couple walked in through the front doors.

"You have a car?" Bill asked, showing his gun.

"Here, the blue one out front," the scared man said, as he handed Bill the key.

"Hospital?" Courtney asked.

"Follow the road down that way and you'll see signs for the military hospital," he replied.

"Thanks. You can pick up your car there in an hour," Courtney said and they rushed out of the building.

"We're smoked," Terry said. "Military hospital? Are you kidding me?"

"Mike is a Colonel, right? We'll drop him off and they'll take care of him. Then we'll find someplace to lay low until we can figure this out," Courtney said. She jumped in behind the wheel and started the car.

When the last door shut, Courtney popped the clutch and spun the car around in the middle of the street. Speed shifting every gear, she drove the car as hard as it could go.

"Almost there, Mike. You still hanging in there?" she asked.

"I'm OK. Got my fingers over both leaks…there's internal damage," he said.

"I know. I'm sorry," Courtney called back to him. "Hang on, going to take a hard left," she said, barely a second before the tires started to howl.

"Up there, on the right," Terry said, as the facility came into view.

* * *

Coming to a stop at the triage emergency doors seemed to take forever, so Courtney yanked up on the emergency brake and jumped out. As the car skidded the last few feet to a stop, she opened Mike's door. Courtney helped Bill get Mike out of the car as Terry ran inside. Moments later, Terry returned with an attendant pushing a gurney, meeting them as they reached the doors with Mike.

"This is Colonel Mike Devon. I advise you to get your best people on him. Stat," Courtney ordered.

"Yes, ma'am," the attendant replied and rushed the gurney down the hallway.

Courtney froze in her tracks. *If you go, you'll be arrested. If you leave him, you may never see him again.* She stood in the hallway, unable to leave Mike behind.

"Mr. Owens, can you hear me? Captain Owens?"

Courtney turned to see a pair of nurses standing over an elderly man on a gurney. "I called his only living relative, a granddaughter, but she won't be here until morning. Until then, I guess we'll do what we must."

What they 'must'? You have to leave him, Courtney. Get moving.

She turned and headed for the car, slowly gaining speed. When she reached it, Courtney saw Terry had gotten into the driver's seat and Bill had joined him up front.

Climbing in behind them, she said, "We need to find someplace to crash for the night."

"Your bag's heavy. Ammo?" Bill asked.

They know.

"There's about twenty pounds of gold in there," she replied.

"That's a lot of gold. Why so much?" Terry asked.

"How do you fund an op in a place that uses currency you don't have? Gold, that's how," Courtney replied. "So, how about getting us out of here, before the locals arrive?"

As Terry pulled away from the curb, Courtney felt a sense

of loss. Don't look back, you won't see anything, she told herself. Courtney glanced back anyway, for a last glimpse of the hospital. The further they went the more distraught she became, feeling as if she had abandoned Mike.

"Head back toward the hospital, this is too far away," she said.

Courtney saw Bill glance at Terry. Pretending not to notice, she said, "There—those apartments—pull in there."

She got out, walked up to a door with no number on it and rang the bell. The door opened and a heavyset man poked his head out. After a few exchanges, he went back inside and she returned to the car.

"One ounce of gold and we can have a two bedroom apartment for the month, no questions asked," she said.

Taking out one roll of gold rounds, she said, "here's four for each of you. Each one is roughly a month's salary here."

"Thanks, I feel better already," Bill said.

"That's good," Courtney said, as the man peeked out the door. "I'll be right back." She paid for their apartment, took the keys and turned as the man closed the door.

Scumbag, Courtney thought, then walked up to the car and said, "Unit twenty three."

"How far to the hospital from here?" Bill asked.

"Less than eight blocks. Come on." Courtney walked over to a staircase and went up, motioning for them to follow. Once they were inside the apartment, she handed Terry the second key. "This one is for you guys, I'll keep the other."

"You think he'll keep his mouth shut?" Terry asked.

"For a few days, I hope, but we'll need to keep an eye out for trouble either way."

"I don't like it," Terry said.

"Me either," Courtney replied. "I'm taking the car back. You guys should do a little scouting. Here's another ten ounces apiece, in case something happens and one of us gets separated. I'm taking the rest of the gold and the spud with me," she said, as she zipped her backpack.

"Maybe we should take the spud?" Terry asked.

"I might have agreed to that if you guys hadn't gone through my bag when I was trying to save Mike's life back there. The trust is damaged, in both directions. It's because of me, I get that. But until I'm sure you guys are over it, I'm going to play it a little extra safe." Neither of them spoke and Courtney was glad. "So, let's do some recon tonight and try to stay in during daylight hours until we can get out of here."

"Roger that," Bill said.

Terry asked, "What time should we expect you?"

"Before sunrise," Courtney said, then closed the door.

* * *

Courtney stopped the car one block before the hospital driveway. She shut off the engine and wiped everything down they might have touched. Pulling the paperwork out of the glove box, she memorized the owner's information. Courtney closed the door with a tissue, locking the key inside. She pocketed the tissue and started walking toward the hospital.

Remembering the unresponsive elderly Mr. Owens, Courtney formulated a plan. She pulled her hair back and got the cap out of her pack. She slipped it on, walked in the main entrance and up to the nurse at the front desk. "What room can I find grandpa Owens in? They brought him in earlier. I guess he's in bad shape."

"Let me look him up," the nurse said, after giving Courtney a strange look.

She didn't like the accent, Courtney told herself. She exaggerated a deep breath, as if she was attempting to calm herself.

"He's in room four eighty three."

"Thank you," Courtney said. She rushed over to the elevator, expecting Mike was in surgery, down the corridor from where she stood.

Arriving on the 4th floor, Courtney walked up to the desk and checked in.

"Your grandpa may not wake up this time dear. It's only a matter of hours or days before his heart stops completely. I wish I had better news for you."

"I just arrived from out of town and I'm exhausted. Can I sleep in his room in case he awakes in the night?"

"Certainly, there's a recliner already in there. Here's a blanket and pillow."

"I appreciate it," Courtney said.

"Supper is over, but I have a couple of meals left."

"I'm fine, thanks though."

"I'll throw them away if someone doesn't eat them."

"Thank you, I will take one," Courtney said and walked into Captain Owens' room. "Hi grandpa, I'm here now," she said and sat down to eat. "Food's good here, grandpa. Let me know when you're hungry and I'll have them bring you something." Courtney finished eating and made herself comfortable in the recliner.

Let's hope he doesn't wake up and start screaming, she thought, then closed her eyes.

A young girl was laughing and playing with a doll in the middle of Mike's living room. Courtney felt a warmth wash over her.

"Micah, whatcha doing?" a woman's voice asked.

"Playing with dolly, Momma," she answered.

"I see that, are you having a tea party?"

"No, we're getting ready to go kill some bad guys with Aunt Courtney. They're going to hurt Daddy if we don't go now."

Jillian? What's she doing with Micah?

Courtney awoke with a start.

What a weird dream. Wait, what's that? Voices. Military. Four or five men, Courtney thought.

She glanced up at the clock on the wall.

Twenty three hundred? You slept three hours—he's out of surgery by now.

Courtney pulled off her blanket and got up. "It's me, grandpa," she said as she walked to the door and peeked out.

She saw several uniformed soldiers talking outside a room, a few doors down the hall.

That has to be Mike.

Courtney closed the door, walked over to the window and looked out at the ledge.

It's plenty wide enough.

She put a chair against the window, pushed it open as wide as she could and squeezed herself out.

Time for a quick prowl.

In less than a minute, she was able to work her way down the ledge and confirm her suspicion. The lights were dim and Mike was fast asleep. Courtney made her way back to the elderly man's room and pulled his street clothes out of the drawer next to his bed. She put his pocket knife in her own pocket and placed the clothes in a plastic bag she found under the sink. Confident she was as prepared as possible, Courtney sat back down in the chair and closed her eyes. The surgery had taken about two to three hours so that meant Mike would be out at least another three hours.

Just before daybreak will be the only chance you get.

Courtney forced herself to relax and wondered if she would dream about Micah again. She closed her eyes and waited.

* * *

Court was locked in a room and shackled to a chair at the SAF building beside the research facility. He was nearing exhaustion after being periodically interrogated for over sixteen hours. Between sessions his captors played the video where the Colonel, Danni and he forced their way into the crystal altar. He watched the video of the first soldier shoot the other and then commit suicide until the images were seared into his memory. Court was nearing his breaking point and knew it. He felt himself start to fall asleep, as his thoughts went to Danni once more.

Tell the truth, no matter what, tell the truth, he kept thinking, over and over.

The video stopped playing again and Court looked up to see who the next interrogator would be. A man stepped inside the room and Court thought he detected a smile on the man's face.

"Court? Are you OK? Have they hit you?" Mr. Skwira shoved

119

the guard aside and rushed into the room. "What have you done to him?" he screamed at the soldier, who stepped back into the hallway.

"I have made my frustrations known to the General. He agreed to release you both into my custody, providing I accept full responsibility," Mr. Skwira said.

"Brian, I hope we aren't causing you any trouble," Court said.

"Forget it. I happily accepted that responsibility. Also, I've engaged a military lawyer to file a complaint regarding your mistreatment. Fat lot of good that will do, but it will get us on the record."

"We never wanted anyone to get hurt," Court said. "Where's Danni? Is she all right? Have you seen her?"

"She's right behind me and she's fine," Mr. Skwira said.

"She told the truth. We both told the truth."

"I know, Court. They said that both of you had told the same story. Also, that it matched the video footage they had of that mess with the Colonel next door in the basement. From what I gather, they're trying to get information on the Colonel and they think you two are the key."

"Brian, I already told them, he's dead. When we followed him through the crystal altar, he was already shot. He died less than thirty minutes after that. I don't know what else to tell them."

"I understand. Guard, take the cuffs off my friend," Brian said, as the soldier entered the room.

"Step out into the hall please," he said.

Court struggled to stand and nearly fell over.

"That's not possible. Look what you've done to him!" Brian exclaimed as he put an arm around Court. The guard removed the cuffs, then the pair went into the hallway.

"Danni!" Court yelled, "You're OK!"

"I'm fine, but you—are you all right?" Danni rushed up to steady him. "What did they do to you?"

"The usual, level one interrogation."

"I'm not sure I believe you, you look terrible," Danni said.

"Mr. Skwira here arrived just in time and stopped them. Otherwise, level two would have begun any time."

"Let's go back to the house so we can take care of you," Brian said. "I've already made arrangements to increase security and we have a nurse available too."

* * *

Perry, the driver, was standing outside the building and rushed to the door when they appeared. "Mr. and Mrs. Lewis, I'm so glad you're both all right," he said, as he opened the door.

"Thanks, Perry. It's good to see you as well," Court said, as they climbed into the back of the limousine.

Mr. Skwira looked at Court as they started to pull away from the building. "Court, it seems Courtney and her friend made it out, but we haven't heard from them since," he explained.

"That is great news, Brian. What about the missing soldier? Is he dead?" Danni asked.

"No, he turned up about an hour later. He was bruised up a little and somewhat confused about where he'd been. He told them he fought with Mike, in Mike's closet. Said he was knocked out and when he came to, he was in Courtney's room across the hall."

"So, he was there all along?" Court asked.

"Now that's where it all gets a little confusing. The room was searched, but no one was inside. Two guards saw him run into Mike's room and heard him crash through the closet door. When they went in to help him, the soldier was gone."

"Oh, I see," Court said.

"Mike's invention?" Brian asked.

Court nodded.

"You two get some rest. When you're ready, we'll have a meeting to clear the air," Mr. Skwira said, as the car stopped in front of the house.

"I need a few hours of sleep, so let's plan on getting together before lunch," Court said, as they climbed out of the car.

"Perfect, that gives me plenty of time to get a few of my affairs in order."

* * *

Courtney watched out the small glass window and kept track of the routines of the guards and nurses.. Each time the nurse came to check on Captain Owens, Courtney pretended to be sleeping in the chair.

She checks on Mike at ten or twelve minutes after the hour. It's about an hour before dawn. You have to try to get him out now.

As soon as the nurse had gone, Courtney was out the window, shuffling back down the ledge toward Mike's room. Through the dim glow of the room, she saw Mike was still laying on his side, facing the door.

She pulled out the pocket knife and jammed it into the latch of his first window to try and force it open. She struggled to get it into the latch but couldn't. Frustrated, she held the knife in one hand and then pounded on it with her other. The window rattled from the blow but she managed to get the knife into the latch. Concerned the guards heard the noise, Courtney quickly darted back to the adjacent room's window ledge. She peeked into the room and saw a guard throw the door open, look around, then close it again.

Close call, she thought.

Courtney relaxed her muscles for a few seconds and then moved back toward the window. Standing in front of her was a groggy looking Mike Devon in a hospital gown. He smiled and waved slowly at the startled Courtney.

"You scared me," she whispered.

"Sorry," he mouthed at her and smiled sheepishly.

Courtney pointed at the latch. Nodding that he understood, Mike reached out and flipped the handle to unlock the window. The door to his room began to open and Mike awkwardly shuffled back to bed. Courtney drew her gun and leveled it at the door. As it opened, she could see the guard had his back turned to her and appeared to be opening it for someone else.

Seeing Mike get back in bed, she moved away from his

window, holding on to the frame of the next window. The lights inside that room came on and Courtney spun her head to see a bandaged young boy on his bed, peering at her. Smiling, Courtney acted like she was wiping off the window, then waved. The boy waved back with a corded controller in his hand, but his face showed concern. Holding a finger up to her lips, she nodded with a secretive look. He nodded back and smiled. Courtney pretended to turn off a light switch. The boy understood and turned off the light. Once again, Courtney was nearly invisible out on the window ledge.

Inching her way over, she peeked around the edge of Mike's window and saw a nurse making a note on his clipboard. After counting out one minute, Courtney checked his room again and saw it was empty. Mike's head popped up and he climbed back out of his bed.

He opened the window and said, "You must get me out of here. These guards knew those two soldiers that died and blame me—well, the Colonel—for it."

"Have you heard how long you'll need to be in here?" she asked.

"They're moving me first thing this morning. I have to get out now," Mike implored.

"I was afraid of that. How bad is the pain?"

"It's not bad, but I'm stiff and weak."

"They are more advanced than us, medically. Probably due to the seventy plus years of war and killing," Courtney said.

"Can you open your window far enough to slip out?" Courtney stepped back so he could try.

Mike shoved on his window and forced it open as far as he could.

"I think I can fit, but hold on," he said, as he made his way over to the door. Standing quietly, Mike listened with his hand on the latch. After a moment he returned to the window. "The cute nurse is distracting my guards."

"Typical men. You're all so predictable," Courtney said.

"Don't make me come out there," Mike teased.

"I wish you would, since we don't have much time."

"Scoot over then, I'm coming to join you." Mike winced as he stepped up on the chair. "The drugs must be wearing off."

"It's the excitement, making you burn it off faster," she explained. "It's better that you feel the pain, otherwise you'll hurt yourself more." Courtney helped Mike out onto the ledge.

"Maybe this wasn't such a good idea after all," Mike said, as he struggled.

"Use this metal strip to hold on and shuffle your feet. We don't have very far to go."

"If they catch us now, we're both dead," he said.

"Thanks for the encouraging thought. Now, smile and wave at the nice boy," Courtney said, as she waved into the dark room.

"What are you—" Mike was interrupted by the flash of the light in their eyes.

"That. Wave, or you're going to scare the kid," she ordered.

Obediently, Mike waved at the startled boy.

Once again, Courtney motioned for him to turn the light back off but he shook his head.

Smiling, Courtney pulled out her pistol, smiled sweetly and nodded. She mouthed the word yes at the wide-eyed little boy, who immediately switched it back off.

"You sure know how to charm a kid," Mike said.

"My tactics seem to have worked on you, too," she said.

"I suppose."

"Here you are, in a gown, wounded, walking a ledge with me. I must have done something right," Courtney said coyly.

"You have a point," he chuckled.

"This is where we get off."

"Good, I'm feeling a bit dizzy," Mike whispered.

Courtney opened the window as far as she could, but it was clear Mike could not fit through. "Hang on while I try another one." Courtney slipped inside and opened the other windows.

"This one is the widest, try it."

Mike gingerly worked his way through the narrow opening. "Oh, this doesn't feel good. I think I'm stuck."

Courtney held the chair anxiously, as Mike worked back and forth.

"We're down to less than five minutes before the nurse's next tour," she cautioned.

"Got it," Mike said, as he slipped his chest in through the window.

"Sit for a few seconds and rest. This is grandpa Owen, he had a bad stroke. Looks like we are going to lose him any day," Courtney said, as she walked over and petted the man softly on the head. Leaning over him, she kissed him on the forehead and a smile eased across his face. "Goodbye grandpa. We love you. Here, put these on," Courtney whispered to Mike.

Mike nodded at Mr. Owen and pointed to the clothes. Courtney smiled and nodded. Shaking his head with a grin, Mike donned the old man's slacks and shirt. When he realized he could not bend low enough to put on the shoes, he glanced up at Courtney. Taking them, she gave Mike a quick kiss on the cheek and then put the shoes on for him.

"I'll go first and you follow right behind me. When we get close to it, you walk right up to the elevator and push the button. Don't look up and don't make eye contact with anyone. Remember, your grandpa is dying," Courtney said.

She opened the door and walked toward the nurses' station, only a few doors away from the guards at Mike's room. Courtney distracted the nurse at the desk by getting a brochure off the wall. She then watched the younger nurse make her way past the guard post. The elevator chimed, but no one heard. Courtney walked down the hall to the elevator and heard one of the guards make a comment as she joined Mike inside.

"Men are idiots and easily neutralized," she said.

"Yikes, you sound a little hostile there, pretty lady," he teased.

Courtney almost punched him in the arm but stopped herself. Mike gasped and let out a groan.

"I didn't even hit you."

"Yeah, the bullet broke one rib and grazed three more. Even breathing hurts."

"In that case, if we walk past a mirror, you need to look away," she replied.

"Why's that?"

125

"Trust me," Courtney said, then took Mike's hand as they walked out of the hospital. "We have about a ten minute walk to the apartment we rented, so go at your own pace."

"Planning to stay a while?" Mike asked.

"We should stay long enough for you to get well."

"I need a few days, then we can go."

"Two weeks, minimum. I know it's risky, but losing you isn't an option anymore," she replied.

"Anymore?" he asked.

"Right, now that we're going to be married," she smiled.

"We could use the spud to back things up a bit, back in time before—"

"We aren't going to start doing stuff like that. Plus, I'm not leaving you behind, unless I have no choice. Besides, we don't know what might happen if we start backing up."

"I see you've already made up your mind. You're probably right anyway."

"Probably?" Courtney teased.

"Oh, um, I meant definitely," Mike said, slowly lifting a hand, as if to defend himself.

"Nice touch, fraidy-cat," she said and laughed.

Mike chuckled, then groaned. "Now that was mean."

"Then watch it, or I'll make you laugh again."

"Yes, ma'am, I will," Mike said, as he patted her hand.

Courtney leaned over and laid her head on Mike's shoulder. "What do you think about naming our daughter Micah?"

"I'd like that very much. Micah Danielle?"

"We'll have to work on a middle name, but it has to be something fitting a beautiful little girl."

* * *

Court could hear Brian talking on the phone as he walked up to the office door. He thought about listening in but remembered that he was under surveillance and knocked.

"Come in."

"I may look like a beat dog, but I'm feeling much better,"

Court said, as he walked into the office.

"I'm so glad the two of you are all right," Brian said. "They can get pretty rough if they think you have a secret."

"It's definitely not something I wish to repeat," Court said. "Brian, I don't want you to take this wrong but how did they know we were all here?" Court watched for any telltale reaction.

"I called the General to go over the deal and arranged for the IDs. He agreed to it, then reneged," Brian said, without blinking.

"See, that's what I don't quite get," Court said. "The General couldn't get four IDs made up that quickly if they were his own. And, if he did do that, why would he need to get counterfeits?"

"Court, I'm sure—"

"The other thing that gets me is why would you confiscate those IDs before the SAF could get them?"

"No, I—"

"I'm guessing that somehow the General caught on to your game. Could there be a leak in your own house? If that's the case, I expect someone is no longer in your employ. If not, then you're currently scrambling to find out who it was." Court paused to let Brian speak.

"Let me show you something, Court." Brian got up and walked toward the bookcase behind his desk which swung open toward them. "After you."

"Now that's something, I must admit," Court said, as he walked past Brian into the secret room.

Brian closed the door and said, "Now we are free to talk. My house is wired for security and the SAF tapped into it. We usually have very little to hide and let them watch, most of the time. When I knew you were coming, we pulled their tap, assuming they'd come by and fix it. What I didn't know was that they had more than one."

"I'm sorry to push you on this, but you understand," Court said.

"I do and you have every right. I would have been livid if something like that had happened to my wife and me."

"Knowing Danni was being interrogated was, by far, the worst part."

"I'm sure it was. For what it's worth, I've disconnected all internal monitoring systems," Brian said.

"That's refreshing to know," Court said. "Do you think we're safe now? And Courtney? Is it safe for Mike and her to come back?"

"No, but they have Mike already and he's the one they really want."

"They have him? How?"

"It seems they got into a gunfight with the authorities at some hotel downtown. There's footage from the hospital that shows Courtney and some man taking him inside. They left him with an orderly and drove off," Brian said.

"When did you hear this?" Court struggled to remain calm.

"Just got off the call when you came in. My sources aren't always the quickest. Funny part is, they left the car right where they told its owners they would," Brian chuckled.

"So, they're close by?"

"Mike is. He took one to the hip and one in the back."

"How bad is he?" Court asked.

"My source said Mike was in surgery for a couple of hours, but that's all she knew. Sounds like Courtney needs our help," Brian said, as the phone on the wooden desk started blinking. "Go ahead." As he listened to the caller, Brian's eyes cut over to Court. "He's gone? As in vanished or dead? Seriously? Now that is interesting. I owe you another one, thanks."

Brian hung up the phone.

"That girl of yours walked right into the hospital, pretended to be the relative of another patient and camped for the evening. My source watched her get Mike on the elevator right under the noses of two SAF guards."

"She's been well trained," Court said with a smile.

"Has her parents' genes, that's for sure."

"They escaped," Court said, trying to imagine her next move.

"If they did, we're going to have company soon. Come on, we need to grab a bite and get ready for whatever comes next."

As they walked back through the office, Brian placed his hand on Court's shoulder. "My friend, if that boy survives, he's going to have his hands full."

"No more than I did with her mother," Court said with a smile.

* * *

It took Courtney and Mike nearly half an hour to make the short walk to the apartment.

Courtney opened the door for Mike and said, "Looks like the guys already managed to get some shopping done." She glanced at the card table, folding chairs and blankets as she walked into the kitchen. "They bought a couple bags of groceries and some bottled water, too."

"Can I have a bottle?"

"Sure," Courtney said, then read a note aloud, "Gone to look around a bit more, back by sunrise."

"Are they safe out there?" Mike asked.

"Safer out there than in here. They have lots of escape routes and we have two."

"Never thought about it that way."

"Enough talking, you need to lay down."

"I'm fine for a while, why don't you get some rest," he suggested.

"You aren't fine. You look like death warmed over and then thrown from a speeding car for good measure. Take this room and get to sleep." She handed him a bottle of water, gave him a kiss and closed him in the bedroom.

After eating an early breakfast and reading for a couple of hours, Courtney heard a noise at the door. She pulled out her pistol and peeked out the edge of the drapes. Terry and Bill had on dark hats and jackets, each carrying two sacks of supplies.

"Great work guys," she said, opening the door.

"We figured you'd try to spring lover boy in the next day or two, so we grabbed extras in case," Bill said.

"Already done," she said.

"Done? You have Mike?" Terry asked.

"He's asleep on your bed actually." She smiled.

"My floor you mean," Terry said. "Poor guy is going to be in bad shape when he wakes up."

"They were going to move him this morning, so I had to."

"How bad is he?" Bill asked.

"From what Mike could remember, one was lodged in his hip, the other went in his right side and out the back. A few stitches, one broken rib and some bandages," she explained.

"That's amazing," Bill replied. "I thought he was a goner at first."

"It didn't look good," Courtney agreed. "Are there any shops nearby where we can get some camping mattresses and other supplies? Wait, where did you get the local currency?"

Bill nodded at Terry.

"Well, Bill flagged down a fancy limo and I offered the guy an ounce of gold for a grand. He pulled out seven fifty and said if we could do another he'd be back with twelve fifty."

"He didn't actually do it?"

"Yep. We didn't think he'd come back either, but he did, in less than twenty minutes," Bill said.

"That's a nice job, guys."

"You're not mad?"

"You thought I would be?" Courtney looked at Terry as well.

"We did bet an ounce of gold on it," Terry said, as he tossed a coin to Bill.

"Thanks for your faith in me, Bill," Courtney said.

"No sweat, it paid well, too."

"We would've bought a few sleeping bags, but the store didn't open for another hour," Terry said, glancing over her shoulder at the stove behind her.

"Perfect, I'll go pick some up," she said.

"Shouldn't Bill go? You and I were inside the hospital and they probably have nice pictures of us in the media by now."

"You're right. Bill, would you mind making a run for me? I'll give you an ounce of gold," Courtney said, smiling as he spun around to look at her.

"You bet. I need all I can get, now that I'm semi-retired."

"I never knew that monkey was so fond of gold," Terry said,

pointing his thumb at Bill.

"I don't have any job prospects on the horizon and selling blood plasma isn't gonna cut it," Bill said, as he put his shoes back on.

Courtney tore off a piece of grocery sack and scrawled out a list. "Put everything in the big backpack and double up the sleeping bags before you roll them up. You'll be just another vagrant to folks out on the street."

"Got it. See you in a couple of hours," Bill said and headed out the door.

Terry said, "You should lay down and get some rest."

"I already got some at the hospital while I was waiting. Besides, I need to find my parents and make sure they're OK," Courtney said. "You hold down the fort and keep an ear out for Mike. He'll be in a lot of pain when he wakes up."

"Roger that. Anything else I should know before you leave?"

"Keep your head down and stay alert. If something goes wrong you need to be very careful. These people are quick to shoot, as we've seen," Courtney said, as she pulled the bag over her shoulders. "Bill's bringing back some liquor for Mike, until we can get him some real painkillers."

"Understood."

"Terry?"

"Yeah?"

"I'm sorry I got you guys into this, but we couldn't do it without you." Courtney smiled and pulled him in for a hug. "It's great to have our team back together."

"Wow, you're human after all," Terry said.

"Thanks," she said with a smile. "I'm going for a quick look around, but I'll be back in an hour, at most."

"OK. Can I ask you a question first?"

"I suppose," she said, as she stepped toward the door.

"How long have you been in love with him?"

"Wow."

"Seriously, how long?"

"I suppose I realized it when he and what's-her-name broke up. Though, it may have started a little before that." Courtney opened the door.

"That's about what I thought. I guess I didn't overlook every secret you had these past few years."

"I suppose you knew I had a crush on you when we first met?" Courtney asked, then closed the door. *That's going to bug him for hours*, she thought, as she walked down the stairs smiling.

* * *

Courtney made her way further away from the apartment and the hospital, memorizing the street names as she went along. She spotted a rundown antique store over a mile from the apartment and decided to make a call to the Skwiras' residence.

Courtney walked inside and saw a little older man behind the counter.

Just as I thought, no security cameras, but I bet he has a gun in his hand, she thought, as she walked up to him.

"I have a bit of gold to sell, do you buy?" she asked the elderly man at the counter.

"I do from time to time, but I don't pay top dollar. For that you'll need to go downtown," he answered.

Pulling three of the gold rounds from her jacket pocket, Courtney set one of them on the counter.

"What would you offer me for this?" she asked.

"I could do twenty one hundred, a thousand in paper, the rest in smaller gold and silver coins. Unless you want it all in paper, then I could do twenty four hundred."

"Paper's fine. Can I make a call, too?" Courtney asked, pulling Brian's business card from her pocket.

"Of course," he said and handed the phone to her.

* * *

Danni was walking down the stairs when she saw Court and Brian walking across the foyer talking.

What are those two up to? she wondered.

"I took the liberty of ordering a heavier breakfast this

morning. I assumed you'd both need something substantial after your interviews," she heard Brian say, as he lead Court to the kitchen.

"That sounds nice," Danni called from behind them.

"Good morning, Madame," Brian said, with exaggerated formality.

"And to you, fine sir," she answered.

Brian smiled, then said, "I hope you brought your appetite."

"I'm ready to eat, that's for sure."

"Brian, would you give Danni and I a moment?"

"Certainly. I'll be in the kitchen," he replied, then walked through the tall, double doors in front of them.

Danni listened as Court relayed the conversation he had with Brian.

"We need to get healing accelerator meds to him. I doubt Courtney even knows they exist."

"Good point. We should get into the archives and grab some meds, so we're ready to roll as soon as she contacts us," Court said.

"Do you trust Brian?" she asked.

"Yes, but I know what he's capable of."

Danni looked at Court for a moment, then said, "I trust your judgment."

She turned and walked past him, entering the kitchen. Brian was seated at the table with Perry, waiting for them.

"Brian? Is something wrong?" she asked. "You look worried."

"We will discuss it later. For now, we have cleared our schedule and are at your service," Brian replied.

"Brian, Perry, we're in a very dangerous situation. We've already put you and your families at great risk," Danni said.

Court added, "She's right, you know. We thought we could slip in and offer a mutually beneficial arrangement. The information we brought would be in SAF hands and we'd be out of trouble. Now—now things are going to get very dangerous and we need to get you out of it."

"I for one am becoming bored with my life and have been looking for another adventure for some time. Perry is my rock.

He keeps my wife and the household safe and secure. You get one of us, but not both." Holding up his hand, Brian said, "Eat up. I'll be back shortly to finish this discussion."

Danni looked at him as she chewed another bite. *Why are your eyes puffy, Brian?*

Brian returned in moments and smiled. "I know you're on to me, which makes it my turn to share a problem. We've been exposed to chemical weapons released by the Nazis."

Court gasped. "What?"

"Over half of the city is sick and about one percent has already died. The Nazis were desperate. We should have predicted they would do something like this."

"That's terrible," Danni said.

"Yes, it is," Brian replied.

"When did it happen?" Court asked.

"In the last day or two, they think. Coupled with the radiation that's been circulating above the earth for five years, it's devastating. Estimates put the worldwide death toll at over ninety percent in two months. We know it's possible as the death rates are climbing by the hour. Mass graves are being dug outside every major city."

"Isn't there something that can be done?" Danni asked.

"The technology you brought may help, but it's too late for most," he replied.

"There's nothing we can do?" Court asked.

"Not here," Brian said.

"That explains why they let us go," Danni said.

"When did the people find out?" she asked.

"The SAF will make the announcement in the morning. For now, they are saying it is an influenza outbreak. There will be a massive panic if we tell them the whole truth, so it will need come out in phases. Once the remaining people are too sick to do harm, they will be told the whole truth."

"What about Courtney and Mike? They weren't here for the worst of the radiation and they only recently came in contact with the biological weapon the Nazis released. They might be OK," Court said.

"They should be removed from the atmosphere right away.

They will need to be tested to be certain they're clean and quarantined for a time. If they're cleared, they'll join those chosen for protection, back when the nuclear holocaust became a real threat," Brian said.

"How can you be sure they can get in?" Danni asked.

"I funded and built enough space for a thousand people myself, I can get them in."

"Then why aren't you and your wife there?" she asked.

"This house is protected from radiation and the air is highly filtered. We're safer if we go into the shelter below," Brian said. "Your usage of the altar and the recent disappearing act by Mike and Courtney, has triggered some new hope within the scientific community. They think you may have the key to our survival."

"How many people know about us, the altar and Mike's invention?" Court asked with deep concern.

"There's a number of them and they want it, along with Mike and Courtney. They'll take everything they want, unless we go to them first," he replied.

"Mike can undo all of this, but we must find him before it's too late," Court said.

"So, it's true? The rumor that the altar can allow time travel and Mike's device does this too?" Brian asked.

"Mike can do it, but I'm not sure about the altar," Court said.

"They theorized it would, but after several people vanished and others were mentally damaged, they locked it away. That changed when the Colonel and you two broke in, started it up and then vanished. You need to stop, or even undo, this great tragedy."

"We understand, but there's nothing we can do without Mike and Courtney," Danni said.

"The SAF is not aligned with the scientific community—yet. There's a meeting to resolve that this morning and we should have news of the outcome soon," Brian said.

"Shouldn't you be there?" Court asked.

"I have a team in there. My presence would only complicate things."

"I'm not going to sit here for long, Court, we have to find our girl."

* * *

Courtney dialed the number and listened intently for an answer.

"Skwira residence."

"Perry, quickly, do you know if my parents are all right?"

"They're both sitting here now, Miss. Here's your mother."

"Courtney?" Danni asked.

"Mom? You're still there?"

"We went for a talk with the SAF, but we're back. You're OK?"

"Yeah, my friend is recovering from a couple of bug bites, but I'm good. I'll call you in a couple of days so stay safe until then," she said.

"Something very bad has happened, on a very large scale. There's an important discussion happening this morning that involves us," Danni said.

"Oh. I'd better go for now. Love you. Tell Dad I love him, too." Courtney felt helpless and her anger began to grow. *This will go badly and you will be killing again, very soon,* Courtney thought.

"We'll talk soon," Danni replied.

Courtney saw the shopkeeper approaching with two small stacks of money as she hung up the phone.

"Would you consider letting two of them go for forty five hundred?" he asked.

"How about three for that? You're going to have some SAF visitors looking for me in five minutes or less. Could your eyesight be extra bad today?" she asked, with two more coins in her fingers.

"You aren't a Nazi, are you?" he asked suspiciously.

"Goodness, no. I've devoted my life to helping win the war," she said. "My friend made the General mad, so the General wants to make everyone my friend cares about suffer for it."

"The General is a very proud and powerful man. Many have

died under his iron fist, my son included," he said, dropping his glasses on the floor. "I'm blind without my glasses."

"Thank you," she said. Courtney then placed the two remaining coins in his hand, folding it closed with her own. She patted his aged hand and stepped out onto the sidewalk, without saying another word. As the door closed, Courtney could hear the sound of engines roaring in the distance. She hurried around the building and crossed the street, entering the alley behind. She flipped her jacket inside out, pulled her hair up and put on a cap. Courtney then slipped on a masculine looking pair of sunglasses and adjusted her stride. With her transformation complete, a young man walked out the other end of the alley.

Out on the main street, two military brown vehicles roared by, screeching to a halt down the block.

Close call. Bet they'll be even quicker next time.

* * *

The next hour was spent meandering toward the apartment. After a few double backs, Courtney figured she was clean. She walked the last block to the apartment and saw Terry's eye looking out the edge of the curtain, as she climbed the stairs. The front door clicked and then opened for her. As she stepped in, she felt her spirits pick up.

"Hey boys, I see everyone's out of bed," she said, especially happy to see Mike was awake. "How is the patient doing?"

"He's in some pain but trying to act like he's not and moves like a sloth," Terry replied.

"Excellent." Courtney smiled. "Has he eaten?"

"He did, but needs to get some more rest," Terry said.

"Oh, and another thing," Mike said, "his hearing works fine and he speaks, too."

"I see his attitude is a bit poor," she said.

"True," Terry replied.

"Hey, you guys be nice to me. I'm in bad shape here," Mike said.

"Oh, then you should go lie down. Take a swig of that liquor, it's all we have for the pain," Courtney said.

"I'm not a big drinker, thanks though," Mike said.

"Look, the pain pills the doctors pass out are opium or cocaine derivatives. You'd take that if we had it, so shut up and have a drink. Besides, I need you rested up in case something comes up," she said.

"But I—"

"Good night, Mike," she walked over and helped him ease out of the chair.

"Enjoy that fancy bed we got you," Bill said.

"I'll try. Thanks again for everything guys," Mike said.

Courtney walked with him to his room. She helped him kneel then roll onto his makeshift bed.

"Get some rest." Courtney knelt beside him and gave him a kiss.

"Yes, ma'am."

Courtney looked at him and smiled, then closed the door and returned to the kitchen.

"I found out that we may have some news later this morning that could be a gamechanger," she whispered.

"What did you hear? Who did you talk to?" Terry asked.

"I called the people we stayed with the first night we were here and talked to my mother. She said there is a meeting that will affect us, so I'll be leaving in an hour to make another call. When I do, we should all be ready to get out of here. Completely out of here," she said.

"The next move is to go to ancient Egypt? Are we ready for that?" Terry asked.

"It is and we're close to being ready. We still need to learn some glyphs and ancient dialects, of course."

"We don't know when though? And if we do, can he get us exactly there? Or then?" he asked. "You know what I mean."

"We know the time to within ten or twenty years. Somewhere near the end of Sneferu's reign or the very beginning of Khufu's, like 2595 BC to 2575 BC."

"So, we go in early and hang out for a decade or two until we figure it out?" Terry asked. "Why not wait here, or in the USA?

Why risk it before we even know if we can survive the attempt?"

"Mike has tested it and proved it several times, so we know it's safe," she said.

"You saw this happen for yourself?" Bill asked.

"There were four of us who saw it," she said. "Well, I should get going."

"Sorry for the grilling. I know you don't like that, but I hope you understand that this is not easy for us to believe," Terry said. "Anything you're willing to share will help our nerves and strengthen our chances."

"You're right, on all counts, but I need more time to think about this," she said, then picked her sandwich up from the table.

Terry walked over to the small stack of books Courtney had set out. "I'm going to do some reading and see if there is something I can pick up with this history problem we've inherited."

"OK. Thanks for lunch, I'm going to hit the shower now," Courtney said, as she walked away with the sandwich in her hand.

When the water was on and he was sure they wouldn't be overheard Bill walked over to Terry.

"We won't survive this will we?"

"Nope, not a chance," Terry answered without looking up. "But, we're in control of our decisions on this path. Back there, we were running scared and hiding. That's no life for me."

"Yeah, me neither," Bill said. "I'll be back in an hour, after I get some fresh air." He picked up his hat and a jacket.

"See if you can find a bookstore with something on this Sneferu guy."

"Roger that," Bill said and closed the door.

* * *

Courtney opened the door, saw Terry reading at the table and asked, "Anything good?"

"Educational. Trying to get up to speed on this whole ancient Egypt thing."

"That's good. We all need to understand as much as possible before we go there," she said as she walked toward the door.

139

"Try to go there, you mean?" Terry asked.

"I suppose," Courtney said. "I should make that call and find out if my parents have some information for us." She opened the door and stepped outside into the sunlight.

"Be careful."

"Roger that," she said and pulled the door shut behind her.

* * *

Danni, Court and Brian were still sitting around the table when the phone rang. Brian walked over to the counter and picked it up. "Go ahead."

Court watched Brian's face and saw his expression fall.

Bad news.

"Be careful. OK, thank you." Brian took a deep breath and looked off into the distance for a moment. "The SAF is sending the healthiest troops into the underground bunkers," he said.

"That doesn't sound all that bad, for us at least," Court said.

"All the scientists that would have helped us were taken with them to work on the poison," Brian said. "Any antidote will be under military control but the general population has been written off."

"They forgot who they're supposed to protect," Court said.

"To top it off, martial law is in effect. Security forces have been ordered to shoot any and all criminals on sight."

"It'll be a bloodbath," Danni said.

"I doubt it makes much difference, but Courtney and Mike are on their list. That's going to make it hard for us to get out of the city."

Court said, "And to think, they risked their lives to help us out."

"The fools destroyed the crystal altar too," Brian added. "There's nothing more we can do. We need to leave now."

"We'll get our things ready, but I'm not leaving until she calls," Danni said.

"Meet back here, with your gear, in ten," Brian said. "Perry, stay by the phone and keep that shotgun in your hands."

Court and Danni rushed out of the room, with Brian on their heels. They made it back to the kitchen in seven minutes and sent Perry out to help Brian.

"I'm not leaving, Court, not until I know she's safe."

"Then let's hope she calls soon."

Court stared at the phone, willing it to ring and when it did, he jumped. "Skwira residence," he said with a forced calm.

"Dad?" Courtney asked, "what's the news?"

"Nothing good. We need to get out of here. Pick a place and we'll be there as fast as we can," Court said.

"Remember my favorite book? Meet me on his avenue and the number of months Mike has known me street."

"Got it," Court replied and hung up the phone. He whispered into Danni's ear, "Her favorite book was?"

"Eva," she replied.

"She said, his avenue and the number of months Mike has known me street," he whispered again.

"Evans Avenue and O Street. Mike hasn't known her for more than a week or two. She's tricking any eavesdroppers and sending them to low numbered streets. That should give us a chance to reach the others, roughly fifteen blocks away," Danni explained.

"She's good, isn't she?" he said, smiling at Danni.

"She takes after her mother," Danni smiled back.

"Heard the phone, was it her?" Brian asked.

"Courtney called, we have a destination," Court said. He turned to see Brian approaching with a massive shotgun and a large drum of ammunition hanging from each hip.

"You look scary packing that cannon," Court exclaimed.

"Yeah, but it's only good inside of a hundred yards, so I hope we don't need to use it."

Perry came in through the kitchen doors and said, "The truck is ready, sir."

"Excellent work, Perry. Take my wife down the back elevator, drop the blast doors when you get her down there and wait it out. You have two years' worth of supplies so relax and get comfortable."

Their host turned and said, "She wanted to say goodbye for herself but she's very upset and asked me to," Brian said. "Follow me."

Court's mouth dropped when he saw the large, all-wheel drive, armored vehicle. The engine sounded more like a freight train at idle than a truck. The large, off-road tires were overkill for city use and looked big enough to roll over a car. Court grabbed hold of the matte-black machine to help him pull open the thick, heavy door. Inside, he saw a bank of electronics that put him at ease.

Brian opened the driver door and smiled. "I see you like it."

"It's impressive, that's for sure."

"The house phone will ring in here now. We have all military radio channels monitored for proximity but we can't hear their words. It's that screen, right there," he pointed as he climbed in. "Anything transmitting will show up as a red dot, we're the green dot in the center. She can take small arms fire with no concern. Grenades, small rockets and the like will do damage but I'm told we can survive a couple of hits."

Court stepped back and helped Danni get in.

"Sounds like she has some power," Court said.

"Yeah, a pair of small turbines that run their own generator. They charge the batteries that power everything. She can run silent for fifteen minutes on the four electric drive motors, one at each tire. Top speed is only fifty, but she hits it in under three seconds." He smiled again as he closed his door, latching his weapon into a rack between him and Court.

"Harness up kids, we're going for a ride," he said, as he clipped himself into the five-point harness.

* * *

Courtney could feel fatigue setting in as she reached the steps of their apartment. She flew up the outside staircase and saw Terry's wide eyes peek from the edge of the curtain.

Courtney said, "I'm fine."

Terry disappeared from view. Courtney heard the lock click

and Terry let her in.

"Good, Bill's back, too. We should leave." Courtney said, breathing hard, "The meeting didn't go well. Mom and Dad are heading to an exfil for extraction, so we need to get there ASAP and secure it."

"Roger that. Cover the front for me while you catch your breath and I'll pack my junk." Terry rushed over to his bags and started stuffing things inside.

"I'll get Mike," Bill said. He hurried to the door and knocked. "Mike?"

"Yeah, I'm awake."

"You gotta get up and pack, pronto," Bill said.

Moments later, Mike stumbled out of the bedroom. "What's wrong?"

"All I know is there was a meeting that had something to do with us and it didn't turn out good. Mom and Dad are heading to meet up with us about a half mile from here."

"I'm pretty sore," Mike said, "I'll slow you all down."

"We have time. You come stand by the front and keep watch while I pack," Courtney said.

She grabbed Mike's hand to give it a squeeze as she walked by, then put Mike's things with hers. Courtney then placed the spud on top for easy access and zipped the large, black bag shut.

"Love my new pack, Bill, thanks," Courtney said, as she walked out.

"Glad you like it," Bill said, "but it looks like you're a little overloaded to me."

"No, I've got it, thanks though," she replied.

Terry stood up with his new bag. "Mine is great, too, fits like a glove."

"We look like a bunch of vagabonds with our backpacks and bedrolls," Bill said with a little laugh.

"Yeah but the quality firepower sets us apart from the common bum," Terry replied. then stuffed his pistol into the holster in his jacket.

Mike walked uncomfortably toward the front door.

"Here, take a big drink of this," Courtney said, handing him the bottle of liquor. "I need you to be able to move."

"Got it," Mike said, then obediently took a drink from the bottle. "That stuff is nasty."

Bill chuckled.

"Everyone ready? Guns, money, gold, necessities?" she asked.

"Can't wait to get out of this town," Terry said.

"We go in pairs, one block apart, Mike and I lead. The letter 'O' Street and Evans Avenue is our destination. It's Northwest of here about half a mile. Any questions?"

Her gaze panned across their faces and got three determined looks in return.

"Here we go." Courtney opened the door and led the way. "Mike, you set the pace."

After a few blocks and speeding up to a fast walk, Courtney asked, "You doing OK?"

"Yeah, the booze kicked in, I can't feel a thing."

Courtney looked at Mike's eyes and noticed they were slightly glazed. "Uh, that must have been a pretty big drink."

"Yeah, I'm a bit dizzy."

"Don't push any faster or you'll regret it," Courtney said.

"How long will it take us?"

"It's about twenty five more minutes if you can hold this pace."

"OK."

They walked in silence, taking a few unnecessary turns in case they were being watched.

"It's around the corner, so sit here with me on this bench," Courtney said. She waved at the other two to join them as she sat down.

Courtney turned to look at Bill and Terry as they approached.

"You guys cross the street and sit on that short retaining wall. If something happens, it'll be when they arrive so be ready," Courtney said, as she covered the pistol in her lap.

Five minutes went by before they heard a strange sound closing in on their position. Terry glanced down at Courtney for direction.

"That's something big. Mike, go stand between the buildings

across the street in case—"

Courtney was interrupted by the roar of countless rounds of gunfire coming toward them. Bullets could be heard striking metal and glass.

"Stay down!" Courtney screamed.

Terry and Bill sprinted across the street, heading toward Mike as Courtney ran past them.

"Keep him safe and have him get that thing powered up!" She screamed at them, as the deafening roar approached and handed Bill her backpack.

The few people that were out in the street had vanished from sight, but a few heads peeked over windowsills. The heads all disappeared when a loud explosion shook the entire block.

Courtney saw a big, military looking vehicle with a large gun sticking out of its roof. It was firing backwards, apparently at something following it. The strange howling machine roared around the corner and Courtney recognized Court's face.

"Over here!" Courtney yelled, waving her arms at him.

The vehicle lunged toward her and Courtney motioned for it to follow her as she ran toward Mike and the guys.

"They're here!" Courtney yelled.

The dark vehicle skidded to a howling stop behind her.

"Get in!" Danni ordered from the rear door.

"That's a freaking minigun!" Bill yelled, as he helped Mike into the back seats. He tossed his bag on the floor and climbed in, with Terry right behind him.

"You and I are on the floor, the others are in the belts," Terry commanded.

"This beast is amazing!" Bill called up to its owner. "Video sighted minigun? I love it!"

"Glad you like her, but she may not be enough," Brian said. "Now hang on!"

Courtney tugged the door shut as the truck quietly hurled forward. The turbines roared to life a few moments later.

"No way—she's electric. Man, what a sweet rig," Bill said.

Brian laughed. "You sound like me when I first saw her."

Courtney asked, "Where to?"

"Airport. My plane is waiting for us," Brian said. "It's about five minutes away."

"But what about your wife? And Perry?" she asked.

"Perry stayed behind to watch after her, so I know they'll be fine." He kept his eyes on the streets ahead of them.

"We've got another transmission, three o'clock," Court warned.

"Lock on as soon as you have it in your sights," Brian ordered.

A military vehicle rolled into the intersection in front of them.

"Got it," Court said and squeezed the trigger on the stick he was holding.

The roar from above was almost as impressive as the fire spraying above the windshield. Courtney watched the computer track the target and train the spray of heavy ammo on the vehicle. The truck was immediately disabled and on fire.

"They wouldn't listen. Stupid fools!" Brian screamed. "Making me kill my own people! I swear, if I get the chance I will strangle that lousy General with my bare hands!"

* * *

No one made a comment as the vehicle roared the few remaining, uneventful minutes to the airport. When they arrived at the gates to the private airport, Brian swiped his pass and drove them over to a white hangar.

"Unload all our gear onto the tarmac off the end of the hangar. Then move the truck out in the open, over there by the grass and leave her running," he said.

They jerked to a stop in front of the large, metal building.

Brian pulled the targeting display unit from the dash and Court said, "Got it."

Court unbuckled his harness and jumped out.

"You, come with me." Brian tugged on Bill and sprinted for the side door.

Danni and Terry helped Mike get out of the truck, then joined Courtney to help unload the remaining items. Courtney

146

saw Court roar off in the truck and park it where Brian had instructed. She heard the hangar doors roll open and looked back to see Bill on one door and Terry on the other. Inside the hangar was a navy blue, twin engine jet.

Brian jumped on a small tractor attached to the nose gear and started it up. Courtney watched as he said something to Bill, then ran back and climbed the stairs into the plane. Bill eased the plane out and as soon as the wings cleared the hangar, Brian had the engines warming. Terry ran over to Bill and helped him disconnect the tractor, then Bill drove it back into the hangar. Brian stopped the plane with its stairs in front of Mike, where the pile of bags, cases and miscellaneous weapons were.

Courtney called out over the sound of the jets, "Bill, get Mike on board! Dad, you toss the gear up to me and I'll hand it to Mom!"

The scream of the truck's turbines spooling up overpowered the idling plane. Courtney looked out the side window to see the Gatling styled minigun tracking up toward the sky. The barrels started to spin and then the gun roared with fire. It spewed ten feet into the air, with brass spilling onto the top of the truck, bouncing all around the tires.

"Are we loaded?" Brian yelled.

"Last bag!" called Terry, as he poked his head in the door.

"Then get in and close the door!" Brian ran toward the cockpit.

Courtney looked out at the truck and could see dirt and grass flying around the truck. Every second or two one would strike the truck, making a flash as molten fragments splattered. Looking up the stream of bullets, Courtney saw a black dot in the distance and a flash of fire.

"Chopper!" she called out.

"Incoming missile!" Terry yelled.

The entire plane shook from the shock wave of the missile detonating on the truck.

Courtney looked back up at the helicopter and saw a large puff of black smoke. "The chopper's going down."

"Court, I need you up here by me," Brian announced over

the intercom. "Everyone else buckle up back there."

Courtney watched the truck relentlessly pummel the helicopter all the way down to the ground. Smoke was billowing out from under the truck and both driver's side doors were hanging off their hinges.

Confident the threat was gone, Courtney sat down beside Mike and buckled in.

"I keep thinking we should use the spud and get out of here," Mike said.

"I know, but it's a little late now," Courtney said as the plane's nose pitched up and the wheels came off the runway. "Besides, we have to get to Egypt somehow."

* * *

"This baby goes," Court said, from the copilot's seat.

"I got the afterburner option." Brian smiled and pointed to the airspeed. "Three fifty," he announced over the intercom.

Thirty seconds later, the plane reached five hundred knots and Brian eased back on the throttles.

"Your German is still good?" Brian asked.

"Yep, I can read them," Court said, motioning toward the control labels.

"Excellent. If anything shows up on the display with a red dot, touch it on the screen, then touch 'aim-lock' and then 'engage', got it?"

"Got it," Court replied.

Brian pointed to the headset on the wall next to Court. When he had his set on Brian said, "There, that's better, huh?"

"Much."

"She'll go supersonic but we need to make our fuel last so we'll hold her to around six hundred."

Court heard an alarm, "What's that?"

"It's the targeting control from the truck and the signal's getting weak."

"Scared me," Court said.

Brian chuckled, "shut it down, would you? It's the switch

148

marked Main."

Court reached down to the box on the floor beside Brian's seat and flipped the switch. He was startled by a loud buzzer and blinking light on the control panel. "Oops, what did I do?"

"Buckle up, we have a visitor," Brian announced, then shoved the throttles forward. Switching off the intercom he said, "It's on your display, look."

"I see two streaks on the horizon at two o'clock," Court said, pointing out the window.

"Court, keep me under a thousand knots and fifty thousand feet," Brian said, pointing at the two gauges. He pulled back on the yoke and then banked away from the missiles. "Four G's on that one," he said over the intercom and leveled the plane back out.

"Seven hundred knots and just under fifty thousand feet," Court said.

Brian reached forward, flipped a switch that turned on a blinking red button, then pulled back on the throttles.

"When you hear a solid tone, hit that blinking red button to release the countermeasures." He pushed a button and the buzzer stopped. "They'll be on us in twenty seconds," Brian said, then flipped the air brake switch.

The plane slowed even faster with the loud air noise, pulling them forward in their seats.

Court didn't take his eyes off the display as the small, red dots approached. "Five hundred knots."

A high-pitched tone sounded and Court released the countermeasures. Four distinct pops sounded and machinery hummed under their feet.

"I can't believe she held up with those tanks still attached," Brian reached out, flipped two switch covers up, then toggled both switches. "External tanks are away." He then pulled back on the yoke, throwing the nose up toward space. "Hang on everybody, we're going over," he warned, then flipped a switch tucking the air brakes back in and quieting the plane once more.

"She's reloaded! Send off another volley if the alarm buzzes again!" he yelled, as he pulled back on the throttles, slowing the jet.

"What do I do?" Court was startled, noticing the skyline was upside down.

"Watch the gauges. She'll tear apart around seven G's, but I can't even take six. Everyone, take deep breaths, clench your muscles and grunt as hard as you can," Brian yelled.

Court released the countermeasures again. The seriousness of their situation was clear when they felt shockwaves from the exploding missiles.

"That was a close call," Brian said. "I need you all to hang on to your breakfast a little while longer while I turn us over."

Brian slowly flipped the plane back over, jerking everyone hard into their seat. "Grunt people!" He then banked hard to the left.

"Five G's," Court said, in a strained voice. "Almost six now."

"Copy. We're back on our heading now," Brian said, as he brought them out of the turn, and shoved forward on the throttles again.

"You can all relax a bit," he announced.

"Have you done that before?" Court asked.

"Yeah, but my pilot was at the yoke."

"Your pilot?" Court asked.

"Yeah. I fly her occasionally, once we're in the air, but I've never taken her up all by myself before," he said.

Court felt his stomach drop as he stared at Brian.

"We had no choice, Court."

Court sat back in his seat and closed his eyes to relax, trying to forget what he had heard.

* * *

UNIT 3: GOODBYE TO OLD FRIENDS

"Hey, Court?" Brian asked.

"Yeah?"

"We need to stop for fuel in about an hour. I need you to keep your eye on things while I look for a quiet little airport along the coast."

"How can that be? I thought we had enough fuel to make it to England, around six thousand miles."

"I wasn't planning on using up over half of our fuel trying to avoid those missiles," Brian replied.

"Sorry, I wasn't thinking. So, what do I do?"

"Sorry to eavesdrop but I can fly her," Courtney offered.

"Hey, Courtney. Did you get some rest?" Court asked.

"At least a half hour."

"How is everyone else back there?"

"Fine. They're all resting," she replied.

"You're a pilot?" Brian asked.

"I've had crash courses in both planes and helicopters, but I wouldn't call myself a pilot," Courtney said, smiling.

"Here, take my seat and I'll show you the controls," Brian said as he stood up.

"Wait, everything is in German?" she asked.

"Yeah, all the good tech comes from the Germans. We steal it, then improve it."

"Your truck?" Courtney asked as she took his seat.

"Mostly German designs, but built in my factory," Brian said. "I'm just learning myself, but here's what I know—"

"Learning?" Courtney asked.

"Yeah, came in handy today," he smiled at Courtney's raised eyebrows.

"Really? So, if you make them better then why not change the labels, too?" Courtney questioned with a half-smile.

"German is the language of flight. Besides, I watch the airspeed, altitude and the horizon." Brian pointed at two gauges and a square display.

"I suppose I'll do just fine then," Courtney said, as Brian released the yoke to her. "Got it."

What an amazing girl. If things were different, I wonder if she and my son, Denny, would have been together?

Brian thought about his son's interest in Courtney as a young teenager. He felt himself drift and heard Denny's voice talking about his next mission. Brian shook himself alert and felt his eyes burning.

Enough of that. He's gone and that's all there is to it.

He glanced up to see Courtney and her father scanning the sky in silence. Brian opened a set of maps and flipped through the pages, struggling to regain his focus.

"I found a nice little community airport but it isn't staffed. They may not store fuel on site, so we could have a bit of a wait," he said.

"We'll call from a phone on the ground then?" Court asked.

"Yep and hope that no one out here in the Wild East wants to kill us," Brian said.

"Wild East?" Courtney asked.

"Yep, every city has its own laws and militia. It can be pretty risky to travel out this way without military support," Brian explained.

"So, we need to be ready for anything," Court added.

"If they try to board us, they'll get the business end of my shotgun in their face. If the locals even look like they want to board, get ready for a fight." Brian paused for a moment. "Enough about that. I'm going to relax for a bit."

"Take as long as you like, she flies easy," Courtney said.

"If you're sure, then I'll take a few minutes to introduce myself to your friends."

"I'm sure."

"What are their backgrounds?" Brian asked.

"They're both ex-military and worked with me in intelligence for the last few years."

"Those are good friends to have and now they're my friends, too," Brian said with a smile, then went into the cabin.

"Gentlemen, I'm Brian," he said, reaching out to shake their hands. "Courtney tells me you're both good in a fight."

Terry and Bill introduced themselves and Brian explained his plan to them and Danni.

After Brian was done, Terry asked, "You want us to set up the perimeter as soon as we stop?"

"That would be perfect. I'll let you handle the security, Terry. It sounds like you know more about it than I do. Oh, and those cases in the back have some toys in them you'll like."

"Roger that," Terry replied. "Let's break out the gear, Bill."

"Danni, would you come back here, too? I'd like to talk with you some more, but I don't want to wake Mike."

While Bill and Terry prepped the weapons, Brian knelt on the seat across the aisle from Danni.

"I want you to call for the fuel delivery, and pay for it too. We'll have you covered from every angle."

"Sounds easy enough," she answered.

"I hope it is, but there is definitely risk," Brian said.

Bill exclaimed, "Terry, check this out," Bill lifted a matte-black rifle with a large scope from one of the cases. "A pair of tactical rifles," he said, as he threaded the barrel into place on the first one.

"Nice. What's in the other cases?" Terry asked.

"Everything you ever wanted," Brian answered.

Bill opened a large, square case and said, "A selection of ammo for Brian's cannon is in this one. Looks like smoke, explosive and shot rounds."

Reaching past him, Terry opened the other long, rectangular case.

"Not much in this one, just a rocket propelled grenade launcher and eight rounds." Terry smiled as he held it up.

"RPGs, miniguns, afterburners? Joe Citizen doesn't get this kind of hardware. You must be connected," Bill said.

"Around here, Joe Citizen does have shoulder-fired rockets and automatic weapons," Brian said.

"Sounds like the way it is in the Middle East, back home," Terry said.

"I must get us on the ground, so you guys get prepped. We'll be down in thirty," Brian said and walked back up to the cockpit.

"OK, my turn now, Courtney."

"Roger that," she said, then unbuckled and got up. "I'll be in my seat if you need me."

The plane lurched downward as Brian put on his headset. "Sorry folks, I'm not the best pilot. We're about twenty minutes out and on fumes. I kept her coasting at altitude as long as I could, trying to avoid ground threats and conserve fuel. We are close now and need to go down there," Brian said over the intercom. "Buckle up."

They were nearing the runway when the left side engine sputtered. Brian reached out and pulled the left throttle all the way back. "Don't need that one to land," he said jokingly.

"Fuel?" Court asked.

"Yeah. I turned off the alarms already," he replied, keeping his eyes on the tiny little runway in front of them. "We'll coast in the rest of the way," Brian announced to the passengers, then shut down the other engine.

"Good choice," Court said.

"Yeah, plus, a silent entrance will keep from alerting the local population. If they're even alive."

The plane descended for several minutes in silence. Everyone knew that an attack on them now would likely be fatal.

"Is it safe for us to breathe the air?" Court asked, as they neared the runway's surface.

"We'll find out," Brian said as he touched down with only a slight bump.

The plane slowed and began taxiing toward the buildings.

"Terry, Bill, you can open the door anytime," Brian announced, flipping the passenger door release switch. A buzzer sounded immediately and he said, "Looks like they were ready."

As the plane rolled to a stop, Brian saw Terry and Bill running toward the front of the little airport.

"OK, girls, you're on," Brian said as he picked up his oversized weapon. He watched Danni and Courtney walk over to a telephone on the wall of the office. After Danni made a quick call, he saw her give a thumbs up and the girls ran back toward him.

"The fuel truck is in town, about five minutes from here."

"I hope he wants to do some business, rather than fight us," Brian said. "With all the deaths, I'm afraid they will want to take our plane and try to get away."

"Here's some gold. I'm guessing it will be four or five of these, but here are two more in case they give you any trouble. No change and no bartering. We pay whatever they ask," Brian said. "The boys already know what they need to do, so hit the deck if someone makes a wrong move. I'll be at the top of the steps, just inside the door. If they want to come in, let them try, but stay back so I have a clean shot down the stairs."

Bill's voice called out, "Glare on your windows, we can't see in the plane from this angle!"

"Got it! Thanks!" Brian yelled back. "Court, put this body armor on," he said, tossing a vest to him.

"Thanks."

"Inbound!" Terry yelled, from the other side of the hangar.

"Mike, cockpit. Stay low," Brian ordered, handing him a pistol.

A moment later, Bill yelled, "Two in the cab!"

"I see it now. It's about thirty seconds away. Everyone, get ready," Brian called out the door of the plane.

"And stay calm," Courtney said, winking up at Brian.

Brian smiled. "Yes and stay calm. Court, you're my backup. If they get inside, unload on them. Clear?"

"Crystal," Court said, as he crouched beside a seat, halfway to the cockpit.

Brian watched the fuel truck pull into the driveway and drive straight up to the side of the plane.

"He's getting out. I don't like his smile, Court, this won't end well."

Danni handed the driver four pieces of gold and then looked up at the second man in the truck, taking a step backward.

"Danni senses something. What is she doing? Court, get ready," Brian said, as he felt sweat trickling down his back. He watched Danni move closer to Courtney, between her and the strangers, as the second man walked over to begin fueling. The driver turned and walked to the back of the fuel truck, out of sight. "Where'd he go?"

"Who?" Court asked.

"The driver. Stepped out of sight, but Bill can see him. Stay ready. There he is! Shoot him, Bill! Shoot that pig," Brian hissed. He watched in horror as the driver reached under the back of his shirt. Courtney saw him, too, and turned to face him as he appeared from the corner of the truck.

Courtney yanked her own pistol out and Brian started to jump from the plane. A misty cloud engulfed what used to be the driver's head. A split-second later, Brian heard a rifle shot. Courtney and Danni dove to the ground. The truck windshield turned blood red and the side window blew out, then they heard the second rapport. Danni and Courtney started to get up from the tarmac with pistols in hand. Then, a third shot sounded that startled them all. Waiting, they all scanned for a sign of danger but could see nothing. Danni ran over to the plane, slightly bent over the whole way. Courtney pulled the pistol from the dead driver's hand, then followed after her mother.

"Brian, I need help with the fuel situation," Danni said.

"You don't even look a bit scared after that?" Court said.

"She predicted it," Brian said.

"Went off like clockwork too, huh?" Danni asked him.

"Just like clockwork. I liked the way you girls kept them out toward the front of the plane so the boys had a nice clear shot," Brian said.

"This is not funny!" Court yelled.

"Danni thought that if they saw men, they would immediately fire on us. She figured they would try to capture women."

"Nice. Turned yourself and your daughter into bait," Court grumbled, as he walked off the plane.

"He'll be fine in a few minutes. Let's look at the fuel," Danni said.

Brian walked over to the fuel truck and checked the meter.

"Courtney, you get aboard and watch the fuel gauges while I fill the tanks. We should be fueled in twenty more minutes, so tell everyone to keep their eyes open," Brian said.

Everyone jumped when they heard a lone pistol shot.

Brian looked toward the front of the airport. "Bill's waving at us. Must be someone coming, get ready!" Brian yelled, then grabbed two spare magazines for his massive gun and hung them from his belt.

* * *

"Multiple incoming!" Bill screamed from out by the road for the third time. "They can't hear me!" he yelled at Terry, then he pulled out a pistol and fired a shot into the air.

"Get your eyes back on that road!" Terry screamed at him, watching the small puff of gun smoke dissipate above his partner. *Fool! You gave away your position.*

"They heard that!" Bill called back.

"Bad guys coming in hot!" Terry screamed.

He looked at the concrete foundation he was laying beside.

"Ought to be solid enough," he said, then laid back down and scoped in on the trucks. "Gunner on blue!"

"Roger, I'm on green," Bill replied.

"On my mark!" Terry yelled. "Three, two…"

The two guns went off in unison, a skill mastered by only the best marksmen. Both gunners disappeared from view.

"Now for the drivers," Terry mumbled, as he sighted in on the driver of the blue truck.

Before he could shoot, the ground in front of him exploded in dust, flashes and asphalt from the road. The deafening barrage of large caliber rounds tore through the siding above the foundation.

Lay still until they stop to reload. They'll be less than two hundred meters out, he thought and dialed his scope in to a hundred. Moments later, everything went silent.

Now! Terry slid forward, sighted in on his truck and dropped the new gunner. Hearing nothing from Bill, he immediately took out the replacement on the green gun. Terry looked at Bill's position.

He saw the Ocean City Delaware Municipal Airport sign Bill had been underneath was shredded. Terry turned back to the blue truck and shot through the windshield. *Headshot.*

Once more, the road erupted from a hail of bullets.

Terry looked over toward Bill and was glad to see him lift up and pull off a shot. That ended the gunfire once more.

Terry aimed toward the trucks and shot another man at the gun on the blue truck. "Don't these guys ever give up?" he yelled. He watched the gun spin around and a man falling over the side of the truck, hanging on to it. As the gunner went over, several wild rounds went off. The green truck swerved, then the back end bounced up slightly.

"Road kill," Terry mumbled.

Terry and Bill fired round after round into the engines, attempting to disable the trucks. Smoke and steam were pouring from under the hoods of the vehicles, but neither had stopped. Terry took his final shot and the blue truck swerved off the road, slamming into the ditch.

Looking over at Bill, Terry realized that he was also reloading. Terry started emptying his pistol into the truck. He hoped to buy Bill some time, but the gunfire from the blue truck immediately resumed.

Bullets were all over Bill and several of the large caliber rounds met their mark. Bill was rolled backwards along the ground, being obliterated by dozens of rounds. Clearly the wounded gunman in the stationary blue truck took out his fury.

Blocking out the anguish of seeing his partner mutilated, Terry looked for a clean shot. The gunner turned toward him and Terry took advantage of the new angle. He pointed at the gunner's nose as rounds started erupting around his own position. He squeezed off the round, hitting his mark.

That'll shut you up.

Terry knew he had to stop the green truck before the attackers turned in to the airport. The truck was less than fifty yards away, billowing smoke. Terry shoved his rifle to the side and reloaded his pistol. He got up on one knee, then rapidly fired his entire clip into the engine. He dropped the clip as he fell to the ground, reaching for his last clip. He snapped it in and rose to see an attacker jump out of the truck, who opened fire at him with an assault rifle.

Don't do it again, you fool! Terry screamed to himself but ignored his own command. He fired back as bullets whizzed past, watching the man fall face first onto the roadway. Terry felt himself spin around and fall over, then a searing pain overcame him.

When he opened his eyes, all was silent. Terry saw a pair of boots approaching at an unbelievably slow pace. The boots each appeared to compress under great load as they touched down.

Only dreams happen in slow motion. This isn't real.

His eyes blinked as he looked upward and he saw Brian. Terry watched Brian in slow motion as he raised his cannon and began firing. Terry felt his body shake after each pulse from the weapon.

Shell casings eject consistently, Terry thought, watching them twirl away in perfect harmony.

That's a well-balanced weapon, less recoil than I expected.

Brian turned and jumped with the big gun in one hand. Terry continued to watch as his eyelids darkened his view again. He saw Brian had a hand in his pouch and the gun no longer had a magazine in it.

Oops, that was twelve rounds. I wonder how long it'll take him to get the next drum in?

Terry felt his body shake again.

This is no dream. You're in shock, dying. Assess your condition soldier! Get up, Terry! He screamed at himself with all his being.

Terry felt immense weight on his feet and then his legs.

Where's the concrete coming from?

He watched as his eyes blinked a third time. As the light came back, he saw traces of bullets and ricochets all around Brian.

* * *

"Dad, take Mike and Mom onto the runway. Be ready to take off without us," Courtney ordered. She threw the fuel nozzle aside and snapped the cover shut, then sprinted toward Bill. She scrambled through the last few feet of tall grass on her belly and saw large pieces of her mutilated friend. Pain hit her gut as she realized nothing could be done for Bill.

Courtney turned her attention to Brian and Terry when she heard the rapport of Brian's shotgun. She heard secondary sounds from the explosive shells and knew they were hitting their mark. Lying in the blood soaked grass, beside her fallen partner, Courtney realized she needed more firepower. She dug through the shredded mass to get at his rifle, then popped out the clip. Seeing it was full, she worked the action and took a deep breath. She pulled up, peeked through the scope and saw the blue truck crash into the building. Opening her other eye, Courtney watched as a large chunk of concrete slammed Brian to the ground. Sighting in on the man with an automatic rifle blazing, she fired off her first round. The bullet struck two feet to the left of the man, into the damaged siding of the building.

* * *

Help! They're shooting at Brian! Terry called out in helpless silence.

Lying there, facing death, he struggled to reach for his sidearm but he couldn't move his arm. He shifted his eyes as far to the side as he could and saw the man firing at Brian. He felt his eyes blink a fourth time.

Please, God, let me die. Please, stay closed. Don't look. Don't you look!

Terry felt tears welling up in his eyes, his throat burned but he couldn't swallow.

His rebellious eyes opened to the horrific scene of Brian being driven into the ground by a large piece of concrete.

Why did you make me see that? Terry pleaded, *Don't make me watch any more of this. I deserve to die, I know I do.*

He watched the man's boot step next to his head and then

the barrel of his assault rifle swung over Terry's face.

Thank you. Thank you for peace.

His eyes closed for the fifth time, then Terry felt the percussion of a gunshot, a slight pause, then a second. Hot liquid gushed across his face, the pain vanished and the world went dark.

* * *

Was that me or the gun? Courtney asked herself. *Gun.*

Aiming two feet to the right of his chest, she watched the man swing his weapon from Terry's face toward her. Courtney fired off two more rounds in rapid succession. Both of her shots hit the man center mass. In the throes of death, the gunman sprayed bullets in her direction. She aimed again, roughly the same distance to the right of his face and fired her fourth round. The gunfire ceased and he fell onto his face, his feet inches from Terry's head.

All was silent as Courtney scanned the area for more threats, spinning around on her knee. Seconds went by, but she did not move from her position. She could hear the plane's engines idling off in the distance but waited. Her heart pounding, finger on the trigger, eyes unblinking.

Get up Courtney! Move it now!

Courtney pried herself up from the ground. Her blood soaked clothes stuck to her flesh. She felt liquid oozing down her neck as she slung the rifle over her shoulder. Pulling her pistol, she pointed it at the fallen attacker, Courtney sprinted up to Brian's body. Seeing the glazed look in his eyes, she jammed the pistol into her waistline and knelt by his body. Courtney picked up his shotgun and inserted the spare magazine, while she watched the wrecked truck. Her senses were pulling in every available bit of information. A slight breeze was coming toward her and she kept getting a hint of body odor.

There it was again, gravel crunched under someone's feet. Heavy, one eighty plus. Just around the corner…

"Don't come any closer!" She screamed at the unseen, approaching person.

161

"I ain't scared of no girl! I'm gonna make you pay for this!" a man screamed from around the corner and fired off several rounds into the truck in front of her.

The percussion caused Terry's arm to jerk and she heard him exhale with a sputter.

Terry's dead, ignore that. Get ready for it…

A gun barrel appeared around the corner of the building, immediately followed by a dirt stained face. Courtney fired. His head disappeared in a cloud of spray and his corpse hit the ground with a dull thud. She set Brian's massive gun beside her and tore at the pile of concrete on top of Terry. She tried to ignore the wet mist raining on her, but noticed it on the backs of her hands. When she rolled a large block off his chest, she heard a wheeze and realized that Terry was struggling to live.

"That gun's loud," Terry wheezed, as his eyelids fluttered open.

Courtney looked into her friend's eyes. "Hey buddy, I'm going to get you out of here."

Courtney watched his face change as his eyes turned toward Bill's last location.

"I know. Bill's gone. Brian, too. You guys took out the three on the gas truck and at least eight on the other two trucks. You saved the rest of us."

"Ribs cracked, left leg damaged, right foot numb, at least one bullet in torso," Terry choked out the physical assessment he took moments before.

"Roger that soldier. Let's get you out of here," Courtney said, as she helped Terry to his feet. His groans told Courtney the pain was unbearable. "Here, you carry this," she said hanging her rifle over Terry's shoulder.

"They had body armor," he wheezed. "Couple of 'em got back up."

"It's over now. Save your energy, I want to hear the story when you're better," Courtney said, as the plane rolled closer.

"Your mom looks worried," Terry said, and they made their way to the tarmac.

"Yeah."

She handed Terry over to Danni and Court, then trudged over to the fuel truck and pulled out the water hose. Turning it on herself, Courtney watched the reddish brown water cascade onto the tarmac.

Mike's coming this way, what are you going to say to him?

She felt her hand twitch when Mike took the hose from her, but she didn't turn.

"How are you feeling by now?" Courtney asked.

Mike stepped in front of her and forced eye contact.

"Me? I'm fine, it's you I'm worried about," he said, as he rinsed her off.

Turning her back to him, Courtney said, "Get the back for me, would you?"

"Sure."

Please, don't talk, she thought.

She leaned her head back and Mike rinsed her hair.

"There are pieces of—"

"I know," she interrupted.

A moment later, Mike said, "That's about all I can do."

Courtney leaned forward and wrung out her hair.

"Thanks. Now let's get out of here, before anyone else shows up," she said as she walked past him, toward the plane.

With every step she took, the distance between her and their two fallen friends grew, as did her anger. Courtney was forcing each step, not wanting to leave their bodies, but knowing they had no choice.

You were weak. You let down your guard and people died. This is your fault.

Her mother met her at the door of the plane with a blanket and wrapped it around her.

Nodding toward the pile of dusty firepower lying in the back of the plane she asked, "We get all the weapons we need?"

"And your mom grabbed a few spares, too," Court replied.

"Excellent. Court, I need you to put us on the far end of the runway while I change into some dry clothes. Danni and Mike, you two get buckled in after you help Terry with his," Courtney ordered and took clothes from her bag. "I'm going to change."

Moments later, when Courtney was returning to the cockpit, she asked, "How is he?"

"Bad enough, but he'll be on his feet in a week," Danni said.

"I'm going to need him ready as soon as possible," Courtney replied.

"He won't be fully recovered for a month or more," Danni said.

"He has about twelve hours, Danni, so I advise you load him up on that accelerator drug of yours," Courtney said.

"This stuff speeds up the process, but not that much," Danni said, holding a bottle of blue pills.

"Twelve hours until we land in Africa. Buckle up." Courtney said, then turned and headed for the cockpit.

"Hey, Captain, we're ready to roll," Mike called down the aisle to the cockpit.

"Here we go," she said into the intercom, then eased the throttles forward.

"Landing gear, flaps, beacon," she pointed as she translated the German labels. "Full flaps for takeoff. We need to conserve our fuel. We don't have spare tanks now so our range is a thousand miles less."

The plane accelerated less aggressively than their first takeoff.

"Dad, I need you to get out the maps right away. I need the coordinates of a small airport, on the Northwestern point of Africa. We're going to Cairo," Courtney said, then eased the craft off the ground.

"We can't go to Morocco, the Nazis were still holding their ground there," Court warned as they gained altitude. "Western Sahara has flat ground, but I'm not sure about a safe airport."

"I understand, do your best," she replied.

Courtney then put on her headset, flipped on the cabin com and said, "We're heading out over the ocean now. I expect no further disturbances for eight to ten hours." Courtney paused for a moment to gather her emotions.

"Bill and Brian both died saving us. We're going to put things right or die trying. Now get some rest, you're going to need it."

"Hassan airport in Laayoune, Western Sahara," Court said,

pointing to the coordinates.

Looking over at Court, she said, "Go on back and get some rest, I'll enter them in when we get up to cruising altitude."

"You sure?"

"I am."

* * *

Danni looked up, saw Court walking down the aisle and asked, "You missing us?"

"Of course," Court replied.

Danni saw his smile fade.

"That girl is tough, but she's hurting," Court said.

"She lost a good friend and you know how hard that is," Danni said, as she worked on Terry's wounds.

"Terry, the bleeding is over, but the holes, bruising and ribs are going to take some time to heal up," Danni said.

"I don't know what you injected me with, but I can't feel much," Terry said.

"You'll get sleepy here in a bit and you won't be able to wake up for several hours."

"Then I better use the facilities before I pass out," Terry said and chugged a drink of water.

"Here, I'll help you," Court offered and helped Terry ease out of his seat. "Put your hands on my shoulders and follow me," Court said.

As they walked away, Danni looked at Mike and said, "Looks like he's in good shape for now. Let's have a look at your bandages."

"Thanks, I think," Mike teased.

"Looks like you're healing up," Danni said.

"I'm trying," he said.

"Take one of these," she said, handing Mike a pill.

He obediently popped it in his mouth and drank some water.

"I want you two resting as much as you can," she said.

"Yes, ma'am," Terry mumbled and eased himself into his seat.

"Here, Court, put this on him," Danni said, handing him a blanket.

Terry exhaled loudly, then made a soft snoring noise.

"Is he asleep already?" Mike asked.

"Yep. I slipped some drops into his first water. I'm surprised he made it as long as he did," Danni said.

"Remind me never to...never to take...drink your water," Mike stammered.

"Next time," Danni said.

"Why...why next time?" Mikes asked.

Danni smiled mischievously, "You already finished that one."

"You...my..." Mike's head fell to the side.

"Goodnight dear, sleep well," Danni said.

"You killed them both?" Court asked.

"Court, that isn't funny," Danni said, as she sat down in her seat.

"Sorry, you're right," he said.

"Now, sit down here and take a nap with me," Danni said. She leaned back in her seat and pulled a blanket across her lap.

"But I—"

"Court, please?"

"Courtney—"

"I can't think about it right now," Danni interrupted. "We'll talk about this soon enough. Come on, let's get some rest."

Court sat down and Danni leaned her head on his shoulder, closing her eyes.

* * *

Mike opened his eyes and struggled to read the dial on his watch.

Seven hours? he thought, looking around.

Mike focused on Courtney's auburn hair in the front of the airplane. He lifted himself from his seat and walked past the three sleeping passengers.

I wonder if she—

"Did you get some good rest?" Courtney asked, turning her head to the side.

She must have eyes in the back of her head.

166

"Hello?" Courtney asked.

"Uh, yeah, but dreaming a lot," Mike said.

"About the firefight?"

"A little, but mostly stuff from Michael and the Colonel. It's kind of creepy, but at the same time I almost want to see more," he said. "How are you do—"

"How are your injuries?" she interrupted.

"Still feel nauseous when I breathe too hard and moving the leg is tough, but most of the pain is changing to soreness. How are—"

"That's a good sign," Courtney cut him off again.

"How are you doing?"

"Fine," Courtney answered.

"The airport, are you—"

"I'm fine. Next subject."

"OK, are you having flashes from the other girls?" he asked.

"No."

"Nothing?"

"That is what 'no' means," Courtney said, without turning her head.

"So, I've been thinking—" Mike started.

"Yeah, me too," she interrupted. "I think we need to cool things off for a while. I can't do my part if I'm always worrying about you." Courtney continued to stare straight ahead while she spoke. "I should have put the plane in the air and not run out there risking the entire operation to save Terry. Mistakes like that kill people."

"That was a mistake?" Mike asked.

"Yes. Terry will agree. I acted out of emotion, not with my mind and it nearly got us all killed."

"And somehow that's my fault?"

"I've allowed myself to be distracted by you. That's not your fault, it's my own," Courtney answered.

"I see," Mike said. He remained quiet for a moment while he thought about his next question. "Do you like yourself better this way? You know, a heartless machine? Not too many people can lie in their best friend's corpse and blow someone's brains out. Then, act as if nothing happened, jump behind the wheel of a jet and fly for a few hours. Oops, I forgot to add, without shedding a tear."

"You're mad."

"That was a question, Courtney."

"What was, Mike?"

"What was what?"

"Now you've confused me," Courtney pretended to laugh. "You might want to cut back on the meds a little, they're starting to mess with your mind."

"I'm glad you found your sense of humor, this is definitely funny," he said. As Mike shuffled his way back to his seat, he noticed everyone was awake. No one made eye contact, but Danni reached out and touched his hand as he passed. Mike paused and held her hand for a moment, then walked on. He stepped over the pile of weapons at the rear of the plane, then grabbed several bottles of water and a bag of sandwiches out of the refrigerator. He worked his way back up to the others with his load. "Here, I figured it was about time for some food," handing it to Danni.

Mike, you should have let me do that," Danni said.

"I appreciate the thought, but I must pull my weight or I might get myself culled from the herd."

"Oh, don't be silly," Danni said.

Mike appreciated the silence while everyone ate. The episodes of deja vu were all but gone now, but his dreams were becoming troublesome. One dream in particular put him into a panic each time. As he thought about it, he closed his eyes and slipped back into the dream again.

Only sixteen seconds left, he told himself.

He was so worried about the time, he held his arm in front of himself and checked his watch every few seconds. Mike was trying to soak up everything he could from the scene around him in the very short time he had. He was very careful to hold his exact position. His feet were frozen in place and he refused to move them for fear he would be killed, or worse. Looking off to his left, he could see someone had spotted him and started toward him. He then glanced to his right and saw more soldiers coming.

Caught between two closing forces, Mike refused to move—he couldn't. Spears began to land nearer and nearer, until one struck the ground past him with a thud.

Seven seconds, he thought as he counted in his head.

Mike glanced back up to see the unarmed stranger had closed the gap to a dangerous distance, then recognized the face.

Me? What am I doing here? Oh no. Mike thought in terror. *I shouldn't have come!*

A sharp pain shot from his wrist and he looked down to see that the spear had whipped back and struck him.

My watch is gone! Three seconds left, maybe?

Fear tore through Mike's gut as he dropped to his knees to find the watch. A sharp pain in his right knee told him exactly where it was. Then the sound and vibration tore at him and Mike scrambled to his feet, driving the watch deeper as he did. He glanced back over to see the look on his own face approaching him. He felt immense guilt and knew he had made the wrong decision.

I shouldn't have tested it, not like this.

* * *

Danni broke the silence. "Terry, when the fuel delivery guys started to make a move on us, who noticed the third guy?"

Mike lurched forward. "What? Did you ask me something?"

"No, I asked Terry a question," Danni said.

Terry answered, "Bill took him out. I couldn't see him from my angle."

"That was a close one," she said.

"Yeah, he might have saved both your lives with that shot," Terry replied. "That girl of yours sure saved my skin out there."

"Yes, and what a gruesome sight it was."

"Strange how time seems to slow down at those moments. Makes time travel much easier to imagine. So, are we all going? Back to ancient Egypt I mean?" he asked.

Everyone looked at Mike.

"I think we should. There's a lot for us to do there and two of us can't handle it all," Mike answered. "Anyone want to stay behind?" he asked. "I guess I'll take the silence as a resounding no."

"So, what now?" Terry asked.

"Well, we'll have to learn the language, or hire an interpreter I suppose," Mike answered. "We need ancient Egyptian, spoken and hieroglyphs both. We'll stand out like a sore thumb at first, so we'll need to be careful."

"That period used Archaic Egyptian. We can get some books on it when we get to Cairo and get started on the basics right away. The more we know before we go back, the better off we'll be," Courtney said, over the intercom.

"That'll be a slam-dunk for Courtney, since she picks up a language in a week or two," Terry said.

"I've seen some of that already. She is amazing," Mike said quietly, glancing toward the front.

"She gets that from her mother," Court said.

"Are you sure you want to go back with us?" Mike asked. "I mean, with the injuries and all?"

"Getting shot is overrated. Heck, I'll be good as new in a week," Terry said.

"That's about all we'll have, I expect," Mike said.

Danni reached out her hand, "Speaking of which, you two need to take your pills and drink a bottle of water. They'll speed up your recovery, though not as fast as you'd like."

"I can get my own water," Mike said.

"This is the water you need to drink," Danni said.

"Really, I'm fine."

"No, you're not. You need to stay on them for another week," she said.

"But they make me sleepy."

"Michael, take this," Danni ordered.

"Yes, ma'am," Mike said, as Terry chuckled.

"Oh, man don't make me laugh, that isn't good," Terry pleaded.

Mike turned to see sweat already forming on Terry's brow.

"Sorry, I know exactly how you feel." Mike popped his pill

and took a drink of the water. "Nite all," he said, as he leaned back in his seat and fell asleep.

* * *

Mike opened his eyes to a dimly lit horizon. "Hey, what's up? Where are we?" he asked.

"We're about to land at a little airport in West Sahara," Danni answered.

"I guess we had enough fuel after all," Mike smiled weakly.

"Not yet, we've been on fumes for a while now," she explained. Mike's smile fell. "Oh."

"Did you get enough sleep?" she asked.

"Yeah, and I slept like a rock. I don't even remember dreaming."

"And how do you feel?" Danni asked.

"Actually, I don't have much pain," Mike said, as he tested his muscles. "Oh, I'm a little sore here and there."

"Excellent, your body is strong. Not everyone does so well with the healing accelerator I gave you guys."

"How's Terry doing?" Mike asked.

"He woke up a few hours ago, in a lot of pain. I gave him another dose and he's been out ever since."

"We need him awake when we land, even if it's only for his eyes, so don't put him out again until we are back in the air," Court said.

"Yes sir, Captain Dear," she said.

"Captain doesn't sound like such an impressive title when you say it that way," Court said.

"Exactly," Danni said, with a smile.

Courtney's voice came over the intercom, "Buckle up, we're making our approach. Mom, wake Terry up. Dad, start handing out guns and ammo as soon as we touch down. Mike, I want you looking for people off in those buildings to the right side of the airport," Courtney ordered.

"I'm awake," Terry said.

Mike's heart was racing and he felt like he couldn't get enough oxygen. *Relax. Breathe deep.*

As soon as the nose gear touched the runway, Courtney called out, "We have company! At least two in the hangar on the left!"

Court was out of his seat and quickly handed Mike, Terry and Danni their weapons.

Mike got up on a knee and stared out the right side of the plane, scanning for trouble. He glanced over at Terry and saw that he was doing similarly on the left.

"We're being waved in," Courtney said.

"Do you think it's safe?" Court called out.

"No, but I know it's not safe to sit on the tarmac in this beauty," she replied.

"Safety off but keep your finger out of the trigger guard. We don't want any accidental shots," Terry said.

"Don't fire unless you hear us shooting," Courtney added.

That was all for me, Mike thought.

When the plane rolled up within a hundred feet of the building, the doors began to roll open. Two young boys, each with an AK-47 strapped over his shoulder, pushed the heavy doors wide open. The older of the two motioned rapidly for the plane to pull inside the massive building.

"Here we go," Court said.

"Everyone be on your toes, but keep the weapons down," Court ordered.

Courtney pulled the plane into the massive building and shut down the engines. "Looks professional to me, they have a pusher and a fuel truck ready to go."

Suddenly, the room went dark and there was a solid boom that reverberated in the hangar. The team nervously waited as their eyes adjusted. The dim light coming through the translucent panels around the upper half of the building was barely enough to see by.

Court said, "I'll take this one," then opened the door and lowered the stairs. "Hello there boys!" he called out.

"Hello there," the eldest said.

"Your English is outstanding," Court said, walking down the stairs. "Are you from around here?"

"We've lived here all our lives," the eldest replied. "Do you like my airport?"

"Your airport? You must be quite a businessman to own a grand airport like this," Court said, as he shook the boy's hand.

"Everything as far as your eyes can see belongs to us, now that everyone else is sick or dead. God has smiled on my big brother and me, too."

"Sick or dead? What happened?" Mike asked from the steps of the plane.

"The illness. They say the Nazis have poisoned the world, but not us, we are too strong," the elder brother said.

Mike looked at Courtney, but she didn't react.

"You expected this?" he asked.

Danni said, "We discussed it while you slept, but weren't sure how bad it would be."

"This isn't the time, Mike," Courtney whispered.

"When were you planning on including Terry and I?" Mike asked.

"You're putting us all at risk," Courtney said.

"It wouldn't change a thing, so why worry you with it?" Danni asked.

"Unbelievable," Mike said. He turned to watch Court and the eldest negotiating for the fuel.

"What is going on out there?" Courtney whispered again.

"Court's buying our fuel." Mike looked back at Courtney and said, "It wouldn't change a thing? Billions of people may have died and we could have stopped it? Are you serious?"

"Mike, we're going there to fix the real problem. You need to keep your focus on the divergence in ancient Egypt," she said.

"So, we let everyone suffer and die? I can't be the cause of all this." Mike sat down in the seat nearest him, feeling nauseous.

"You aren't the cause of all this. That's absurd. Look, I understand what you're going through, but these people aren't who they should be. These worlds are fractured, they're perverted versions of the one, true reality. We must set things right or we'll never know what our lives should have been," Courtney said.

"What if the Nazi timeline is the real one? Maybe someone

went back to change the past and that's why things are this way."

"Mike, you're losing your focus and starting to sound a little crazy," Courtney said.

"We could go back far enough to—"

"Quit it. Keep your mind on what you know and stop letting silly dreams take you in other directions," she said.

"What do you know about my dreams?" Mike asked.

"We're all having them."

"Terry?"

"Yep me, too," Terry said.

Courtney continued, "We have to go all the way back, Mike. You think we could put all this in motion and get this close, if we weren't meant to finish the job?"

"I didn't think you believed in destiny," Mike said.

"I suppose I do, in some ways."

"It actually sounds like you're using my own beliefs against me."

"You may have swayed me," she said.

"Swayed?" Mike asked.

"Shifted?" Courtney replied.

"Is that a question? I'm trying to understand where you stand and dodging my question seems counterproductive."

"First of all, I won't be forced or coerced into answering any questions. Second, if you think you're some sort of a skilled interrogator, then you're in for a rude awakening."

"Sounds like you're threatening me."

"If the tone of this conversation doesn't improve, it's over. If you want to know something, then ask," Courtney said. "I'll choose whether or not to answer it. Period."

"I want to know what you believe," he replied.

"I no longer believe that I'm in charge of my own life. My decisions yes, but my fate seems to be out of my control. So, yes, I have changed my opinion. Happy?"

Reaching his hand out, Mike whispered, "Still wanna get married?"

"Let's wait and see what fate has in store for us before we get all mushy again," Courtney said.

Mike pulled his hand back as Courtney walked off the plane. As she reached Court's side, Mike noticed her eyes glance back toward him. *She still cares, but you're going to have to give her some space.*

Mike stood inside the door and listened to the group negotiate.

"So, they want the AK-47's we picked up, and any ammo we have to go with the AK's. That, plus eight ounces of gold will get us six thousand gallons of fuel," Court told Courtney.

"It's a deal, but we need to get going so we can make the four hour trip to Cairo before dark. Here's two ounces to get us started and at each thousand gallons we'll pay another ounce of gold."

With big smiles, the boys pulled the fuel truck alongside the twin engine jet and began pumping.

"Fuel's flowing," Mike said.

"Roger that," Terry said, without taking his eyes off the side door into the hangar.

"See something?" Mike asked.

"No, but I have a bad feeling about that door."

"Bad feeling or deja vu?"

"Bad feeling, that's all," Terry said.

"Good. Besides the dreams, some of us are also having—"

"I know," Terry interrupted, "and no, I don't want to talk about my own."

"So, you're—"

"You didn't hear me?" Terry raised his voice. "I thought I made that clear."

"Sorry, I'm a little out of sorts right now," Mike grumbled.

"I don't want to talk about that either."

Mike stood in silence, watching the boys and the Lewis family talking back and forth. He started to feel like an outsider and decided to join them.

The younger boy screamed at him, "Don't move!"

Both boys swung their rifles and pointed them straight at Mike.

Mike froze in place.

"Put that gun down!" the elder brother ordered.

"Mike! Put that gun on the step and get back on the plane," Court ordered.

Mike dropped his weapon and listened to it bounce down the steps to the concrete as he entered the plane.

"I messed that up," Mike said.

"Yes, you did," Terry agreed.

"I'm out of my element."

"Yes, you are, which is why we're here."

* * *

The plane flew along in silence for over an hour when Mike broke the silence.

"You've been bouncing furiously between those two books for a while now. Did you find something?"

"I might know when it all started," Terry replied.

"Let's have it," Mike said.

"The brown book says no one knows what happened to Sneferu, but this book says Sneferu was taken by The Messenger of the Gods. Pharaoh Khufu's reign began roughly ten years later, in the brown book. So, it would make sense that someone interfered and killed Sneferu," Terry explained.

"But, what if someone interfered and prolonged his life? Or even gave him some technology?" Danni asked.

"I didn't think about it that way," Terry said.

"We have a couple more books here on Sneferu. You can read them if you like. I initialed the books from this timeline, so you can't mix them up," Danni said.

"Thanks," Terry replied, taking two of the books.

Mike asked, "What if we were the ones who did it?"

"Then why would we be trying to fix it now?" Terry asked.

"We're doing two things when we go back there. We're living our current lives and changing the entire timeline," Mike said.

"I'm pretty sure I didn't follow that," Terry said.

"Our current lives are messed up because the past changed, even if we're the ones who changed it. We could be going back for the first time to fix someone else's mistake. What if we're doing this for the second, third, or even fourth time?"

"Now that's a mind trip," Terry said. "How can we know for sure?"

"I don't have a clue," Mike replied.

"Wait, if that's true, then we aren't real. We're merely living out a history that never happened. That would mean we're just part of a timeline and not, well, us?"

"Time travel has always been avoided due to the concern that one simple act could destroy nations. They call it the Butterfly Effect," Mike explained.

"Then how do we know that we won't make it worse, not better?" Terry asked.

"We don't know that either."

"Not exactly reassuring, but we must try," Court said. "There shouldn't be three different realities. Something went horribly wrong somewhere in the past and we're the only ones who can fix it."

"And we need to figure out when it happened, so let's compare ideas. I'll do the writing, while you each read the discrepancies we've marked in the books," Danni said, as they settled in to do more research.

Later on, Courtney's voice came over the intercom.

"That's enough. You've been at it nearly four hours," she said. "We'll be landing in about twenty minutes so get your gear ready."

"We're trying to solve this mystery," Danni said.

"I heard. Court, I need a quick relief before we touch down."

"On my way," he called and went to the front of the plane.

Walking through the group, Courtney said, "Get everything ready in case we don't come back to the plane. Oh, and you may want to take a quick look at the pyramids if you haven't seen them before."

Though she looked in Mike's direction, he felt as if she didn't know him. *Give her some space*, he reminded himself. Mike got up and looked out at the pyramids. "Am I the only one who hasn't seen them?"

"We've seen them a few times," Danni smiled, "they're impressive."

"I've been here several times myself," Terry said. "To the area, that is."

"These may be different than the ones back home," Mike joked.

"Compared pictures in the books already. No difference," Terry replied, rising to stand.

Mike walked up to the cockpit for a better view. "They look huge compared to everything around them."

"Just wait until you're standing in front of them, that's when you really get a feel for their size," Court said.

"I can hardly wait," Mike said. "I've wanted to make this trip all my life." Mike heard Courtney walking up behind him. "I'd better get back to my seat."

Mike stepped aside for Courtney to pass and noticed Terry's face react as Courtney walked by him.

What does that look mean? Courtney said something to him.

Mike sat down, but couldn't stay quiet for long. "Terry, what did Courtney say that got to you?" he asked.

"Her opinion of our situation," Terry replied.

"Which is…" Mike prompted him.

"None of this is real."

"I think she meant that when we go back in time and fix what was changed, our own histories will no longer be real," Danni said.

"I like the way you said it better," Terry said. "But, could it be true?"

"What we did and will do is all real. If future events are changed after things are fixed, they aren't less real," Mike said. He looked at Courtney. *If that's true, then our friendship and your feelings aren't real either.*

* * *

"We'll be landing at the Cairo airport in five minutes," Courtney announced over the intercom. To her father, she said, "I'll take it in from here, thanks, Court."

"She's all yours," he said as he released his yoke.

"There's no air or radio traffic. You think it's that bad already?" she asked.

"It's that bad. Though, folks built a lot of tunnels and bunkers back when the Nazis started using tactical nukes."

"So, fifty percent?" she asked.

"No, maybe five to ten. Knowing how passionate the Nazis are about murdering, I expect they found ways to get many of them also," he said sadly.

Courtney said, "Brian told us that they expected the global death toll to reach as high as ninety percent. That includes the diseases that would follow from unburied dead and starvation estimates."

"From the looks of things here, they weren't far off," he said.

"The poison only maintained deadly potency for a few days, so it must have been heavy around here," she said. "Or the high temperatures, low humidity and lack of rain around here may have made it worse."

"True," Court said.

"Interesting, but it won't matter soon."

"As long as we're successful."

"We cannot fail, no matter what happens," Courtney said. "Which brings me to an important question. Are you ready to let Mom or me die to complete the mission?"

"That's an unfair question and I won't answer it," Court said.

"It's very fair. Will you kill women and children?" she asked.

"I don't think that will be necessary."

"That may very well be necessary and you better not let us down." Courtney turned and stared into her father's eyes.

"I hope it doesn't come to that," Court answered, "because I'm not sure I could do it."

"But it could and we can't fail."

Reaching back up for the mic, Courtney said, "Everyone be ready for anything. Mike, get the device ready in case we have to make a quick exit." Pausing for a moment, she added, "We may need to do some things we won't be proud of, but failure isn't an option."

Courtney landed the plane and taxied up to a row of hangars.

"Not a soul in sight," she said softly, then got up and turned to join the others.

"Everyone ready?" she asked, then grabbed Brian's shotgun.

"I hope so, can't carry another pound if I must," Court said as he muscled his pack onto his back.

"Thanks for the refill," she said to Terry, as she picked up the two spare clips for the shotgun and hung them on her belt.

"Court and Danni did it, not me," Terry said.

"Thanks guys." Courtney grabbed a pistol and her backpack, then turned and said, "Lead the way, Court, but let Terry set the pace."

"Roger that," he said and headed down the steps.

"Let's take that van," Courtney said, and they made their way over to a shuttle on the tarmac. She jogged past the others and opened the driver's door. "This area must have been hit extra hard since there are no maggots or flies."

"That's not a good sign," Mike said.

"OK, let's clear the vehicle," Courtney said. She grabbed the body seated inside her door and dragged it out onto the concrete.

Court pulled the first passenger out, gagging loud enough that Courtney heard.

"You going to make it?" she asked.

"I'm not used to the smell of human corpse, baking in the sun," he said.

Immediately, Mike dropped to one knee and vomited.

"Sorry, Mike. Hang in there, we're almost done," Court said over his loud groans.

Courtney climbed in for the third body, a young woman in her twenties.

Unbuckling the corpse, Courtney said, "Makes you want to go nuke those pigs right now."

Once Courtney had the last body clear of the van, she rolled down the passenger side windows. Court rolled down the driver's side, then started the engine.

"Over half a tank," Court said.

"Excellent. There's a lot of room in this, so let's pull over by the plane and load anything else we might need," Courtney said.

"Danni, follow me," she said and ran back to the plane.

"Grab the water, more ammo, bedding and anything else you think we need," Courtney said, as she pulled an ammo crate toward the door.

After the van was loaded, Court said, "Cover your noses and climb in. We're going downtown to fill Courtney's shopping list."

"I cut up a blanket. Here's something to breathe through," Danni said, handing out folded pieces of cloth.

"Be on the lookout for crazies," Courtney said, as they drove away from the airport.

* * *

Why is this so familiar? Sure, the pyramids are, but why the rest? Mike wondered, as they drove into downtown Cairo. *Here comes an orange building on the right, with a pink arch*, he thought as the van neared a corner. As they rounded it, he saw the building come into view. *Think, Mike, think. What does this mean?*

"These little shops should have everything we need," Court said. "Everyone find two simple looking robes. I'll get some more water. Mike and Terry, keep a lookout."

"Got it," Terry said.

"Also, check the bookstores. We need anything on the time of Khufu, Sneferu, the fourth dynasty, hieroglyphics, or the ancient Egyptian language," Court explained.

"Remember, there could be people holed up in these buildings. Shoot to kill and stay focused on the mission," Courtney said. "From the looks of the broken windows, there was a skirmish here recently."

"We leave in one hour. Questions?" Court asked, then paused for a moment. "Nothing? OK, then, let's get at it."

Mike watched the team scatter into the various shops and buildings. One by one, they stepped back out onto the sidewalks and tied their blanket pieces over their faces.

After only thirty minutes, a large pile had accumulated next to the van. Courtney was searching through the items, but tossing much of it aside, when Mike walked up.

"Keep it coming, there's some great stuff here," she called out.

"I stacked the books I thought were the most interesting over there, on the left," Mike pointed.

"Thanks."

Mike noticed something out of the corner of his eye. When he turned to look at it, the object disappeared.

Relax, you're getting jumpy, he told himself, then walked toward it to investigate.

"That's far enough," a female voice said.

Mike sidestepped and bumped against the building. His eyes scanned in the direction of the voice.

"Where are you?" he called back. *Smart girl. Now where could you be?* Mike thought, as he glanced back toward the van. *Where are you guys?*

"What do you want?" the voice called out.

Educated female, Asian maybe? Why are you in Cairo? Mike decided to tell her more, knowing it could make Courtney angry.

"We're trying to figure out what happened. Can you help us?" he called out, glancing once again to the van.

She's moving. Should be popping out about there, he thought, as he trained his eyes on the ally between two buildings. *Bingo!* Mike saw one eye peek around the corner of the closest building.

"We were gassed," the girl said.

"How many survived?"

"Not many," was her reply.

"How did you?"

"We were down inside one of the pyramids when it happened. Five of us. When we tried to get back out at the end of the day, we were stopped by dead bodies near the opening. We stayed inside for two more days, until one of our own died," the Asian girl explained.

"Tourists?"

"Egyptologists," she said.

"That's amazing. We can sure use your help," he said.

"Help you with what?"

"It's complicated. Can I come closer?"

"As long as you stay out in the street," she said.

"My name's Mike. There are five of us."

"I'm Lynn. I have a gun and I know how to use it," she warned.

"I have a gun, too, in my waistband. I don't know how to use it," he said with a smile, as he walked toward her.

"Show me."

Mike turned to show her the pistol and saw Courtney staring down the street at him, gun drawn. He waved at her. *Relax, don't spook this girl.* Mike felt relieved when Courtney waved cautiously back.

"All right, but keep your hands in front of you," Lynn said.

"Thanks. This problem is global and few are expected to survive," he explained.

"That explains why everything is down. We haven't even seen a plane in two days."

"Would you come with me and meet the team? They'll be excited to meet you."

"Me?"

"You're exactly what we need for our mission."

"What exactly is your mission?"

"We need to deal with the Nazi problem, but we think it all started back in ancient Egypt," he said. *Don't tell her too much, yet.*

"Mike, people have been crazy lately, I'm not sure I can trust anyone."

"I completely understand, but if I told you all the details, you would think I was crazy, too."

"Try me."

"Uh, that wouldn't be helpful. Not yet, at least."

"It's that bad?"

"Worse," Mike said.

"Give me an overview, as we walk to your van," Lynn said, stepping out from the edge of the building as she pointed her gun toward the ground.

As Mike and Lynn walked up the street, he started explaining the basics of the spud to her. He shared a few details about the group, and Lynn discussed her background. As moments passed their familiarity grew, and each felt drawn to the other.

* * *

"Three timelines? You're not crazy, but you sure sound it," Lynn said.

"I know. I think I might be crazy, too," Mike said. "Once you've seen it in action you'll understand. Then, we can explain the plan in more detail."

"I would like to believe you, really. Then, we'd be able to escape all this," she said.

"Right, escape to one of the other worlds," Mike agreed.

"How many people can go?"

"First things first. Let's introduce you to the team and we'll go from there."

Mike watched Lynn look toward the group, one block away.

"OK, let's do this," Lynn said, slinging the gun's strap over her shoulder.

Mike smiled at the waiting group and waved as they walked the remaining distance.

"Everyone, this is Lynn."

"Hi, Lynn," Danni called out. "Nice to see another survivor."

"Yeah, same here," Lynn said.

"She's a grad student from USC. An archaeologist," Mike said.

"Bill was stationed there, in L.A., and lived right next to the campus," Terry said. "You could have lived within a few blocks of each other."

"Archaeologist?" Courtney asked in amazement. "Sorry, Terry, that is a coincidence."

"Yes, it is," Lynn said, as they joined the others at the van. "There were others who were underground when it happened. All but four of us went outside too early. We were lucky."

"Exactly how good are you with history around Sneferu and Khufu?" Courtney asked.

"Fairly good. They're important historical figures since they were the fathers of Egyptian technology."

"Technology?" Mike asked.

"The batteries, chemical reaction power plants and the timekeeping devices appeared at the end of Sneferu's reign," she said.

"Is that theory?" Courtney asked.

"No, but it's not widely known," Lynn said.

Mike looked at Courtney. "Fate?"

"It's not a coincidence," Courtney said. "All the books we found won't add up to an hour with this girl."

"That reminds me, I have a big load of supplies I need to take back to our camp. I told them I would be back in an hour, so I need to get back."

"We can be ready in five minutes since we have everything we need now," Courtney replied.

"Super. I'll go get my truck now. It's down there a few blocks." She pointed toward the direction where Mike had met her.

"Be careful," Courtney said.

"I will. Mike, would you like to ride with me?" she asked.

"Sure, let's go," he said and glanced at Courtney. *Did I just detect a bit of jealousy?*

"Mike is still recovering from an injury, he should probably stay here," Courtney said.

"Actually, it feels good to walk a little." *Yep, jealous*, Mike thought, holding back a smile until he turned to walk away.

"I feel safer already," Lynn said.

"No sweat," Mike said. *I bet Courtney is mad now.*

* * *

That skinny little archaeologist drives too slow, Courtney thought.

The half hour drive following Lynn to her team, in the rancid van, was becoming nearly unbearable. Off in the distance, Courtney could see a campsite and noticed people moving about. She slowed the van and put some distance between them in case the camp was concerned about the unknown guests. Lynn got out a hundred yards ahead of them, and by the arm waving, guns and posture, they had definitely startled Lynn's team. Courtney stopped the van.

"Stay calm everyone, they have their guns out," Courtney said, hearing a few weapon clicks inside the van. "Easy now, we don't want to worry them any more. Terry, that goes for you, too."

"Copy," Terry replied.

After a few tense moments, Lynn waved for them to approach.

As they pulled up to park, one man with a rifle walked over to their van.

"Hey, there. Sorry about that, everyone is jumpy."

"No problem. We totally get it," Courtney said.

"It's nice to see we aren't the only ones who survived," he said. "Name's Tom."

"Hi, Tom," Courtney said, reaching out to shake his hand. Seeing him wince, she said, "Yeah, it wreaks in here, sorry."

"Let's get you out of this thing then," he said.

Courtney watched Tom walk up to Lynn and the others.

Lynn waved at them to follow and parked beside a large tent.

"We'll leave everything in here for now," Courtney said to her parents, then climbed out of the van.

After introductions and nearly an hour of questions and answers, Courtney's patience was fading. She wanted to wash up and collect her thoughts, not listen to them chatter.

"I'm glad we found each other. Your expertise in all things ancient Egypt will be helpful in the coming weeks," Courtney said. "We should—"

"It's amazing, actually," Mike said. "You'll be instrumental in undoing this terrible situation."

"Undoing? What's that supposed to mean?" Tom asked.

"It's not a good time to go into the details right now," Courtney said.

"We believe we know how to fix this," Mike said, ignoring her objections. "All of it."

Courtney noticed Mike glance at her. *Don't do it. Not yet.*

Mike unzipped his pack and reached inside.

"I'm not sure they're ready for that," Courtney said.

Tom stood up. "We don't even know if we will be alive tomorrow. If you have something that can help, we all need to know."

"I need to show you something, to help you understand," Mike said. "You won't believe me otherwise."

Stupid move, Mike. Too early, Courtney thought.

Mike pulled out the spud.

Courtney stepped back from the group and slipped her pistol out of her waist-band. She clicked off the safety and watched the others intently.

Mike walked several yards away from the group, then vanished from sight. A moment later, he reappeared on the opposite side of the group.

Courtney knew he had achieved the desired results by the gasps all around.

"The device works off the Earth's gravitational and magnetic fields. It's the same phenomenon that causes solar flares to eject millions of miles into outer space," Mike told his amazed audience.

"Are you talking about an X-point generator?" Tom asked.

"Yes, that's basically what I have," Mike said. "I see you payed attention in physics class. The ancients had a much larger one—the crystal altar—that they used for the same purpose. We're almost certain they damaged our timeline with it, sometime in the past. When they changed time, they caused reality to fracture into three separate timelines."

"Impossible," one of the archaeologists said.

"I know it's hard to believe, but we have been to the other two timelines. Though eerily similar, they're also very different. In my opinion, this is by far the worst one of the three timelines," Mike explained.

"You can get us out of here?" Tom asked.

Of course, they want to run, Courtney thought. *This was a waste of time.*

"We need to go back in time and stop the event that caused the divergence," Mike said.

"Can you take us to one of the other timelines?" Tom asked.

"We'd like to see for ourselves. If it works like you say, we're in."

Courtney saw the others stand up with Tom. They were speaking but Courtney was watching their faces. *Scared children. Lie. Lie. Fear. Disbelief.* She looked at Mike.

"Sure, but only once. We need to conserve the power cells," he said.

I should shoot them now and get it over with, Courtney thought.

Mike walked a few steps away, adjusted the spud, then turned it back on. "We'll go to the best of the three, current date."

"Does it hurt? Do we jump?" Tom asked.

"No. All you need to do is step through the hazy field right there and keep walking a few feet to make room for the people following you. Wait for me before you do anything or go anywhere. The last thing you want to do is meet yourself in one of the other two timelines."

"That's bad?" Lynn asked.

"Deadly for you, dangerous for the rest of us," Mike said.

One by one, the archaeologists stepped into the haze, then Mike jumped through and joined them.

* * *

"Thirty minutes? What's Mike thinking?" Courtney asked, as she looked at her watch again, calculating how much time passed since the group stepped through the haze. "Five more minutes and I am going to ransack this place."

"Give them a little more time," Danni said.

"Five minutes," Courtney grumbled.

"Ten, and then I'll help you," Danni said.

"Deal," Courtney replied. "He knows we'll be worrying. This was a bad idea."

"Courtney, that's not fair and you know it," Danni said. "Mike may be too trusting, but that's not always a bad quality."

Ignoring her mother, Courtney said, "First, he tried to make me jealous, and now he's putting the entire op in jeopardy."

"You haven't been very nice since Bill's death, and blaming Mike for your issues is ridiculous," her mother announced.

"That skinny little archaeologist is part of the problem, too," Courtney said. "If she's to blame, I'll break her pretty little nose."

"Courtney! Listen to yourself," Danni scolded.

Courtney opened her mouth to speak, as Lynn stepped into view. Lynn turned around and Mike stepped into the camp and bumped into her, putting his arm around her.

Nice move, you little snake. You can kiss that perfect nose of yours goodbye, Courtney thought.

"Sorry," Mike said, stepping around her. "The others wouldn't come back with us."

"Knowing how important this is?" Court asked.

"Of course. They were scared and ran away. What did you expect?" Courtney asked Mike.

"Not that," he said.

"What kind of problems will that cause? I mean, what's going to happen when they're discovered, or if they find themselves there?" Danni asked.

"If we accomplish our goal, it won't matter. If not, they can't possibly make things worse than they already are," Mike said.

"I see your point," Danni said.

"We tried to talk them out of it, but they refused," Lynn said.

"*You* did?" Courtney asked, pointedly.

"Actually, Tom knocked her down when she tried to drag him back with us," Mike explained.

"I'm sorry, I don't know what to say," Lynn said.

"It's not your fault. They're adults after all. Besides, if they were that worried about staying here, they wouldn't have been much help," Court said.

"You're here and that's what counts," Danni said, as she walked up to her, patting Lynn on the shoulder.

Court said, "This isn't their fight."

"It *is* their fight! It's everyone's fight!" Courtney yelled.

Danni said, "Don't be angry at your friends for being scared, Lynn, it's only natural."

"I'll help you stop the Nazis," Lynn said with misty eyes.

I think I'm going to puke, Courtney thought.

"That means the world to us," Danni said, putting her arm

around Lynn. "Finding you was a miracle, and you'll be an immense help."

Fate maybe, but a miracle? Courtney forced herself to calm down. *She's weak, but she's the best we have,* Courtney told herself. *You can always kill her when this is over. Or if she screws up . . .*

After a few moments passed, Lynn asked, "Do you think this device is powerful enough to move us that far back in time?"

"We don't even know if we can get there. You know, back that far. All I know for sure is that I can control it in short bursts, to move minutes or even a day. I haven't really tried to go years, much less millennia," Mike said.

Haven't really? Courtney noticed Mike blink several times. *Liar, you've gone back further than that, but when? Aunt Margie's?*

"If it doesn't work, I guess we could always join the others back in your world," Lynn said, wiping her eyes.

"Maybe," Mike replied. "But we've been leaving a lot of trouble behind us.

"We really don't have any other options," Courtney said. "Let's go inside, there's a lot more we need to work out." Her mother pulled on her arm as Courtney was about to enter the tent, and lead her several feet away. "What, Danni?"

"Stop calling me that. I don't like what you're trying to do," she whispered.

"It's your name."

"I know what my name is, and you know what I mean," Danni replied.

"What do you need, Mother?"

"Losing your cool back there was way out of line. You're upset you lost a friend, but stop taking it out on the rest of us," Danni said. "We all lost someone we cared about."

"I guess I don't see it that way," Courtney replied.

"Then you're blind, but I still love you." She smiled, gave Courtney a hug and went inside the tent.

Doesn't anyone else understand what's going on here! It's like dealing with a bunch of children. Courtney took a deep breath and relaxed. *Control. That's much better,* she thought.

Courtney stepped inside the tent and saw Lynn searching

through the papers on the makeshift conference table which held some lighting and small fans. The walls, too, were covered with hieroglyphic charts and photographs of matching examples.

"Ancient Egypt is what we do—or did," Lynn said, as she gestured to the walls around them. "As I see it, you'll need to know the basics of the language, enough to stay out of trouble, as long as we stay together."

"That would be great if we were going back for a few days. We're not exactly certain when we need to arrive and may need to live there for a year or more," Courtney said. "Take a seat and we'll get you up to speed."

"OK, but I thought I was the expert on Egypt," Lynn said.

"I'm sure you are, about *your* Egypt, but there are two versions of Egypt you don't know a thing about," said Courtney.

"I'm sorry, you're right. In that case, I'll track the information by world. Once we have everything listed out, we'll let the data tell us what to do."

That should keep her busy for a few days. "That works for me. Dad, can you grab the books from the van, please?" Courtney asked.

The hours flew by as the group scoured the books for details about the three histories of Egypt. As they rattled off items of note, Lynn jotted them down, commenting on similarities and anomalies. One by one, they finished with their share of the books, and left the tent until only Courtney and Lynn remained.

"We should call it a night," Courtney said. "I want to get started first thing in the morning."

"Sounds good to me," Lynn said. "I will organize a few things to get ready for morning."

Courtney slept for a few hours, then awoke and noticed a light through her tent wall. Peeking her head out of her tent, she saw the main tent was glowing.

Someone's up. Walking over to the tent she said, "Knock-knock?"

"Hey there, come on in," Lynn answered. "I've added some more details to the lists. You should come see."

Courtney walked over to the large presentation tablet Lynn

191

had been working on. She was impressed by all the information and Lynn's hard work. Courtney flipped back through the pages, to the beginning.

"You can be my guinea pig." Lynn smiled. "Stop me whenever something doesn't make sense to you so I can elaborate."

Courtney sat and listened as Lynn recounted what she had gleaned from the various books. After several minutes, the similarities and discrepancies began to form in her mind.

"That gets us down to a two year period," Lynn said. The problem is that calendars were adjusted. That makes it possible for us to be off by as much as a few years. There were many lies told over the centuries to make one king look greater than another. We are at the mercy of 'his story' or 'history'.

"Lynn, this looks great," Courtney said. "Did you know the calendar systems where we come from are much worse than here?"

"Really?"

"Yes. A powerful church state dominated much of our world for centuries, like in Ancient Egypt. They reworked our calendar several times to rewrite history."

"And the people knew...but why?"

"Of course. They did it to cover their sordid past and pay homage to their gods," Courtney said.

"Keeping the truth from the commoners."

"Exactly," Courtney said. "You look like you need some rest."

"I can keep going."

"No, we need you rested, to help prepare us for the trip." Turning off the lights in the tent to show the predawn light, Courtney said, "The sun will be up soon."

"I suppose you're right, but don't let me sleep for more than a few hours."

"I won't let you sleep too long." Courtney smiled.

"All right then, see you in a few hours," Lynn said and stepped out of the tent.

* * *

Lynn awoke to the noonday sun and the group eating lunch outside in the shade.

"Courtney, you didn't wake me," Lynn said.

Smiling, Courtney replied, "No, you needed the rest. Besides, we have plenty of time to get ready for this and a few hours won't make a difference."

Terry was sitting in a folding chair, eating his lunch. Lynn looked over and noticed he was staring at her.

"He doesn't talk much," she said, nodding at Terry.

"I don't keep him around for his brain," Courtney said.

"Don't have much to offer at this point." He gestured at himself, bruises and bandages plainly visible.

"You must be pretty good at something or you wouldn't be here," Lynn said.

"I suppose."

"Did the other guy win?" Lynn smiled.

Court said, "The other guys. Terry and his partner took out a dozen men. They saved our lives."

"I'm very sorry," Lynn said.

"For what?" Terry asked.

"The loss of your friend."

"Oh, they told you?" he asked.

"No, I can see it in your eyes," Lynn said. "Plus, I saw it in my dreams this morning." Lynn leaned in closer. "Can I ask you something about the fight?"

Terry nodded.

"Was there a blue truck and a green truck, with guns in the back?" Lynn was startled by the sharp glance Terry cut at her. "I told you, I had a dream," she whispered.

"You, too?" Terry asked.

"What do you mean?"

"We've all been having them."

Lynn felt the ground under her feet start to move and everything around her with it. She looked into the distance to steady herself and watched as the horizon tilted down to the left, then leveled out. Chills ran down her spine.

The only way this makes sense is if someone messed with the past. We have to fix this soon, or I'll lose my sanity.

* * *

By their fifth day at the pyramids, their week was nearing an end. The team could feel the pressure of the dangerous task, full of unknowns, that lay ahead of them. It was palpable, but no on spoke of it. Their busy days were filled from the time they awoke until they fell asleep, mentally exhausted. Early mornings were spent reviewing progress with the ancient language and its symbols. Courtney had surpassed everyone by day two and began helping Lynn teach the others. Before lunch, everyone helped take care of the needs around camp, before it got hot. The afternoons were used to learn new words, phrases and a few hieroglyphic symbols. Their evenings were usually spent listening to Lynn tell a story about the reign of a Pharaoh. It was a great way for them to learn about the culture and wind down from the busy days.

Mike avoided Courtney and spent most of his free time reading Michael's notebooks. He spent many hours trying to crack the code that hid some portions of the last notebook.

"That's it!" Mike said.

"What, Mike?" Court asked.

"Sorry, I was thinking out loud."

"Sounded like more than that," Court said.

"I finally figured out Michael's code," Mike replied.

"You're serious?"

"Yeah, give me an hour and I'll have it translated."

"I can't wait to hear it. Good job, Mike."

Mike closed his eyes for a moment, *What does that mean? He saw Terry, Courtney, and me? Where is the place he's referring to?* Mike heard Terry and Lynn talking as he fell asleep.

"That was so much fun, we'll have to go out again tomorrow,"

Lynn said.

"Glad you liked it. She's my baby," Terry said, reaching over the side and patting the boat.

"No wonder you two come out here every summer," Bill said. "It's absolutely amazing the way the sun shimmers on the water like that."

"It's sad to think that this is the first time we could all make it together," Jill said.

"I know, we should do it again," Courtney said.

Mike tried to talk but no words came out. *What's wrong with me? Am I dreaming?*

A little girl's voice called out from the cabin behind him, "Would Daddy have loved it too?"

Mike watched as Jillian looked right past him and smiled as a tear rolled down her cheek.

Courtney turned and looked straight through Mike, toward the girl's voice. "Yes, sweetie, your daddy would have loved it out here. Especially since he would have been here with you."

No! Let me wake up! Mike felt a sharp pain in his throat as he tried to scream. *I'm here! Over here! Can't you see me?*

"Terry, something is wrong with Mike," he heard Lynn say.

See! I told you I was here! Wait, where did everyone go? Why is it so dark?

"I think he's having a bad dream, let's wake him."

"You think we should?" she asked.

Wake me! Do it now! Mike screamed in silence.

Mike felt a hand on the back of his shoulder and gasped in a large breath of air. "I…I," he stammered.

"You were dreaming. Is everything all right?" Lynn asked.

"Fine, just fine," Mike said, still breathing hard.

"You look like you've seen a ghost," Terry said.

"I do?"

"Uh, yeah. That crazy look on your face is starting to scare me," Terry said, then chuckled.

"Sorry. It was so real."

"We're going for a walk, wanna come?" Lynn asked.

"No thanks," Mike said.

"Back in a bit," Terry said.

Mike watched as he and Lynn walked off together. *Looks like old times. I wonder if either of them remembers?*

* * *

When Terry and Lynn returned, Mike called for everyone to join him in the big tent.

Once everyone was seated, he said, "I know what caused the problem, who did it and even the day he did it on."

"How can that be?" Court asked in disbelief.

"It was you," Courtney blurted out. "Your experiments were in time travel, not propulsion. You split the timeline."

"My research has always been in propulsion," Mike said defensively.

"Right, but that's in this timeline, not before the timeline was split into three," Courtney countered. "The *you* before all of this, was working on time travel," she said. "No secrets, Mike."

"I'm sorry. Yes, I think you're right," Mike admitted. "How long have you known?" Mike asked.

"Just a hunch, until now," she said.

"I see. Well, when the Colonel and Michael died, I was flooded with random memories I couldn't account for. I understood and knew things I shouldn't have. My dreams were so vivid. I knew they must be memories, but I wasn't convinced until I cracked the remaining pieces of Michael's code. Now, it all makes sense," Mike said.

"We're listening," Court said.

"In the original timeline, on August twentieth, I went back in time to the Euphrates Valley in Iraq numerous times. I was trying to pinpoint when the fusing of the sand had occurred," Mike started to explain.

"What fused sand?" Terry asked.

"There are several places around the globe where the sand is fused into green glass," Lynn answered. "Please continue, Mike."

"My team and I were looking into the sand and other archaeological anomalies. You know, like the megaliths at Stone Hedge and Easter Island, the Antikythera mechanism—"

"Wait, the what?" Court asked.

"Antikythera mechanism. It's a mechanical computer for predicting the position of the known solar system. It was built many hundreds of years before the technology was supposed to exist."

"That is a varied list of interests," Danni said.

"We now believe that technology was injected into the ancient cultures. We wanted to find out who did what and when they did it," Mike said.

"Sure, no one believes the ancients could have done these amazing things without help. That's because they aren't creative enough to offer simple solutions themselves," Courtney said.

"And that's another school of thought," Mike said.

"The only reasonable one," she said.

"Anyway, after the glass research turned up nothing, my team decided to focus on the construction of the great pyramids. We had been in the desert for eleven days, then on August 31, 2014, we were successful. From what I can figure out, the day I went back in time to was the fourth day, of the third month, of the ninth year of Khufu's reign. At least, there were a few references to that date in Michael's ramblings."

Danni asked, "Michael? You think Michael knew what you did?"

"He saw it in his dreams," Mike answered.

"How do you explain Michael seeing this and not you?" Terry asked.

"I think my original invention, before the real timeline was split, was more like Michael's. Last night, I had dreams about a large ring of resonators we assembled in the desert. We had several locomotive engines to generate the massive amounts of power it needed," Mike explained.

"Why the desert?" Terry asked.

197

"So we could experiment undetected. Michael had detailed visions of it and developed his system from those memories."

"Why have you kept this from us for so long?" Danni asked.

"I haven't. Everything just came together for me from Michael's notes. I tried to talk to Terry about some of it on the plane, but I thought I was going crazy so I dropped it. Now that we've been here at the pyramids, the brief flashes have become vivid dreams. No, they're more like memories."

Mike paused for a moment but everyone remained silent.

"Continue with the original trip back to the pyramids, please," Court requested. "This is interesting, but I want to know what happened."

"I went back several times, but my system wasn't powerful enough for me to stay more than a few seconds. Those trips could be the reason all this is happening."

"How can you be so sure?" Lynn asked.

"Almost exactly from that point on, everything was forever altered. Michael had dreams about it and now I do. Our futures were altered since history was altered."

"You caused all of this?" Terry asked.

"We didn't have anything to do with it, did we?" Lynn asked.

"We all had a part in it, even Bill was there," Mike said.

"You're nuts," Terry screamed. "There's no way you're going to pin this on the rest of us! Bill had nothing to do with it and you know it." Terry calmed slightly. "Someone shut him up before I break his neck."

Mike saw Lynn put her hand on Terry's shoulder and whisper in his ear.

"Why doesn't anyone else remember any of this?" Court asked.

"I'm not sure that's true. I only know, or remember, bits and pieces because I was there when the other two died. Somehow, when Michael and the Colonel died, it triggered some sort of collective memory for me. Otherwise, each of you should have similar memories."

"Is it because you were the only one who used the X-points to travel in time, when the original event occurred?" Lynn asked.

"That's not completely accurate," Mike said.

"One of us was with you then? Is that what you're saying?" Courtney demanded.

"Terry and Bill were on the original team, assigned as our security detail. The research was far too valuable, so the Defense Intelligence Agency, or DIA, had assigned a team to watch me. One of the agents befriended me to get closer," Mike explained.

Mike watched Court and Terry look at each of the three women, then Courtney's head fell.

"That's why I have been so drawn to you. I thought they were just fantasies, or that I was daydreaming. Now I know they were fragments of memories of a life I lost. I lost my family. I lost my baby girl," Courtney sobbed.

Danni rushed over to her side.

"I don't believe this and you're really starting to upset me," Danni told Mike.

"Don't you remember my baby girl?" Courtney asked.

"I know you all think we're crazy, but you were all there. Lynn too. She was working to crack the secret codes the ancient Egyptian scientists used," Mike said.

"I do feel like I've known you all for a long time, but that happens with people sometimes," Lynn said.

"Enough already," Terry said. "What are we supposed to do now?"

Mike said, "Go back and fix it."

"Fix what?" Terry asked.

"I had a dream that I lost my watch in the sand. I was taking heavy meds then, so I'm not positive that's it, but it could be," Mike said.

"A watch? In ancient Egypt? That would be a serious problem," Court said.

"I know," Mike said. "And there's one more thing I need to tell you.

"Please, don't stop now. We're learning so much," Terry said in exasperation.

"It happened three days from now, on August 31st," Mike said.

"Three days ago? That would be the twenty fifth," Court said.

"No, I know what day it is. What I'm saying is that the original split in the timeline will occur three days in the future," Mike said quietly.

"What? What does that mean? This guy is nuts! I've had all I can take!" Terry yelled, then stormed out of the tent with Lynn following.

Keep your mouth shut and give them time. You owe them that, Mike told himself.

* * *

"Wait, Terry, please," Lynn said, as she caught up to him on the opposite side of the camp.

Terry spun around, frustrated and asked, "What now, Lynnie?"

"Lynnie? Why did you call me that?" she asked.

"I...I," Terry hesitated.

"You call me that in my dreams. I have had dreams about you ever since we met. It feels like I've known you forever. Like we have something beyond this relationship. Don't you feel it?" she asked, with tears in her eyes.

"Lynn, I feel something for you, I do, but I don't think Mike is all there. He's losing touch with reality. Lack of sleep? Stress? That machine? Who knows," Terry turned to walk away.

"Wait, ask him something for me, please," she pleaded with Terry.

"What could he possibly know that would change any of this?" he asked.

"Ask him what you called me there, then...you know what I mean."

Gently, Lynn reached for Terry's hand and led him back to the tent.

"I have a question," Terry said, as he followed Lynn into the tent. "Mike, is there anything else you can tell us about Lynn, or myself maybe?"

"Yeah, but I don't know what good it will do," Mike replied.

"Step out here while we have a quick discussion about something, then you can come back in," Terry said.

Mike stood up and obediently joined Terry.

"We are going to see if Mike knows some things we have seen in our dreams."

Lynn scrawled on a sheet of paper so everyone but Mike could see.

"Come back in here," Lynn called out to Mike.

"Tell us something you think we would find interesting. Something about Lynn and me," Terry said, as Mike stepped through the flap.

"The two of you were close, if that's what you're asking."

"I'm a good fifteen years older than her! She'd be interested in someone much younger than me."

Lynn saw Terry's face go pale.

"What? What's wrong, Terry?" she asked.

"Someone more like Bill's age," he said slowly.

"No, I remember you, Terry. You called me—" she stopped and looked at Mike.

"Lynnie. Bill called her Lynnie, so Terry did, too," Mike said.

Lynn felt the earth turn under her feet. *What? Bill?* She stood silent and watched Terry stumble out of the tent. She lowered herself onto a chair. *Remember something! Anything.* Lynn felt someone's arm around her shoulders.

"I'm so sorry, Lynn," Mike said.

"Is any of this real?" she asked.

"It is, Lynn, it's all real," he said.

"But it's wrong," she said.

"Yes, I think so," Mike agreed.

"Then we need to go today. Now. We need to get packed up and go now," she said.

"We still have three days," Mike said.

"This is all wrong and we know it. Three days isn't much time. We need get there and be ready for when you show up."

"You're right," Mike said. "Everyone get your robes on and meet me on the backside of the great pyramid in thirty minutes. Bring nothing else but gold and those plain wool blankets.

I understand if someone wants to stay behind, but we're not waiting any longer." Mike got up to walk out. "The portable spud gives us the ability to stay as long as we like, but the limitation of power supplies is a concern."

"What do you mean by that?" Terry asked.

"We could get trapped with no way to return," Mike replied, then walked out.

The group was quiet for a few moments.

"I'm so angry at him. How could anyone do something so stupid?" Courtney asked.

"Sweetie, he's a scientist and an inventor. They push the limits and are often decades ahead of the rest of us. I imagine you would have supported or even encouraged him, if it really did happen that way," Court said.

"You're right, Lynn, we're wasting time. We need to get back there as quickly as possible to stop Mike from screwing everything up," Courtney said.

Lynn watched as she stormed out of the tent.

"That's one amazing girl," Lynn said.

"I wonder what she would have been like if we hadn't lost her," Danni said.

"It's too late for that now," Court said, "if we don't get ready now then we won't be part of the solution."

Lynn felt overcome with joy as she rushed toward her tent. *We'll see you soon, Bill.*

* * *

UNIT 4: OUT OF TIME

Mike was dressed in his Egyptian robe and reading Michael's notebook at the picnic table, when the others walked up. One by one, they sat down at the table in silence.

Mike looked up. "Where'd you get the makeup?"

"Lynn did it for us," Danni said.

"It looks pretty authentic to me, nice job, Lynn." Mike said.

"I don't want to sound overly confident, but I think it's a fine replication of period fashion," Lynn replied.

"You won't say things like that back there, of course," Court teased.

Lynn chuckled, "No, of course not."

"Looks like we're all going then," Mike said.

"We figured that without us, you'd screw it all up. And, if that happened we wouldn't be alive," Terry teased halfheartedly.

"Based on my past track record, I'd say you made the right choice," Mike said, as he got up from the table. "Let's go."

The six of them walked silently along the pyramid. Court and Danni were holding hands while they hiked nearly a mile Southwest of the Great Pyramid.

"This is the bank of the old riverbed," Lynn said, as they came to the edge of a plateau.

"There will be many hundreds of workers all over that entire area. I think this area will be fairly quiet," Mike said. "Lynn and Terry are going to the merchants to buy a tent, a couple of knives and some new clothes while we wait."

"I gave everyone enough gold to last a year," Courtney said.

"Is there anything else we should be thinking about?" Mike asked.

"Pretend like you've seen it all, many times before. Pretend you're bored," Courtney said.

"Great advice. We don't want to arouse suspicion. Our robes, skin and hair will already do that. We must make sure they see us as harmless outsiders," Mike added.

"We may be searched or even imprisoned if the guards take notice and decide to interrogate us," Lynn said. "Once we have a tent or two and can get out of sight, we'll have a better chance."

"Okay then, we're ready," Mike broke in. He uncovered the spud from beneath the blanket he was carrying. "I'll run it as long as I can on the first power supply."

"How will we know the date?" Courtney asked.

"We'll pause a few times at night, I hope, and check for the position of the constellations and planets. I've estimated it needs to run for seventeen minutes and fifty one seconds to get us within one hundred years."

"Sounds reasonable," Courtney answered.

"OK, then, get comfortable and stand close so we don't lose anyone," Mike said, as he adjusted the settings.

"We should face each other so it looks like we're talking," Courtney said.

Mike flipped the spud on and a thick ball of haze appeared around them. He was nervous. By the way the others were holding hands, he knew they were, too. Mike saw Danni nudge Courtney.

She's not going to do it, Danni, but thanks for trying.

Mike looked down at the timer on the spud and watched the minutes crawl by.

"That's strange," he said.

"What?" Court asked.

"The power level dropped quickly at first, but now it seems to be leveling off."

At exactly seventeen minutes and forty seconds, Mike switched off the power and watched as the haze cleared.

* * *

Lynn was in awe as she saw the towering pyramids glowing off in the distance.

"They're so white," Terry said.

"It's limestone, the original coating," Lynn said. "It was stolen from the pyramids when Egypt fell to the Nazis."

"Not back home," Mike said. "They were stripped hundreds of years earlier than that."

"Interesting, I didn't see that in your books," Lynn said. "Why would anyone want to damage such amazing structures?"

"What do you think the date is, Lynn?" Mike asked.

"The pyramids are all here so it has to be after Menkaure. He built that smaller pyramid, with the lower section in granite and the three little ones that sit beyond it. I'd guess we're near 2400 BC," Lynn said.

Mike said, "One thousand and sixty seconds at full load got us about forty three hundred years. We need to go back another hundred and fifty years and check again."

Courtney said, "Thirty five seconds, give or take."

Thinking for a moment, Mike said, "Thirty five seconds it is."

He powered the spud back up and they were engulfed in a ball of haze for the second time. As the seconds ticked by, the power indicator began to blink. One second before Mike was going to shut it down, the power supply failed.

"Thirty four. This should be closer," Mike said.

As the haze cleared, the light faded to a clear, starlit night. A few moments passed as their eyes became accustomed to the darkness and the pyramids came into view.

"You went the wrong way," Terry said, "the limestone is missing."

Danni gasped. "He's right, the Great Pyramid looks normal again. Look, you can see the steps up the side where the limestone blocks used to be."

Lynn said, "Look, 'Menakure is Divine' is gone and I don't see 'Great is Khafre' either. If 'Khufu's Horizon' is still under construction, we're near our destination. I don't see the worker camps, though."

"We have some time while I change the power supply out. Lynn, can you and Terry go and try to find someone who can tell us the date?" Mike asked.

"I don't think it's a good idea for us to get separated," Courtney argued.

"I understand, but a man and woman traveling is less troublesome than six people. Why don't the rest of you follow them for backup," Mike asked.

"I agree with Courtney," Lynn said. "But, culturally, Mike is right."

"I would like it much more if we all went, after you have that thing ready to go," Court said.

"Yeah, we should stick together," Courtney agreed.

"Hey, the river is much closer to the pyramids here," Terry said.

"That theory turns out to be correct," Lynn said. "I argued for it in school, but our professor refused to give in."

"What made you so sure?" Terry asked.

Lynn explained, "The river was life to them and they didn't usually live far from it, nor build far from it. Plus, there was other archaeological evidence that the riverbed was here. For whatever reason he didn't agree, I assumed it was his pride."

"OK, I'm ready," Mike said.

"Shall we try that tent up ahead?" Courtney asked.

"I don't see why not," Lynn said, "but we'll need to approach very carefully."

Lynn lead the pack toward a glowing campfire and tent only a few hundred feet away. As they drew nearer, Lynn called out to the tent dwellers in their native tongue.

"Hello? I'm a stranger looking for help. Are you awake? Hello?" Almost immediately a man came out of the tent with small oil lamp in his left hand and a sword in the other.

"Halt! Who has invited you to the land of my great Pharaoh, Khufu?" the man demanded.

Lynn whispered, "He didn't buy my accent." Then, she replied, "My name is Lein, servant to fisherman Be'an of Adz Jhutar."

"I do not know this fisherman," the man replied.

"He has sent me up the great river, Nile, for supplies to buy. I have been gone for many days now, can you tell me the date on Great Khufu's calendar?" Lynn asked.

"It's the first day of the eleventh month of the tenth year of our beloved Khufu's reign," he replied.

"Why has the construction ended on Khufu's Horizon?" Lynn asked.

"You ask many questions. Come closer, so I may look upon you," he said.

Lynn nervously walked the rest of the way to him.

"I wanted to see the great construction we have heard so much about. Khufu's Horizon is truly great, but I see no large encampments. I hoped to trade some gold there for some meat and salt," she said.

"The gods have given the Great Pharaoh a gift and shown him great things. Khufu has ceased construction on his great pyramid. It has been nine weeks and one year now, while his builders make machines that foretell the future. With his new knowledge, it is said that Khufu will rule the world for a thousand years. Go and tell your spy friends on that fishing boat that they should run in fear of Khufu's greatness."

Lynn bowed and backed away from him. "I assure you, we mean no harm. We are only simple fishermen in the great land of Khufu." Lynn said, as she struggled to keep from running back to the others.

"Did you guys get that?" she whispered. "Sounds like it's already happened."

"We did. Let's hurry back to where we can safely use the spud," Mike said.

Making up the rear, Lynn said, "One year and two months back? Can you set it that accurately?"

"I will do my best to get close," Mike said.

As they walked back to their arrival point, Courtney said, "You'll have to drop the power or we'll overshoot our target. Maybe forty percent for one second?"

"Thanks, but I was thinking about twenty five percent for

207

two seconds and then we can fine-tune it more if we need to," Mike said.

Lynn said, "The two of you are behaving like schoolchildren, from our perspective." *Oops, that was a bit much.*

"I'm trying to focus on the mission and avoid distractions. I'm sorry if I sound rude, but ask Terry, this is the real me," Courtney said.

As the group looked to Terry, a large man jumped out and grabbed Courtney, putting a knife to her throat.

"Gold and small coins now," the man commanded in Greek.

Lynn watched as Courtney grabbed his hand. She moved the knife from her throat and spun around to face her surprised attacker. Courtney then kneed him in the groin, twisted the knife free and thrust it up to his throat. The man hunched forward with such speed and power, that he helped force the razor-sharp knife through his neck and into his skull. Lynn winced at the sight. A bloody mist sprayed Courtney in the face. She grabbed his hair and yanked his head forward but was already covered in his blood. Lynn spun around to keep from retching at the sight. A noise behind her caused Lynn to turn back, in time to see a second knife bearing man headed for Danni. He paused for a moment as his partner fell into the sand, then pulled out a sword. Lynn started to scream as Terry pulled a long-barreled pistol from his blanket. With a quiet crack, the second man knelt in the sand.

Lynn watched the scene in shock, her screams never came out and she was unable to move. She heard the gurgling of the first attacker in the sand and the slow wheeze of air leaving the second man's lungs. Lynn felt herself jerk as the second man fell face first into the sand at her feet.

After a few seconds went by, Courtney said, "we were clear about no weapons, Terry."

"I had the silencer on it."

"No weapons. We agreed to that," Courtney reminded him.

They don't even seem bothered by it, Lynn thought in amazement.

"I can't defend the group barehanded, against swords, knives and arrows. It was only for emergencies, like this one," Terry said.

He ejected the spent bullet casing and slipped it into his pocket.

Lynn managed to say, "Terry just saved us."

"He might have caused a bigger problem, too," Mike said.

"Mine was handled without modern tech, yours could have been, too," Courtney said. "Who else has technology here? A cell phone perhaps?"

"I have the spud and spare power supplies, that's it," Mike said.

"I brought two wound kits with me," Danni admitted.

"Dad?" Courtney asked.

"I have a knife strapped to my calf," he replied.

"Wonderful. OK, no one can lose a single item, so keep track of them. If you drop something we must know immediately," Courtney said. The group nodded in unison. "Good. Now check all your contraband and make sure you still have it, before we go any further."

Lynn said, "Courtney, you need to get washed up. Your face and robe—"

"I know. Dad, take that guy's robe off him for me. Lynn, help me get their sandals and water pouches. Terry, you make a fire over by those rocks so we can burn the modern sandals and my robe. We'll stay here for a few hours to rest, since we know there aren't any more thieves nearby. Not living anyway."

"You want to make camp right here where we just killed those two men?" Lynn asked.

"Thieves. And yes, I do."

What have I gotten myself into? Lynn wondered.

The group set about following her orders while Lynn helped Courtney dig a hole with the knives. Once the bodies were in their shallow grave, Courtney and Lynn walked back to the blood soaked area and kicked fresh sand over it. Confident the event was undetectable, Courtney and Lynn joined the others by the fire.

"Matches, too?" Lynn asked.

"Haven't needed them in years," Terry said. "So, Courtney, won't those two bad guys' current status cause trouble in the future?"

"Probably."

Mike added, "We're still in the future, after the fracture. The pyramid's construction was halted for some technological breakthrough. My guess is that I caused it since the timing is about right. If that never happens, then these guys are never here and we never killed them."

"Wait, so they aren't going to be dead if we fix this?" Lynn asked.

"Basically," Mike said.

"If you're OK with it then I guess I am too," Terry said, then shook his head. "There is no end to the craziness of this stuff, is there?"

"No end. I never should have come back here, it was a stupid and unnecessary risk," Mike said.

"No more talking, everyone needs sleep, especially you two, so let's get some shuteye," Court said.

He and Danni used one blanket for a pillow and covered up with their second. Lynn moved closer to Terry to do the same, then said, "Courtney, you and Mike should share blankets, too," Lynn said. Courtney's expressionless glance almost made her smile. *Gotcha.*

* * *

Terry awoke, to see the sky was starting to turn blue in the predawn light. He looked over and saw Mike sitting up, reading one of Michael's notebooks.

"Guys, we should be going soon," Terry whispered. "Lynnie, time to wake up."

Lynn's eyes fluttered, making him smile.

"You can do it, Lynn, just a little more," he chuckled.

"I'm trying," she mumbled.

"We should go to Cairo, now," Mike said.

"I see you've been doing a little thinking," Terry said.

"We need to find a good place to set up for our trip. Plus, we all need food and fresh water before the heat comes again."

"Let's get moving then," Terry said, as he got up.

Terry went to the river's edge to hire a boat for the trip across.

"I wish you could see this, Bill, it's amazing. We couldn't have made it here without you, buddy," Terry said. "I'm missing you—and your annoying ideas."

He heard voices coming up behind him and turned to see Lynn walking down the trail toward him, with the others in tow.

"They're here now, gotta go. But, if this goes like I'm thinking, I'll be joining you soon."

"Hey, Terry, see anything yet?"

"Just the kid in that little boat over there."

Lynn waved slowly toward the young fisherman. When he looked toward them, she yelled out in his native tongue, "Can we travelers hire you for passage across?"

He waved back, then pulled in his net and rowed up to the shore.

"Two for two pieces," he said.

Pulling out a chunk of their smelted gold, Danni reached out and asked, "This for all six?"

The boy's eyes lit up and he nodded quickly. Two by two, the boy ferried the group across the Nile River. As they walked away, he paddled quickly up the river.

* * *

Upon arriving in Cairo, Courtney leaned across Terry and whispered, "Lynn, you look like a kid in a candy store. I know this is exciting for you, but you have to put it in check or we're all at risk."

Ignore the stares, Terry, you aren't the only pale travelers in the market. Breathe and let Lynn do the talking, he told himself. "Hey, guys, let's sit over by that well and let Lynn shop."

"Good idea," Courtney said.

After having a few drinks at the well, they sat on a stone wall and waited for Lynn. Within a few minutes, she returned with a few robes and some bread. Ten minutes more and she was back with the rest of their shopping list filled. One by one, they went behind the building and changed into their new clothes.

"We'd better get going. Is everyone ready for the next leg?" Mike whispered.

Terry stood up and the others did too. He followed Mike behind the stable, noticing they looked much more Egyptian.

Mike powered up the spud and set it slightly above the low power setting he used when he was at Aunt Margie's barn.

"Should we go five percent for eighteen seconds?" he asked Courtney.

"Your call."

Once again, the six were surrounded by an orb shaped ball of fog, but almost immediately it was gone.

Nothing Terry could see around them had changed.

"Let's walk," Mike said softly. "Lynn, get today's date from the first person you can."

They passed several people, then came upon a little old man sitting near the well with a clay pot in front of him.

Terry noticed a few small, silver coins in the bowl. A blind beggar.

As they approached, his head turned toward them. He lifted his face as if he were looking at the group and Terry's hunch was confirmed.

"What is today?" Lynn asked as she dropped a small piece of gold into his bowl.

"I—I know not your day," the elderly man stammered.

"What concerns you, elder?" Lynn asked.

"The six of you," he said softly.

"We are but five and do not wish to do any harm."

"You have lost two then," he mumbled.

"What could you know about five strangers?" she asked.

"Nothing. You must go. You endanger us all with your presence."

"But will you—"

"No, I won't go with you. Go back and change nothing."

"We don't want to take you away, we have come to see Khufu's Horizon," Lynn said. "Will you at least tell me what the date is."

"It is the fourth day of the third month of the ninth year of Khufu's reign. Go now, or I will call the soldiers." The old man began to shake.

"May peace find you," Lynn said, as she led the group back toward the river to recant the conversation.

"That was weird," Terry said.

"I wonder if they're on to us," Lynn said.

"Focus on the mission," Courtney said. "So, it's going to happen today then."

"We should go back one more day to prepare, just in case," Mike suggested.

"Let's take a look first." Courtney said, then turned and headed toward the river bank.

"Look, they're working on the pyramid!" Lynn exclaimed.

"We need to get across the river, to the back side, as soon as we can," Mike said.

Lynn called out to the first two boatmen, but they refused to help them. Then they saw two women rowing up to them.

"May I buy your boat?" Lynn asked.

"We need this boat," one of the women replied.

Reaching out her hand with a large piece of gold, Lynn asked, "Will this be enough to replace it?"

By the wide-eyed look the women gave her, Terry knew the boat was theirs.

"Let's at least try to go all at once," Terry said.

As they got in, sitting on the floor of the small canoe, he realized they wouldn't all fit.

"Terry and I will get another ride, the rest of you go on ahead of us," Lynn said.

"OK, but hurry," Mike said.

* * *

The group was halfway across the river when Mike heard a commotion behind them. Terry was screaming broken Egyptian at a man wearing a shiny, golden cloak.

"No sale! No sale!" he called out over and over.

To their horror, the group saw Lynn pulling herself on to some crates near the man's feet. He pointed at Terry and yelled something. Two men grabbed him and one of them drove a sword right through Terry's side.

"Oh no. He's going for his pistol!" Courtney exclaimed.

Mike could see Terry was messing with the folds of his blanket as the men shoved him off into the water.

"Where'd he go?" Mike asked, as the group looked on in horror.

"He pulled out his gun right when he hit the water," Courtney said. "If they see that thing, we'll have a big mess on our hands."

"But, that guy stabbed him!" Mike yelled.

"Quiet down or you'll get us all killed," Courtney hissed. "He's going to come up in those reeds and kill as many of them as he can."

"Then what?" Danni asked.

"Then we go back further and stop ourselves?" Court asked.

"I'm not sure," Courtney said.

Mike scanned the water around the barge. "Look, a bunch of bubbles, right where he went in."

"If he's smart, he'll find a rock and roll it onto himself," she said.

"Are you serious?" Mike asked.

"He knows what to do. The question is, will he do it," Courtney said.

"They'll spear him if he comes up," Danni said.

"I'm sure they will."

"What about Lynn?" Mike asked.

"If not, she's going to wish they did," Courtney replied.

"Look, more bubbles in front of the boat," Danni said.

"I think I see blood in the water," Mike said. "It's been too long, he's not coming up."

"Row. We have a job to do," Courtney said.

Mike felt a sense of hopelessness as the canoe continued toward the shore, leaving Terry behind.

* * *

Hitting the warm, crocodile infested water, with blood gushing from his side, Terry knew what he had to do. He swam down to the river bottom, then jammed his gun into the river bottom. Feeling a rock against his arm, Terry dug at it and was able to get hold of it. Reaching back toward his gun, he found it and pulled it free. With all his might, Terry punched it under the large rock, wedging his hand along with it. His lungs burning, Terry inhaled the warm, soothing water in one long breath. He felt his life slipping away as he wondered about Lynn.

Bill, I'm here.

* * *

Mike glanced back toward the barge as they landed the canoe on the shore.

"Focus on the task at hand," Courtney said.

"But, I—"

"Me too, but we need to focus. This is all a game, so let's finish up here and get our real lives back," she said.

"Courtney, it's all real," Mike said.

"I don't have time for this. I'd like to get my life back," Courtney said.

"We all would."

"Are you an asset or a liability?" Courtney asked.

"What if I am a liability?" he asked.

"She's gone, so get over it. Now, answer the question."

Mike felt his heart sink. "I'm here to get this thing done."

"Excellent, then act like it or I'll take care of your mess myself."

Mike turned and walked up the shoreline until he was past all the workers moving the limestone.

"We need to get around back. That's where I was when I came to see the construction," Mike called over his shoulder. Mike noticed several of the workers in the limestone finishing area staring at him.

Oops, that was in English, he thought.

One of the workers called out and a soldier rushed over. He

separated Mike from Courtney and her parents as several workers approached.

Get out of here, Courtney will take care of them, he thought as he broke into a jog.

Within a few strides, Mike heard screams and looked back. He could see all three had gotten away from the locals and were heading toward him.

What's that? Humming!

"He's here!" he called back to the others. Mike rounded the corner of the pyramid and saw the new arrival. He looked further and noticed an Egyptian girl running toward him, so he headed in her direction. As the gap closed, he saw the guards were chasing her.

The vibration started up again, only stronger. Mike watched the visitor drop to his knees and dig around frantically in the sand.

It's under your right knee, he thought. *Wait, Lynn?*

Mike yelled back toward Courtney, "That's Lynn!"

Mike saw the visitor stand up and look around at the sand under his feet, then he was gone. He watched Lynn arrive at the spot first with the Egyptians barely a football field behind her. One of them took a long throw and landed a spear less than twenty feet behind her. Another guard took a turn. His spear made it all the way to Lynn, landing beside her. His companions cheered him on and one gave the man his own spear.

It had barely left his hand when Mike heard Courtney yell, "That one's on the mark!"

Mike reached Lynn, with the other three only a few seconds behind.

Courtney screamed, "Lynn, go right!"

Lynn looked at her then dove to the side. The spear struck a few feet beyond where she had been kneeling only a moment before.

"Quick, Lynn, beside me!" Mike yelled. "Hurry! Everyone!" as he fumbled with the spud. He saw the bubble forming, but Court was outside of it.

The third guard reared back with his spear, then let it fly. The other two guards pulled out bows and fired two arrows each, in quick succession.

Mike flipped the switch on the instant Court was within the perimeter of the X-point bubble. He walked over to the hazy edge and pulled on an arrow that was sticking through part way.

"Close one, Court," he said, then yanked it through.

"Lynn! We are so glad to see you!" Courtney gave her a hug and Danni joined them.

"We saw them catch you. How did you get free?" Mike asked her.

Lynn was panting as she told her story. "I explained to the governor that in Ethiopia it was forbidden to kill a man and take his concubine. Our law requires the surviving brother be paid for me. I doubted the brother was going to be a problem, but that it was my duty to inform him. Lucky, or maybe unlucky for me, some Ethiopian dealers were there. So, he dragged me over to them by the hair, to ask if I was lying."

"Lynn, you did great," Courtney said.

"What happened with the Ethiopians?" Court asked.

"When he told them he killed my owner, I tossed down some of my gold. I told the Ethiopians they had killed my owner for his gold but hadn't gotten it. The Ethiopians were angry and then the yelling started. That's when I jumped into the river and knocked some kid out of his canoe," Lynn explained.

"You're amazing!" Danni said.

"I didn't think I would make it, until I looked up and saw the other Mike digging around in the sand." As she knelt to catch her breath, she laughed once, then cried.

Danni reached out and put her hand on Lynn's shoulder. "You're fine now, sweetie."

"Terry died trying to save me," Lynn said, as she sobbed.

"He died saving us all," Danni said. "We all came here for a cause much more important than ourselves, knowing we would not likely make it back alive. Terry died exactly how he wanted to die, fighting for something bigger than himself." She knelt and held Lynn.

"But we didn't get the watch," Lynn said.

"It's about two to three inches down, Mike said.

"What?" Lynn asked.

"Remember the high spot in the sand where we came in? We brought a few inches of sand with us and now we're taking some of that same sand back with us." Mike said, as he dropped near one side and began to dig carefully around the spear. "Whatever you do, don't dig into the barrier."

Several minutes into their search, Courtney said, "You don't think we left it behind, do you? Surely they'll find it."

"It's possible," Mike said. "We are getting close now, I'm shutting the spud down in about ten minutes." Bumping into the spear for the third time, Mike stood up and began to wiggle it from side to side. "This thing is in tight." Prying on it even harder, he felt a crunch, then pulled it free.

Mike read aloud, "Patek Philippe 3940. It's a perpetual calendar watch."

"You had a Richard Mille RM208 last I knew," Courtney said.

"Uh, yeah, good memory. I beat watches up and break leather bands, so I went with the tougher Richard Mille watch with the metal band. Actually, I did look at this exact watch." Mike chuckled as he remembered the argument he and Jillian had about him spending so much on a watch.

"A watch," Court said.

"The movement alone would have been a major advancement for them," Lynn said. "The calendar would have only made it worse."

Standing up, Mike bent down and looked at the power supply. "We might not make it," he said.

"Have you been watching the power meter?" Courtney asked.

"I forgot. We have one last power supply," Mike said. He counted down, "Twelve, eleven…" and the spud shut down.

* * *

Mike switched off the power supply and looked out of

the haze to see tall buildings and a few, scattered trees. There were people all around and modern vehicles were visible in the distance.

"Did we make it?" Court asked.

Lynn said, "It looks like we ran out of power very close to modern day, but this doesn't look like Egypt."

"We didn't run out of power, we stopped, then I shut it down," Mike explained.

"What does that mean?" Courtney asked.

"We're back home now," he said.

Glancing at a newspaper box across the street, Mike said, "USA Today. The divergence must be repaired!"

Mike changed out the power supply, adjusted the spud and turned it on.

"Let's see if we can go to Supreme Britain," he said, powering the spud and making a few changes. "Nothing happened. The divergence doesn't exist any longer!"

"What about the SAF? Can we go there?" Court asked.

"No. We can't change timelines," Mike said.

"We did it?" Lynn asked.

"I don't want to get too excited yet, but it looks that way," Mike said. A flood of emotions hit him, and he felt dizzy for a moment.

"This is the park down the street from your apartment, Mike," Courtney said.

"Come on. Let's go check it out," Mike said and started to jog.

As they got near a small group of people, Lynn asked, "Why do those people all have hoods on?" Then she gasped, "Do you see what I see? They're albino!"

Another hooded person on a bench beside them said, "Wow, look at them! Their skin is all colorful!"

"They didn't mean anything by it. They probably haven't seen a whole group of people with achromia before." She smiled forgivingly at Lynn.

"Oh, yes, she's right. I'm sorry," Lynn said, embarrassed. "Could I ask you what the date is?"

The girl replied, "Sure, August 31st."

All five of the survivors gasped at the same time.

"We made it!" Danni exclaimed.

"Come on, hurry," Mike said. "That's it, right up there."

* * *

The group walked up to the front of Mike's building and the doorman rushed up to them. "Mr. Devon! How nice to see you. How've you been? Janie has been so worried about you." He shook Mike's hand. "And, Miss Courtney! Very nice to see you too. Hurry up, that little girl will be so excited to see you all," the doorman ushered them into the elevator. Welcome, folks. Sorry to be rude, but Janie has been calling down here ten times a day."

"Uh, yeah, we—"

"No time, hurry on upstairs," the doorman said.

As the elevator doors closed, everyone started asking Mike questions at the same time, but he heard none of them.

"I don't know any more than the rest of you. I don't even know what to say, or think," Mike said. He lead the group off the elevator, into the hallway.

"Here it is," Mike began, then jumped back as someone yanked the door open.

A small girl screamed, "Daddy! Daddy!"

"Janie, sweetie, calm down, Daddy has had a rough couple of weeks it appears." The man went on, "Hello, son, we have been worried about you."

With tears running down his face, Mike leaned down and snatched up the little auburn haired girl.

"Hey, sweetie!" he said, causing Janie to scream and giggle with joy.

"Aunt Courtney! Thank you for bringing my Daddy home to us!" Janie squealed, reaching out for Courtney.

Mike choked back tears with all his might. "Dad? Yeah, there was a misunderstanding. Courtney thought I—" Mike started to make up a story but was interrupted by his mother opening the apartment door.

"Michael James Devon. You have worried your mother to death. Getting a call from preschool saying no one had been by to pick up Janie? And they couldn't reach you? I haven't slept in two weeks," she said. "We called Terry's wife, but all Terry had told her was that he had to leave on an emergency trip. Bill told us Lynn, Terry and Courtney had been helping you with some special project in Egypt. We tried to get more out of him, but he refused to say anything else."

"Yeah, right. Sorry Mom, can't talk about it or I would have to—"

"Don't say things like that or I'll pinch your head off and use it for a soccer ball."

"Ugh, that's disgusting, Mom," Mike said. *Where did she get that?*

"Now get in here and close the door, we want to hear about this mysterious trip."

"Mrs. Devon? Who are you talking to?" A voice called out from the bedroom.

"Jillian! Mike's home!" His mother called out. "I almost forgot, Jillian was in the shower."

Mike and Courtney made eye contact. She fought to hide her disappointment from him but was unsuccessful. Mike's mouth dropped open.

I told you, she mouthed to him.

"Mommy, Daddy's home! Daddy's home!" Janie screamed as a robed Jillian hurried out toweling her hair dry.

"Mike, I was so worried! Why didn't you tell us you were leaving?" Jillian had tears welling up in her eyes. "*They've* been here the whole time." Jillian made a strange face, almost as if she was afraid.

"I'm sorry, I—" Mike started.

Jillian wrapped her arms tightly around him.

"I'm sorry, it was an emergency. I tried to leave a message," Mike said.

"I never got it, maybe Janie erased it or something. We're so glad you're all right. Once again Courtney, Terry and Lynn have kept you safe for us! Oh, before I forget, Denny called and was

221

looking for you, Courtney," Jillian said.

"Denny?"

"Denny Skwira, your husband. Does he and Micah know you're home safe?"

"Yeah, sure. I mean, no, I haven't called yet. Sorry, it's been a long trip," Courtney said.

"Court and Danni, great to see you again!" Mike's dad said.

"Yeah, Mr. Devon, you, too," Court said.

"Lynn, Bill said to call him the instant we heard something," Jillian said.

"Bill? He's OK?" Lynn asked.

"As far as I know," Jillian replied. "What do you say we invite everyone over for lunch tomorrow? We have a lot to talk about."

Mike walked over to his bookcase and flipped through a couple of his books.

"Will they play duck, duck, goose with me mommy? I love it when uncle Bill chases me!" Janie said with excitement.

Jillian walked up and wrapped her arms around an unresponsive Mike. "Can you forgive me for being so angry at you?"

"It's gone." Mike said with concern.

"What's gone?" she asked, letting go of him.

"My book on the Antikythera mechanism, by Michael Wright and Allan George Bromley," Mike said. "It's not even listed in this book on ancient tech, either. That's not right."

He put the books back on the shelf and walked up to Courtney. "We have a big problem."

* * *

—THE STORY CONTINUES—

222

EPILOGUE
Excerpt from Book 3:

MIKE DEVON: DISCLOSURES

"Courtney stared out the window and listened to a soft hum resonating in the distance.

"What do you think?" Mike asked.

"It's not right. Too much has changed."

"Things are different, but how do you know what's *right?*"

"It can't be right," she said softly. "Look at your parents. They look strange, almost dead in the eyes."

"I haven't seen them in over ten years."

"Look again. Look into their eyes and tell me what you see," she whispered. "And Jillian seems genuinely afraid of them."

Mike's mother and father turned in unison to look at her.

Courtney turned her back to his parents. "That was creepy."

Mike nodded.

"You married Jillian? Seriously?"

"It looks that way," he said.

"She drove you crazy. From the smirk on your face, I know you remember."

"I do, but that was different. Maybe she's nicer now?"

"And that noise…"

"Wait, you hear that hum too? I thought it was just me," Mike said, then walked toward the window.

"What are you doing?" his mother demanded. "Get away from the window or they could misunderstand your intentions," she said, pushing him backwards with one hand and closing the blinds with the other.

"Easy, Mom," he said.

"They who?" Courtney asked her.

"The scanners, of course. This is our year, don't you remember?"

Courtney made eye contact with Danni to get her attention away from Jillian.

"Excuse me, Jillian, I need to ask Courtney something," Courtney heard her mother say.

"So, it's our year to be scanned for?" Courtney said, loud enough for Danni and Court to hear as they approached.

"Contraband, of course," Mike's mother, Janet, said. "Cease talking about it. They can hear you."

"We're bugged?" Danni asked, as she reached Courtney's side.

"Bugged? Of course not. The crawlers are scanning the buildings," Mike's dad, Ron, said.

"Don't talk about it!" Janet hissed.

Mike peeked out the edge blinds. "What in the world? There's a little machine on every second story window of those buildings across the street. They look weightless or something."

"Michael, get away from those blinds or I will report you!" his mother demanded.

Courtney looked at Mike and raised an eyebrow. *What do you think now, Mike?*

Mike nodded slightly at Courtney, then said, "Lynn, could you come over here?"

"Sure thing. What's up?" Lynn asked happily, as she walked up to them. "Hey, what happened?" she asked, as her face dropped. "Oh no—"

"We have to go, this place is all screwed up," Mike said.

* * *

ABOUT THE AUTHOR

JW Couch was schooled in the field of industrial maintenance and engineering by his father, from an early age. As an adult, he continued in the field, working regularly with technologies that include thermography, vibration and sound analysis and structural resonances, which appear in his books.

The *MIK3 D3VON* books are his first series and based in part on the real world tech he works in.

Born on a farm and raised on *Star Trek,* he has always shared his father's fascination with technology and time travel.

ACKNOWLEDGEMENTS

PRIMARILY responsible for the continuation of this series is my first readers, our oldest three children. They enjoyed the first book so much, I had to continue. I hope you also enjoy the stories.

Lastly, I would like to acknowledge Google, Wikipedia and NASA for their contributions as well. Details on magnetic reconnection, satellites, history, etc., were verified and made more accurate by web research and white papers on topics inside which you will mistakenly identify as 'Science Fiction'. Now, I don't want to scare anyone, but there is more 'Science *Faction*' going on in these pages than you may realize…